SKIP QUINCY, SHORTSTOP

(Bottom of the Ninth, book 6)

Jean C. Joachim

Moonlight Books

A Moonlight Books Novel
Sensual Romance
Skip Quincy, Shortstop
Bottom of the Ninth series
Copyright © 2017 Jean C. Joachim

COVER DESIGN BY DAWNÉ Dominique
Cover Art Photography: Kristi Hosier, Photography
Edited by Sherri Good
Proofread by Renee Waring
All cover art and logo copyright © 2017 by Moonlight Books

PUBLISHER
Moonlight Books

SKIP QUINCY, SHORTSTOP
(Bottom of the Ninth, book 6)

Jean C. Joachim

Chapter One

SEPTEMBER EVENING, Hingus Stadium

It was too cold to be running around naked on a baseball diamond. With a towel tucked around his waist, Skip Quincy, ace shortstop for the New York Nighthawks, padded barefoot out to the field. Since there was no game, the stadium was dark. Mimi Banner, the photographer, had bright lights set up on the grass.

Skip gripped the towel, keeping it in place. Too cold to worry about popping a boner in front of this lady.

"How many women have you slept with, Skip?" Mimi asked as she examined her camera.

"I don't know. Enough."

"Then being naked in front of me shouldn't be a problem."

"I've never posed for pictures. You're not gonna take one of my dick, are you?"

3

"Nope. Art becomes porn if I'm not careful."

"What are you going to do with these?"

"Exhibit them. In a gallery."

"Why me?"

"I told you. Your body has just the shape I'm looking for."

"What about the rest of the team?"

"I took their photos for Nelson Hingus. He's paying me a mint. Those portraits are going to hang in the stadium."

"I mean what about some of *them*, uh, naked?"

"Nope. You're the only one who's got what I'm looking for."

Ordinarily, those words would be music to his ears, and he'd move right in on her. But not this time. He shook his head. "Let's get this over with. It's damn cold out here."

"Don't worry. I told you I'm not shooting your, uh, private parts. Let's get started."

He stepped in front of the lights and dropped his towel. "Did Rowley know you did this? Take shots of naked men?"

"I didn't do it when he was alive. He'd have killed me."

"Can't blame him. Where should I stand?"

Mimi instructed him, then adjusted the lights, looked through her lens, readjusted the lights, and took fifteen shots. He diverted himself by memorizing her body. His gaze scanned her curves again, and again, settling in the most inappropriate places when she wasn't looking. When the chill wind skittered over his skin, it pebbled, like it did in a horror movie. A shiver shimmied down his spine. He reached up and touched the end of his nose. It was as cold as a dog's.

"Got enough? I'm freezing."

"I know. It's showing."

"Hey, nothing I can do about that. Besides, you said my dick was off limits."

"Not that, your skin, your arms, belly. Goosebumps are visible."

"That means we quit?"

She nodded. "I guess so. Can we do this again?"

"Nope," he said, heading back to the locker room.

"Okay, okay. You've been pretty good about it."

"Damn right. Now how about I take you to dinner Saturday?"

"Okay." Her lips formed a half-smile.

"Well, don't fall all over yourself with enthusiasm."

She laid her hand on his arm. "I'm sorry. I haven't been dating since Rowley passed."

He shrugged his shirt over his impressive shoulders and hugged her. "I'm sorry. Of course. If it's too soon..."

"It isn't. Everybody's been telling me I need to get back up on the horse," she said, then stopped, blushing. "I mean start dating again."

"And I'm just the horse for you." He shot her a grin.

"Down, boy."

Skip raised his hands and his eyes. He'd been staring at her chest far too long. "Just dinner."

"Right. I know you guys. Dinner in a restaurant, dessert in the bedroom."

"Mimi, I never push women. How about just dinner?"

She nodded. "Where?"

"Freddie's? Say, seven thirty? Shall I pick you up?"

"I'll meet you there."

He pulled up his pants and fastened the waist.

"Thanks for doing this. I'll send you a couple of shots."

"Don't bother. I can see it in the mirror after every shower."

She laughed. "Suit yourself."

He zipped up, grabbed his jacket, and placed his palm on her lower back.

"Come on, let's get out of here." He picked up the larger equipment cases and carried them to her car.

"Thanks, Skip. I appreciate this," she said, kissing him on the cheek.

He raised his eyebrows. "Happy to help, Mimi. See you tomorrow." He brushed his lips against hers, then strolled to his car, whistling.

When he got home, he smiled. Mimi had taken his mind off the playoffs next week. He still had three days to relax before the incredible pressure of playing on a team in contention for the pennant kicked in. He toed off his shoes and turned on a movie, hoping it would put him to sleep. Sleep, hmm, what would it be like to sleep with Mimi Banner? Knowing Rowley had been screwing her every night made him uneasy. Banner had once been on the Nighthawks, but they suspended him, and subsequently, released him for domestic violence.

Skip had never been with a woman whose husband had beat her up. Just the idea made him cringe. Mimi was a tiny thing, five foot two on a good day. And Rowley was a big guy. Skip burned at the idea that asshole had hurt her. Hell, he was dead now, so, there was nothing for her to fear. Certainly not Skip, nicknamed "teddy bear", by his high school cheerleaders. He'd never hurt a woman and that would never change.

He grinned at the idea of showing little Mimi how a real man behaved with women. He'd teach her lovemaking 101, Skip Quincy style.

THE TEAM HAD NO GAMES Friday, Saturday, and Sunday, but daily practice continued. They needed to stay sharp, and in shape for the playoffs. Friday night, Bobby Hernandez and his fiancée, Elena, threw a party. Skip picked up half a dozen six packs and headed over to their place.

He threw his jacket on the bed, then joined his teammates and their women in the living room. Bobby hugged Skip and ushered him into the kitchen.

"Beer's in here," he said, before returning to his fiancée.

Francie Whitman, Elena's best friend, greeted Skip. He bent to kiss the top of her head. She was only five-four to his six feet two inches.

"Beer?" Francie asked.

"Yep."

She nabbed one from the fridge. "Food's in the living room."

Matt Jackson, the Nighthawks' catcher, stuck his head in. "Poker in the back room."

"Strip poker?" Skip wiggled his eyebrows.

"I'm in," Francie added.

Skip ruffled her hair. "I don't play strip poker with my little sister."

She frowned and gave him a shove but wasn't able to budge the big man. "I'm *not* your little sister."

"One of the guys?"

"Play strip poker with me and find out."

Skip laughed.

"Mimi Banner's not here, Skip. Only guys playing cards in the back." Bobby joined them.

"Hell, I can see what they got in the locker room."

"Mimi Banner?" Francie trained her gaze on him.

Skip felt color rise to his cheeks.

"Yeah. She's his girlfriend," Bobby said.

"Is that true?" Francie asked.

"We're friends."

"You were naked with her in the stadium last night," Bobby piped up.

"Can't you keep your mouth shut about anything?" Skip frowned.

"Sorry. Cat's out of the bag now."

"Oh?" Francie cocked an eyebrow.

"She wanted to take some pictures. She's a photographer. Totally innocent. I never touched her," Skip said.

"Sure, I get it," Francie said, exiting the room.

"What the fuck did you have to go and say that for?" Skip pushed Bobby against the wall.

"Francie's Elena's best friend. She's a good kid. I don't want you messing with her."

"Is that your business?"

"It is. She needs to know you're hound-dogging Mimi."

"Who says I am?"

"Are you going out with her?"

"Just dinner."

"See?" Bobby took a beer.

"It's a free country. I can have dinner with whoever I want."

"Right. But just not Francie. Not when you're banging Mimi."

"Who said anything about banging?"

Bobby laughed. "I know you, Skip."

"Yeah, well don't jump to any conclusions."

"You have a thing for Francie?"

"She's like my little sister."

"You don't have a little sister."

"Exactly."

"Leave her alone. Her life is rough enough. She doesn't need a broken heart."

"Yeah? How so?"

"None of your business. Stay away from her, Skip. I mean it." Bobby shook his forefinger in his friend's face.

"I'd never break her heart."

"Good. Then leave her alone."

"Fine. She's the little sister I never had."

"Good." Bobby twisted the top off the bottle of beer and left the room.

Skip leaned against the wall. Little Francie Whitman, short, with dark-brown hair, gray eyes and a slim figure was just his type.

At thirty, Skip was still serial dating. He'd never had a relationship because he was devoted to his career. All his energy went into baseball, starting at a tender age.

One minute, he'd been riding in the car with his mother and father, the next thing he knew, he was in the hospital, then shuffled along to an orphanage. Adopted at age ten, Skip had learned from his new father that career came first. Shortstop was the toughest position on the field, next to pitcher and catcher. He had to be sharp, every single day. He started out in Little League, under the guidance of Bart Quincy. "Shortstop's too hard. Play first. Any idiot who can catch can play first base. You don't have to field any big fly balls. If you're gonna do baseball, no video games, no junk food. Just baseball and school." Traumatized by the loss of his parents, he'd been too scared to disagree with his new ones. His new father made it clear, they could return him to the "Little Angels" orphanage any time they wanted. Skip obeyed everything, trying to please so they wouldn't give him back.

When Bart and Ellen Quincy, a childless couple, picked him from all the children hoping for new homes, Skip had been grateful. He did what they said. Bart turned out to be right. Year after year, hard work, coupled with Skip's natural athletic, talent produced a smart, quick, dynamic shortstop, who had become the lynchpin of his team's defense.

As a teen, in the off-season, he had dated around. His family had never approved of one single girl. He kept looking, determined not to settle for anyone who wouldn't meet his parents' rigid standards. Believing he'd dodged a bullet with each female they had given him the thumbs down on, he kept looking. Skip had not questioned their motives until he left high school.

Once he'd made the minor leagues, he had realized they only wanted to control him, not assure his happiness. He'd regretted breaking up with a few who'd met with their disapproval. By twenty-one, he'd matured enough to stop bringing women home and having to explain. He simply separated his life from theirs.

FRANCIE WHITMAN, BARELY twenty-six, was getting her master's degree in studio art at City College. Her stepmother controlled a trust fund her father had left when he died. A frugal woman, Alice

Whitman, counted every penny, sending Francie to a public university, and putting her up in a tiny studio apartment. When she became twenty-seven, control of the fund would shift, and Francie would steer her own way. Because she was still in school and four years younger, Skip considered her a kid. Although he was strongly attracted to her, he kept his hands off, settling for bantering, teasing, and kidding, instead of dating.

She had seemed okay with their friendship until today. Her willingness to play strip poker shocked him. Not that he wouldn't have jumped at the chance, had they been alone, but she'd never gone beyond harmless flirting with him before. The minute she had said, "strip poker" blood had pumped to his dick. It stopped when he teased her and backed away. Her frown also surprised him. He'd expected blushes, stammers, and recanting. Instead, she'd faced him with a bold stare, daring him to take up her challenge.

Rather than sort through his mixed feelings, Skip focused on his date with Mimi. He expected to take a lot of shit from his teammates if he started seeing her seriously. Hell, she was the widow of one of the most hated guys in baseball. Even though they had attended his funeral, every single Nighthawk had despised Rowley Banner. Skip had pitied the guy and his addiction to steroids. But that was no reason to stay away from his beautiful widow.

Entering the living room, he took stock of the activity. A Nighthawks game film, with the sound off, was playing on the giant flat screen television. Men and women, dressed in jeans and casual shirts, stood around talking and drinking. A liquor cart by the window had several open bottles of wine, a six-pack of beer, vodka, gin, and a few mixers. Glasses occupied a shelf below.

The coffee table sat loaded with snacks—chips, dip, raw veggies, pigs in blankets, and a platter of cheese and crackers. After checking out the women in the room, Skip wandered over to eat. He piled veggies, hors d'oeuvres, and cheese on a plate and eased down on the sofa. Francie joined him.

"Mind if I sit here?"

"Don't you see the sign that says no strip poker players allowed?" He cocked an eyebrow.

She laughed.

"Do you play a lot of strip poker?" he asked.

"Not often. But I usually win when I play. My dad taught me poker," she replied.

"Really? You always win? But that depends on what you mean by winning." He'd dropped his voice an octave and wiggled his eyebrows.

She giggled. "You've such a dirty mind."

"Ain't it great?"

"Don't you ever think about anything else but sex?"

"Baseball. Oh, and food," he said.

"How long have you been playing?"

"Ever since I can remember," he said, picking up a carrot stick.

"How old?"

"Since I was maybe four? Five?"

"That's a long time."

"Yeah. I love it. Got the knack for it, too."

"Shortstop is hard," she said.

"Yep."

"You're good."

"Thanks. I train all the time," he said, dunking a carrot in dip.

"I paint all the time. Paint, draw, sketch."

"You're an artist, right?" he asked before putting the veggie in his mouth.

"Yep."

"That's hard. Born with the talent?"

She shrugged. "I guess so."

"What do you paint? Can I see your stuff?"

"Landscapes, portraits. Stuff like that." She dipped a pig in a blanket in mustard, then popped it into her mouth.

A little dab of mustard lingered on the corner of her lip. Skip considered licking it off but decided it was a bad idea. Instead, he swiped it off with his pinky and put it in his mouth.

"Mustard."

She nodded, a slight blush stealing into her cheeks. "Thanks."

"Nudes?"

"What?"

"Do you paint naked people?"

"Sometimes. Do you model?"

He shook his head. "Well, once. For a photographer. Froze my balls off. Not doing it again."

She nodded. "Too bad," she muttered.

"What?"

"Nothing." She reached for a cherry tomato, averting her gaze from his. The color in her cheeks deepened slightly. Although he couldn't exactly hear what she had said, he had a feeling it was almost a pass at him. He smiled. This little girl was hot. She intrigued him. He'd never dated an artist before.

"How old are you?" he asked.

"Twenty-six."

Too young. Still in school. Better as a little sister.

"Were you a baseball star right off the bat?" she asked. "No pun intended."

He shook his head. "I had to work at it. But I've always been pretty good at sports. Always liked to play and stuff. I spent hours and hours playing ball, getting advice from my coach."

"You mean Cal?"

"My high school coach. College, too."

"You went to college?"

"Of course. You think I'm a dummy?" He bristled.

Francie placed her hand on his arm. "I don't. Really. I don't. I didn't think baseball players had time to go to college."

"It was tough. I only had time for schoolwork and baseball."

"Hard to believe you gave up girls," she replied.

"Hell, at thirteen, I didn't even know what a girl was."

"How old were you when you started dating?"

"You mean when I first got laid?"

"I wouldn't have put it that crudely, but if you want to tell me—"

"Actually, I don't. My first date was the junior prom. I was a late starter. By then, I had been playing ball for three years. First freshman, ever, to make the varsity team."

"Did you always play shortstop?"

He shook his head. "My father said it was too hard. He started me at first."

Her eyebrows rose. "Too hard?"

Skip's lips turned down. "He didn't think much of me."

Francie moved closer, giving him her full attention. "What happened?"

"I was a lot better than he thought. End of story."

"Don't want to talk about it?"

He shook his head.

"I get it." She slid her hand over his. He gripped it hard, then released it.

"What about you? Been an artist all your life?"

"I take after my mom. She passed when I was twelve. Dad remarried. He died when I was twenty. I have a stepmother now," she said, making a face.

"A wicked stepmother?" Skip raised an eyebrow.

"Not wicked, just misguided. Thinks she needs to run my life. She doesn't."

"I'm sorry." He squeezed her hand.

A busty blonde sashayed over, eyeing Skip. "You two look so morbid. Somebody play something. I wanna dance." She held her hand out to Skip.

He shrugged, smiled at Francie, and pushed to his feet. When the music came on Skip moved to the beat. He glanced over his shoulder. A quiet Francie, dwarfed by the large couch, sipped a glass of wine and watched him.

She looked sad, alone. His heart squeezed. He knew that feeling. But if she was needy, he was the last guy to rely on. Skip had baseball and Mimi Banner—that was enough.

Will Grant, their newest rookie, plopped down on the sofa next to the artist. He turned toward her, handing her a brownie. She took it, removing her gaze from Skip. His stomach clenched.

Chapter Two

Sweat gathered on Skip's forehead. He sat up in bed, taking deep breaths to calm down. A bad dream woke Skip at six. He shut his eyes, trying to block out the memory but failed.

It took place on the first day of Little League tryouts. His biological father had taught Skip to throw when he was two. A game of catch between father and son had morphed into baseball by the time he was four. By age six, his dad had declared him a natural. His accuracy, even at a tender age, had been amazing.

His adoptive father hadn't planned to sign the youngster up for Little League until Skip had begged him. Mr. Quincy had voiced concern about how it might reflect on the family, if his "new" son failed.

"Adopting you was Ellen's idea," he'd said. "I was perfectly happy with the way things were. So, if you're gonna be my son, for God's sake, don't embarrass me."

Skip had simply stared at the man.

"You know what I mean. You're a scrawny string bean. You'd better do good at the tryouts or this is over for you."

Bart Quincy had used the boy's love of baseball to keep him in line. Any infraction and Bart threatened to end Little League. It had worked, most of the time. Skip had been a model child.

After that, Skip had taken the baseball from his old house and snuck down to the town tennis courts at six in the morning. It had been cold, but he didn't care. He pitched that ball at the backboard again and again and again. Then he'd back up five feet and throw again, then another five feet, then another. Every day for a month, he'd worked out in the morning, then after school, when he could sneak away.

As he had waited in line for his turn to catch, throw, and hit, a wave of loneliness had swept over him. How he'd wished his "real" dad could have been there. A few encouraging words would have gone a long way to reducing the tension, the fear in the boy. He loved baseball like his father did. It was in his blood. His "real" dad had played semi-pro ball before an injury had sidelined him.

"Quincy! You're next."

Skip had pounded his fist into his glove a couple of times, defining the pocket, as he walked to the plate.

"First base."

"Sir, I'd like to try out for shortstop."

"Son, all the boys are doing first base. If you learn how to do that, then you can try out for shortstop."

"But I can do it now. I can. Please."

Bart Quincy stepped forward. "Skip, do as the man says!"

The skinny boy cringed but stepped closer to second base.

"Okay, if you think you can do it. But you've gotta have the strongest throwing arm on the team, next to the pitcher and catcher. Think you've got that?"

The boy nodded.

"Okay then."

Skip had taken his position, punched his glove pocket one more time, then crouched, ready to field.

"Jones, give him a grounder."

A bigger boy got up to the plate and hit a ground ball. It took a bad hop, but Skip was on it. He fielded the ball, then rifled it to first, beating Jones by a mile.

"Very good. You've got short. Gordon? Step up, son."

Bart Quincy didn't say anything until they got in the car.

"Where'd you learn to field like that?"

"My dad taught me. He used to play semi-pro."

Bart nodded. "I see. Been practicing?"

Skip nodded.

"Where? I haven't seen you."

"Down on the tennis court."

"Tennis court?"

"Yes, sir."

"You'd better keep up your schoolwork. Baseball and schoolwork. No video games. I ain't havin' a dummy for a son."

"Yes, sir."

That story had haunted him, sometimes before every practice. Once he hit the pros, fear of not being good enough and getting traded drove him. He'd learned about hard work at ten. By the time he hit high school, he had become driven. Baseball was his life.

Now that he'd made shortstop for the Nighthawks, the pressure never let up. Bart Quincy didn't drive him, Skip did it to himself. Playoffs were coming, and he needed to be in shape. He shook off the memories and ripped the bedclothes down.

After hitting the shower, he fried up four eggs, downed a huge glass of juice and one cup of coffee before heading to the stadium. Fanatical about staying in top condition, he monitored his diet carefully.

Horny from the night before, he figured Mimi would satisfy that hunger after dinner. Hell, she'd been married, used to getting it often. Rowley Banner had probably been slipping it to her every night. She must miss it, he said to himself, as he slid behind the wheel of his car. He'd be happy to take care of her needs, several times until he got it right, he snickered.

With a twist of the key, the engine turned over, and he steered onto the back road leading to the stadium.

"WHERE THE FUCK YOU been, Quincy?" Bobby Hernandez, his best friend and Hawks' second baseman asked.

"Nowhere. I'm here now. So, shut the fuck up." Skip opened his locker and changed into workout clothes.

Vic Steele, Nighthawks' trainer, poked his head in. "Infield, you're up. Stretching, then two laps then the weight room. Let's go."

Skip, Bobby, Jake, and Nat donned sweats and headed for the field. They loped along, staying in a group until they'd done the warm-up, then they headed inside to pump iron. Skip loved the challenge of the weight room. He was reduced to adding reps, because Vic wouldn't let him take a heavier weight. To avoid pulled muscles, the trainer insisted they stretch before working out.

"Keep going. Push yourselves, just a bit. One more rep. Two more. But no pulled muscles!"

Sweat soaked Skip's T-shirt. He stopped to down a bottle of water, then jumped on the bike for cardio. Feeling his body perform, work, stretch, and grow stronger stoked his fire. Each session readied him more and more for the contest with the Washington, D.C., Wolverines. Playoffs were next week. He'd be ready.

The men took a break. There was a buffet spread for lunch in the dining hall. Bobby got behind Skip in line.

"What happened to that Banner chick? You didn't bring her last night."

"Right. I'm taking her out tonight."

"Big night?" Bobby nudged him in the ribs and wiggled his eyebrows.

"None of your beeswax, jerkoff."

"Just thinkin' it might be nice if you got a little, for a change."

"I'm gettin' plenty."

"Yeah? From who?" Bobby picked up a plate.

"None of your damn business."

"Not from Francie?" Bobby's voice rose.

"No way. I keep tellin' you, she's like my little sister." Skip speared a piece of ham and put it on his dish.

"Good. Leave her alone."

"Says you?"

"Yeah. She's too nice for you."

"Fuck off. I'll go out with whoever I want."

"She's got enough problems, without you messing up her head with your dick."

"That's weird, buddy. What you just said? Very weird."

"You know what I mean."

"Okay, okay. But if she wants me, who am I to say 'no'?"

"Don't flatter yourself, asshole."

"She was comin' on pretty strong last night."

"Schoolgirl crush."

"She may be goin' to school, but she's no schoolgirl," Skip said.

"Yeah?"

"Hell, she's twenty-six."

"So?" Bobby quirked an eyebrow.

"Back off, Bobby. She's a big girl. She can take care of herself."

"As long as you stay away from her, I'm good."

"It's none of your business."

The two men had filled their plates to overflowing with ham, roast beef, baked potatoes, brussel sprouts, and salad. They took their places at the table.

"If you think I'm such a bad guy, why don't you sit somewhere else?" Skip scowled at his friend.

"I don't think you're a bad guy. But Francie is Elena's best friend."

"Hey, I'm not about to hurt her. She's fun. We have a good time, kidding around and stuff."

"She flirts with you."

"So do a lot of women. Doesn't mean anything," Skip said, slicing his meat.

The men focused on their food while Cal Crawley talked about the Wolverines.

"Eddie Weeks is gonna be trouble," Cal said. The manager warned about Cullen Murphy, the pitcher, too. While the men ate, Cal flashed film of the Washington team on the flat screen. Then he discussed strategies. The men listened. Grateful the manager spoke so Bobby shut up, the shortstop focused on the film. To be totally honest with himself, Bobby wasn't far off. Francie intrigued Skip. He had to find out more, but he wasn't about to tell his buddy. Skip had a *thing* for artists, even though he didn't know one end of a crayon from the other.

If Francie had feelings for Skip, fine, he'd pursue it, but treat her with kid gloves. Skip had never met a girl like her. First, he had to satisfy his craving for Mimi Banner. Tonight would be the night—if he got lucky.

After practice, Skip headed for the shower.

"Hey, engaged men first. We've got women waiting," Matt Jackson, the catcher, said, giving Skip a playful shove.

"You've already got someone. Doesn't matter if you stink to high hell. I've got a date." Skip elbowed his way ahead.

Jake and Bobby blocked his path.

"Who's the hot chick?" Jake asked.

"None of your business," Skip replied.

"Oh no? Wait a minute. If you won't tell, then I must know her, right? Who is it?" Jake backed Skip to the wall.

"I said, none of your business."

"I'm makin' it my business," said Nat Owen, first baseman.

"Fuck off. All of you."

"Come on. Tell us. We won't give you a hard time," Matt said, trying not to laugh.

"Yeah, right. I'll never hear the end of it." Skip tried to dodge his teammates.

"We're keeping you here until you tell us," Jake said.

"Aw, leave him alone," Bobby piped up.

All heads turned to the second baseman.

"Wait a minute. We don't need Skip to tell us. I bet Bobby knows," Nat said.

Bobby Hernandez backed away, his palms up. "No, no, I don't. Honest. I don't have a clue."

"Yes, you do. Dickwad over here tells you everything," Matt said, narrowing his eyes.

"Mimi Banner! Okay! Jesus Christ! Can't a guy keep anything to himself?" Skip threw a towel in the dirty towel bin.

The men turned their gazes on him, but none said a word.

"What are you looking at?"

"You're dating Banner's widow?" Matt asked.

"So?"

Matt shook his head. "Banner'll come right up out of Hell and cut your balls off."

Skip laughed, along with his teammates.

"Aren't you, like, intimidated? Even a little bit?" Nat asked.

"He's dead. Maybe he was a stud, maybe not. But he's gone, and she's probably missing it. I can fix that."

Bobby shook his head. "Playing with fire."

"Why do you say that?"

The third baseman shrugged. "Don't know. I heard he beat her up a couple of times. She might not be real interested in getting it on with another athlete."

"I'd never hit her. Besides, he took steroids. Maybe that had something to do with it," Skip replied.

"I dunno." Jake shrugged. "Seems there are plenty of other fish in the sea without messing with that hornet's nest."

"Maybe, maybe," Skip said. "I gotta go. You guys are making me late!" Skip shoved his way to the front of the shower line and stepped under the hot spray. Visions of Mimi taking off her clothes drifted through his head as he soaped up. After rinsing off, he dried himself and dressed faster than usual. Skip beat it out of the locker room before the rest of the team could air their opinions.

Next stop—the barbershop. The man neatened up his hairline. Skip liked to look his best when attempting a seduction, it weighed the odds more heavily in his favor. He stopped home to change. After unwrapping a fresh blue shirt from the laundry, he slipped on the Italian custom suit he saved for special occasions. Sure, he had to wear a suit and tie coming to and leaving the stadium, and on all road trips, but he had a fistful of cut-rate, off-the-rack suits for those occasions. He saved the good stuff for the ladies. This was his *lucky* suit. Charcoal gray, tailored to his body and fit like a glove. How could he miss? He smiled to himself. Mimi was in for a big surprise—a magic carpet ride with Skip Quincy.

A PARKING SPACE WAS available two doors down from Freddie's, the Nighthawks bar and restaurant hangout, near the stadium. He parked, checked himself in the mirror, smiled at the handsome face looking back at him, and went in.

Saturday night and the place was already filling up. Tommy, the owner and the late Freddie's grandson, greeted him, giving him the once-over.

"I need a table for two," Skip said, straightening his tie.

"A date?"

Skip nodded.

"Hmm. It's a little busy. Wait, wait. I've got just the thing. Back here," he said, leading Skip to a quiet table tucked away in the back of the restaurant. Skip nodded and sat down. Since he had arrived half an hour early, he ordered a Coke. Tommy brought his drink and a basket of bread.

"You gonna win next week?"

"You have to ask?" Skip cocked an eyebrow at the restaurateur.

Tommy grinned. "That's what I thought. I hate the Wolverines."

"Makes two of us," Skip said, picking up a roll. Tommy smiled before rushing off to attend to other diners.

Skip sat facing the door. His mind drifted back to his senior prom. Overwhelmed with baseball and studies senior year of high school, he'd only dated a few girls. He had gotten laid after senior prom—lost his virginity the same time as his date. He chuckled remembering how ignorant he had been. She had been no help, either. *The blind leading the blind.* They'd been two kids fumbling around in the backseat of a car on a warm night in June.

Glancing up, he spied Mimi, hesitating at the front of the restaurant. She wore a low-cut black dress. His gaze zeroed in on her chest. He marveled that such a petite woman could have such large breasts. He wondered if they looked bigger because she was so tiny. When he finally looked up at her face, he frowned. She looked lost. Skip raised his hand to catch her eye.

She smiled and headed for his table. He rose and pulled out her chair. She smoothed her skirt over her thighs and sat down.

"No one's done that for me in a long time," she said.

"Rowley didn't pull out your chair?"

She shook her head.

"You were his wife."

"Didn't seem to make much difference."

"Don't mean to speak ill of the dead, but he must have been kinda stupid."

"Thanks." She shot him a warm smile.

The conversation was going exactly where he wanted. He needed to come off as a thousand times better than her dead husband if he wanted to warm her bed. Soft, brown curly hair caressed her shoulders. He wanted to touch it but suspected she was skittish and would freak out if he reached across the table to comb his fingers through her locks.

Rowley had smacked her around and been suspended, and eventually fired, for it—and for steroid usage. According to the coroner, steroids had caused the heart attack that killed him.

"You must miss Rowley," Skip said, signaling for the waiter. "What do you want to drink?"

"Just ginger ale."

Skip raised his eyebrows. "I have a game, but you have no reason to avoid a drink."

"I stopped drinking two years ago."

"Why?"

"Alcohol made Rowley more violent. I needed to stay sober to keep my wits about me when he was drinking. It just became a habit."

Switching to her choice, Skip ordered two ginger ales. He couldn't imagine what it was like to be chained to a guy like Banner.

"Makes sense. Are you hungry? All the food here is good. Trust me. I've eaten everything on the menu."

"All at once?" she asked with a twinkle in her eye.

He laughed.

"What are you going to have?" she asked.

"This close to a playoff game, I usually have steak. The biggest, juiciest one I can find."

"Steak? I'm more of a seafood person."

"Lobster? Order whatever you want."

She smiled up at him.

His adoptive father had drilled into him to be careful with his money. Therefore, Skip had plenty put away. One thing, though, he never skimped on food.

"The lobster's too much. Just a few scallops. And, maybe, a salad?"

The waiter arrived with their beverages and took their orders.

"Why is it women always eat like birds?" Skip asked, taking a sip.

"Always watching our weight."

"And if you put on a few pounds, just more to love."

"Most men don't feel that way."

He raised his glass. "Here's to getting to know you." She joined in the toast.

"Of course, you already know a lot more about me, than I do about you," he remarked, his gaze hot.

"Photographers usually leave their clothes on when they take pictures." She shot him a sly glance.

"Unfortunately."

Now it was her turn to laugh.

"How are you doing, now that Rowley's gone?" He took her small hand in his large ones.

"I'm all right. It's been an adjustment. But things weren't great between us."

"I understand he got nailed for domestic violence, at least twice."

"Yes." She lowered her gaze and slid her hand from his.

"Hey, we don't have to talk about that if you don't want to. I don't want to pry."

"It's old news."

"Why did you stay with him?"

Her gaze connected with his. Her eyes were cold.

"Just curious."

"Do you really expect me to tell you in fifty words or less?"

The conversation was headed south, and he'd better do something fast.

"Excuse me," the waiter said, setting down a plate with a large steak on it. Relief flowed through Skip. After the server left, Mimi picked up her utensils.

"Have you ever hit a woman?" she asked, in a quiet voice.

"No! And I never would." His brow furrowed.

"Good."

"Do you feel uncomfortable with me because I'm bigger than you?"

"A little. Rowley was a lot bigger than me, too."

"Let me tell you right now. You have nothing to fear. I'd never, and I mean, never, hit you."

She stabbed a scallop with her fork, avoiding his gaze.

"I mean it!" He took her hand.

Her head snapped up, her eyes flared. "What are you doing?"

"Nothing."

"You yanked on my arm."

"A gentle shake, just to make my point."

"You did make a point, but not the one you wanted." She withdrew her hand from the table.

"Aw, come on. You're not going to say that hurt, are you?"

She answered slowly. "Almost."

"Almost doesn't count. Hey, I'm a strong guy. It was a little tug. I didn't mean for it to injure you."

"You didn't."

"Good."

Skip focused on slicing and eating his steak, sneaking a look at her from time to time. Perhaps dating Mimi wasn't going to be as easy as he thought. If she felt this way about his touch, simply used to emphasize his words, then how could he make love to her? Lovemaking sometimes included a tight grip here or a strong thrust there. Would he have to worry that his lovemaking was too rough? He'd never had that complaint before—not from one single woman. His brain mulled over the problem while his mouth chewed his food.

"Look, Skip. I like you. A lot. But I'm not ready for any hot and heavy romance."

"You're here with me, as a friend?" His heart sank.

She shot a flirtatious glance at him. "Not really. But can we take it slow? Real slow?"

"Like a turtle or a snail?"

"Maybe a turtle."

He tried to smile. "Okay. I guess."

"What did you have in mind?"

"More like a rabbit."

She grinned and shook her head. "Not happening."

"At least you're upfront about it."

"Does that mean this is our last date?"

He hesitated. How could he drop her because she didn't want to jump into bed with him?

"Of course not."

She let out a breath. "Good. I was afraid you had sex on the brain."

"Hey, what athlete doesn't have sex on the brain?"

"One who's on steroids," she said. "Steroids made Rowley infertile," she blurted out.

Boy, that was much more than he wanted to know. He shoved a potato in his mouth.

"We wanted to have kids, but it didn't happen. Couldn't happen. Damn drugs."

"You don't have to tell me," he said, showing his palm.

"It helps to talk about it."

Skip picked up his water glass. He feared that the conversation was about to get a whole lot more personal, calling to mind that expression *TMI—too much information.* He sat back, prepared for an info dump from Mimi that would make his face red. Trapped, he motioned for the waiter. Since this looked like it was going to be a long session, he requested the dessert menu.

MIMI AND SKIP HAD AN early evening and, after seeing her home, he went to bed alone. Her reluctance to get close to him had whetted his appetite, not squelched it. He took a shower and got a good night's sleep. In the morning, he arose early and headed for the stadium.

After stretches and running, he settled down to a long-toss with Bobby Hernandez. The men threw the ball to each other, then backed up several steps. They increased the speed and the power, too. Skip loved those exercises, warming up and strengthening his arm and his accuracy. When they took a break. Skip downed three bottles of water and plopped down on the bench.

"Did you do it with Mimi?" Bobby asked, twisting the cap off a fresh bottle.

Skip shook his head. He normally kept his conquests to himself, but this woman he'd talked about so much, he had to answer.

"Losing your touch?" Bobby quirked an eyebrow at his teammate.

"Nope. Rowley smacked her around. She's got issues."

"Hell, who wouldn't?" Bobby said.

"Hey, I'm not criticizing her. Just sayin'. It's kinda slowing things down."

"Why don't you give up?" Matt Jackson, the catcher, asked.

"What the fuck? Why is everyone trying to control my love life?"

"Since when does love have anything to do with it?" Snickered Jake Lawrence, third baseman.

"Fuck you!" Skip threw his shirt in his locker.

"Leave him alone. The guy's only trying to get laid. Doesn't have a great woman like I do," Dan Alexander, the pitcher, put in.

The men laughed.

"My life is none of your business," Skip shouted.

"You mean sex life? What sex life?" Nat Owen, first baseman, said.

Skip slammed his locker door. Bobby put an arm around his teammate.

"Hey, cool down, buddy. We're just joking."

"Yeah. We want you to get laid every day," Jake said.

"Might cool down that temper," Dan muttered.

Skip took a breath and shook his head. "You assholes should shut the fuck up. Who asked you? Last time I ever tell you anything." He looked directly at Bobby. The second baseman shrugged. "Sorry, man."

"Yeah. Yeah." Skip closed his locker and headed for his car. Sexual frustration gnawed at him, and his teammates' kidding around didn't help. He stopped at Freddie's and picked up two burgers to go. When he got home, Skip flipped through movies. He found an old favorite porn flick and watched while he ate. Then he relieved his tension, manually, took a shower, and picked up a magazine, but it didn't hold his interest. He paced through the apartment like a caged animal. Playoffs started tomorrow. He needed to get to sleep early, but he wasn't tired. Instead, he dialed Francie.

"Hey, baby, what's up?" He lounged on his sofa, resting his legs on the coffee table.

"Skip?"

"Yeah."

"How are you? Playoffs tomorrow?"

"Yep. You coming?"

"I'll be there with Elena. I get to sit in the family section if I go with her."

"Awesome."

"I won't be going to D.C., though."

"School?"

"Yep."

"Any news on that art school thing. Was that in France?"

"You mean the École des Artes in Paris?"

"Yeah, yeah, that's the one."

"Nope. Alice still refuses to release the money. She says it's a waste. That my art school education in New York is enough."

"That sucks."

"I know. I'm going to send in the application anyway. If she won't give me the money from the trust fund, then I'll get a loan."

"It's that important?"

"The people running the Grand Prix des Artes competition won't accept anyone who hasn't taken that one semester course."

"And what's so great about the competition, anyway?"

"The winner gets to exhibit her work at the Guggenheim Museum. You get a name. It's a prestige thing."

"Do you need that? I bet your work is good enough without that."

"Thanks. I want to go to the school. I need that to get to the next level."

"Next level in art?"

"That's right."

"You ever sell your stuff?"

"Haven't had too many sales. A couple."

"Bet your dad would be proud," he said.

Silence greeted him. He waited. There was a slight quiver in her voice when she responded.

"He would. He'd give me the money to go to Paris. I have the recommendations and an idea for a painting I could send them."

"You have to present a painting to them to get in?"

"I know it sounds like a lot of work, but it's standard. Everyone has to do that."

"That's a giant pain in the ass."

She laughed. "Exactly."

"You got something to send them?"

"Not yet. But I'm working on it."

"Can I see it?"

"I never show anyone a work in progress."

"Aw, come on. It's me."

"No way. You nervous about tomorrow?"

He smiled at her feeble attempt to change the subject. He'd go along.

"Nah. The Wolverines are a bunch of pussies—no offense."

"None taken."

"We'll wipe the floor with them."

"Good. I like high scoring games more than pitchers' duels."

"I'll do my best."

"I'll be rooting for you."

"Yeah?"

"I always do."

"For me, or the Nighthawks."

"Both. But definitely for you."

He grinned. "Good."

Silence lay heavy in the air. Finally, he spoke.

"I gotta get to bed."

"Too bad I'm not there."

"Yeah? And if you were, what would you do?"

No response.

"Come on, come on. You can tell me. You can tell me anything."

"I'd give you a back massage."

"That's all?"

"That's a lot."

"You're right. Gotta go, baby. Have a good night. See you tomorrow."

"Good luck, Skip. 'Night."

"'Night."

He put the phone down and wandered over to the window. It was dark outside. He gazed at the twinkling lights that seemed to stretch out forever. The skyscrapers of midtown, elegant in their silver and gold spotlights, towered above shops and restaurants.

With a sigh, he thought about the game. His stomach clenched. Butterflies always hit before a big game. And the first round of playoffs qualified. A sharp stab of fear spiked through him. This ritual was left over from his first Little League playoffs.

Skip had been alternating between shortstop and second base. When the other boy doing the same got the measles, the spot was all Skip's. His adoptive father had lectured him.

"That's the most important position. Try not to screw it up. I know you have two left feet, boy, but do what you can. Don't mess up and make the team lose, or it'll be your fault. You can't blame it on Tommy for getting sick. It's all on you and you'd better deliver."

Bart Quincy had never been a fan. He'd made it clear that adopting Skip had been his wife's idea. Ellen had wanted a child, but by age forty it hadn't happened.

Skip had been orphaned so quickly, he'd thought he was dreaming. His life had turned upside down in a heartbeat. He had cried for his parents every night for three months. Six months had passed before Ellen Quincy laid eyes on him.

Bart had pushed for a younger child, but Ellen insisted on Skip. He didn't know what to think, except that someone's home had to be a better place than the orphanage. He'd been terrified the entire time he'd been there.

He'd made one friend at Little Angels—Billy Holmes. Billy had been three years older than Skip and had taken the younger boy under his wing. He had taught him how to behave to get the best treatment and seconds on dessert. Billy had protected Skip from the others.

When he went home with the Quincys, Skip had missed Billy terribly. Bart's words, spoken out of Ellen's earshot, had scared him. He'd never forget what his new father had said on that first night.

"If you don't behave, if you give Ellen even one night of grief, you'll be back in that orphanage so fast you won't know what hit you. This isn't permanent, we can give you back. It's not like it's legal yet or we signed any papers. We didn't."

Even now, the memory of that conversation still made him tremble. Skip had believed Bart. Skip had behaved like an angel as much as he could, motivated by the fear of losing his new home with good meals and a room of his own.

Ellen had attended every game, while Bart would show up at the end, wearing a dour expression and smoking a cigarette. By the time he was fifteen, Skip had given up trying to please Bart. He knew he would never be the perfect son his new father wanted. He rebelled, got into trouble, and headed for the dark side of life, accompanied by his buddy, Billy.

Coach Sal Guardino had reached out to Skip, spent time with him, and trained him. It was his coach, not his father, who gave Skip the confidence to work toward pro ball. Skip grinned to think how happy his coach would be to see him in the playoffs, heading toward the World Series.

"This one's for you, Coach Sal," he said.

Padding back to bed, he slid between the sheets and doused the light.

Chapter Three

F rancie awoke early. She was excited to be Elena's guest at the first playoff game. They'd be sitting with Bobby Hernandez's father, too. Elena didn't like the old man, but Francie planned to be friendly, hoping to help mend the rift between him and her friend.

Happiness flowed through her to be watching Skip Quincy, the best shortstop in the league. Although he might argue about his status, his game stats convinced her that he was number one. At least he was with her.

"It's been three years since Rob. You should be over it already. Time to find someone new," Elena had said to her. Francie had not told her friend she'd had a crush on Skip for the past eight months. The first time she met him, her heart rate doubled. Although he was much taller than she, he didn't make her feel small. Instead, he'd been friendly, joking with her, and flirting. His thousand-watt smile, coupled with his broad shoulders and slim body, started her blood pumping. She'd been hooked right away.

Francie had kept her feelings to herself, like she did most things. Oh, she knew how to have a good time, laugh, drink, and party with the best of them, but reveal her true feelings? Not Francie. Since she'd lost her father, she hadn't been the same. Her stepmother treated her coldly. She got how the woman didn't want to be in charge of money she couldn't touch, but did she have to be stingy?

Francie opened the drapes and gazed outside. The sun was shining, a good omen. Attacking her closet, searching for the perfect outfit for the game, the young woman tossed out several before settling on snug jeans and a black T-shirt. After a shower, she applied makeup highlighting her gray eyes and heart-shaped lips. A quick brush through her short dark hair and she was ready to go. Her cell jingled. It was Elena.

"Ready, girlfriend?"

"Ready."

"I dropped Bobby at the stadium. I'll drive down and pick you up. Leaving in five."

"Great. I'll be outside."

Jealousy had never been a problem for Francie. She was happy that her best friend was engaged to Bobby Hernandez, second baseman for the Nighthawks. Elena's life had been hard. Finding love with Bobby had not been a smooth road either. Francie had held Elena's hand and encouraged her. Would the artist's turn for true love happen? Probably not, she figured. She didn't have the curves, the long hair, or the flirtatious ways men loved.

She'd pinned her dreams on taking an advanced art class in Paris, even fantasized she'd meet a sexy French artist or professor, fall in love, and settle in the city of romance. Those scenarios didn't happen for little girls like Francie, and neither did love with a star baseball player, but she could dream.

She grabbed her red jacket, tucked her camera under her arm, and headed outside. Easing down on the stoop, she kept her gaze on the cars. Within fifteen minutes, Elena's Silver Lexus pulled up to the curb. Francie climbed in.

"You look hot today. Any reason?" Elena asked, her eyes twinkling.

"Just the first thing I pulled out of the closet."

"Liar."

The women laughed.

"How's the new book coming?" Francie asked.

Elena was more than happy to chat about her progress on the new romance book she was writing. Then the topic changed to the wedding. Francie was to be the maid of honor. As they wended their way through the traffic, they exchanged ideas on dress color for the bridesmaids and what kind of flowers. Elena and Bobby hadn't set the date yet, but that didn't stop the young women from making plans.

Elena pulled into Bobby's spot in the parking lot, and they headed for the stadium. As the ladies took their seats, the pitchers were warming up in the bullpen. Francie adjusted her camera.

"What's that for?"

"To snap any cool shots. Close plays. That stuff?"

Elena sported a sly grin. "You mean to get amazing shots of Skip Quincy, don't you?"

"Skip?" She raised her eyebrows and shook her head.

"You are such a little liar! Girl, I see right through you. I know you have a thing for him."

"He's involved with Mimi Banner. We're just friends."

"Bull. I know you. You can't hide from me. I think Skip would be amazing for you."

"Really? Looks like you're the only one who thinks so."

"Don't be so sure. I see the way he looks at you."

"The way a guy glances at his little sister," Francie replied, frowning.

"I saw him checking you out. Staring at your cute butt."

"Come on, no he didn't." Heat seeped into Francie's cheeks.

"He did! I swear!" Elena traced a cross with her finger over her heart.

"Then he didn't like what he saw."

"Why do you underestimate yourself all the time?"

Francie shrugged.

"Is it your ex? Just because he was a stupid idiot doesn't mean all men are."

"They are when it comes to me."

The announcement of the players, as they ran out on the field, interrupted their conversation. Francie searched for Skip. He was taller than the other infielders, so she picked him out right away. She studied him, his straight posture, broad shoulders, and nice butt. When he took his hat off and held it over his heart, she stood up. The Star-Spangled Banner played. Francie sang along, her hand resting on her chest. At the end, the Nighthawks took their places on the field while the Wolverines came up to bat. Her gaze zeroed in on Quincy at shortstop. He crouched low, his glove in front of him as the first Washington batter came to the plate. Her heartbeat sped. She lifted her camera, zooming in on him, and snapped. Sure, he was way out of her league, but she could dream and enjoy her pictures in privacy.

"Strike!" The umpire called.

SKIP CROUCHED DOWN, his eyes on the ball as Dan Alexander went into the windup. The sun beat down on his back. He hadn't expected the heat. After swiping at the sweat on his forehead with his sleeve, he lowered his hands, glove open, facing the batter, his weight on the balls of his feet.

He took a tip he'd read from Derek Jeter, another tall shortstop. Jeter said he got down low to come up on the ball, rather than sink down and stab at it. Skip found the idea worked for him, too. The batter was D.C.'s first baseman, a right-hander. Matt Jackson had given Skip, Bobby, and Jake a signal indicating the batter might be pulling the ball more toward third. Skip shifted, side-stepping a few feet toward third. Jake was a foot away from the base.

Sure enough, the batter smashed a grounder that bounced toward Skip. He kept his eye on the ball, running to meet it. Centering his gaze on Nat Owen, Skip plucked it swiftly from his glove and fired to first. He aimed chest-high and got it there in plenty of time. He felt good, His arm was warm and strong, ready to play, and Skip's nerves kept him focused. One away.

They threw the ball around the circuit before it went back to Dan. Skip crouched down again, but the second batter struck out. Skip loved every strikeout—an easy out from a fielder's point-of-view— and one he couldn't mess up. His fear of making an error intensified in a playoff game.

Next up was their centerfielder, a man with a great eye who could it hit out of the park. Dan threw a strike, then two balls.

"Don't walk him," Skip muttered. This guy could run as well as hit. Seemed as if Dan wasn't paying attention because that's exactly what happened. Umpire called ball four and Eddie Weeks took first base.

The 'Hawks shifted. Bobby moved closer to second, Nat took a few steps toward second, behind Weeks, who took an insane lead. Skip shifted toward second as well. He watched Matt, the catcher, give the sign. Dan rifled one to first, but Weeks dove back in the nick of time. He brushed the dirt off his uniform and shot a shit-eating grin at Dan—which obviously pissed off the pitcher. Skip crouched low, ready to move at lightning speed should the asshole attempt to steal second.

If? When was more like it. Weeks led his team in stolen bases and was top five in the league. Skip glanced at Bobby, then turned his attention back to the ball. That was key, keeping his eye on the ball. The count was two to one. Dan went into his windup, and Weeks broke for second.

Dan swiveled and fired at Bobby, who was between first and second. Skip ran to second, anchoring himself with his back foot up against the bag, and stretching out toward the second baseman with his other one. Bobby tossed it to Skip, who bent down and tagged Weeks' right foot as he slid into base. The bastard raised his left foot, aiming his cleats at Skip's back leg, but the shortstop dove forward, into the dirt, bending his back leg at the knee, barely avoiding the spikes. And he kept hold of the ball, nestled snugly in his glove.

"Out!" The umpire called, making a fist and pumping it toward the ground.

Weeks jumped up and immediately argued with the umpire. Skip smiled and loped toward the dugout. He knew he'd tagged him before hitting the ground. One glance at the Jumbotron, which showed a re-play, and Skip shook his head, his grin widening. Eddie Weeks, once an asshole, always an asshole. Skip hit the dugout and nabbed a bottle of water, downing it in almost one gulp.

Cal Crowley sidled up to him. With one nod and a pat on the shoulder, the manager said, "Way to go, Skip."

"Thanks."

After several teammates high-fived him, he sat down, waiting his turn to bat. Nat was up first, then Bobby, who was in the on-deck circle. Skip couldn't wait. Confidence flowed through him. This was going to be his game. He felt it, in his bones. All the weeks, months, and years of endless practice would come together on this field, starting today.

He stood up, walked to the front of the dugout, and glanced at the stands. The seat he'd bought for Mimi Banner was empty. Swinging his gaze to the left, he spied Francie Whitman, sitting next to Elena Delgado. That was all he needed to know.

BY THE BOTTOM OF THE sixth, the two teams were tied, three to three. Nat drew a walk. It looked like the Wolverines pitcher might be getting tired. Bobby stepped up to the plate. He hit a checked-swing dribbler down the third base line, catching the other team by surprise. Skip chuckled. Bobby had surprised himself and the rest of the Nighthawks, too. That had been unplanned, a mistake, but he managed to put on the speed and beat out the throw.

Skip sauntered to the batter's box. This was a golden opportunity. He narrowed his eyes at the pitcher. The man wiped his arm across his face, sopping up the sweat gathered there. The unexpected heat of the day had taken something out of all the players. Skip wondered how the pitcher was still throwing 95 mile-per-hour fastballs.

Shouldering the bat, bending his knees and then straightening them, Skip watched the man on the mound. He kept shuffling the ball from hand to hand, rubbing it, fitting his fingers around it. Skip recognized the signs of nervousness. Hell, he'd displayed his own crazy moves to cut the tension when the game got intense. It was a dual between the pitcher and Skip. With two men on base, one home run, or even a solid hit could bring in the winning run. He knew the strategy. Make the pitcher throw more. The more he tossed, the more tired he'd get, increasing the chances of either a fat pitch right down the center or enough out of the strike zone to walk Skip.

He glanced at the third base coach who threw him the signs to take the first two pitches. Skip shouldered the bat, narrowed his eyes again and drilled his stare right into the man on the mound. As much as he looked like he was getting ready to whack the ball out of the park, it was all show. He had no intention of swinging, no matter where the ball was.

With furrowed brow, the pitcher shook off two calls from the catcher before he released the pitch. Skip figured that was a good sign. When the pitcher is shaking off signs, it means he's losing control and can't throw the fancy pitches. He's getting tired.

Two balls and a strike were called. Skip stepped out of the batter's box and looked at the third base coach again. The sign was batter's choice—or Skip could do whatever he wanted. If he got his pitch, he was to go for it. He stepped up again, turned to face the pitcher and tightened his grip on the bat. Skip made up his mind to swing. The windup, the pitch, yessiree! There it was, right down the fuckin' middle.

He swung with all his might and connected. The ball soared high and far, heading for the top tier seats. Son of a bitch, he'd hit a three-run homer! Bobby and Nat waited for him at home plate. Skip enjoyed his lope around the bases to the cheering of Nighthawks' fans. Nothing like a home run to make his heartbeat double and his grin widen. Skip had always been a short ball hitter, dependable, but not known for homers. That made this one even sweeter.

He had more high-fives and butt pats than he could count. Even Cal slung an arm around him for a moment, and his manager was not known as the huggy type. He beamed, turning to check out the stands. Again, his gaze went to the empty seat reserved for Mimi. He frowned. As he turned back, a frantically waving fan caught his eye. It was Francie. She was bouncing in her seat, making thumbs up at him, and grinning. He chuckled. Damn, she was one energetic chick. He doffed his cap to her.

"Think you can get over yourself long enough to get back out on the field?" Matt Jackson asked.

"Sorry, sorry," Skip mumbled, picking up his glove.

Bobby joined Skip, running out to their respective positions for the top of the seventh inning. Skip pounded his fist into the pocket of his glove and crouched down into position. He caught the signal from Matt and shifted to the left. Matt signaled that the batter, a lefty, would pull the ball. Skip was squarely between second and third base.

Sure enough, the D.C. player smacked a line drive right at Skip, who simply straightened up and opened his glove. The ball hit hard, but he felt it only a little. His calloused hands had been fielding line drives since he was ten. They were used to the ever-increasing speed and force of a fly ball.

One away—only eight outs away from a first game win for the Nighthawks—courtesy of Skip Quincy. However, anything could happen with eight outs left in the game. Skip, a seasoned player, didn't take it for granted that they had it in the bag. He narrowed his eyes, trained his gaze on Matt, and shifted to his right. Thank God Matt Jackson was so good. His memory of each batter was a key factor in the excellent fielding that made the Nighthawks famous. Skip's chest swelled a bit with gratitude for his teammate, an unsung hero of the game.

The next batter hit one out of the park, making the score six to four. Skip licked his lips, rotated his arm, and sweated. Was it the sun or the pressure of the game causing him to perspire?

THE NIGHTHAWKS SQUEAKED out a win, seven to six in the bottom of the tenth inning. Jake Lawrence had knocked in the winning run. The team headed for the locker room. The men were exhausted. Skip peeled off his soaking wet jersey, and his undershirt, too. He stopped short when he remembered he'd left his watch in the dugout. He brought that timepiece with him to every game. His parents had given it to him the Christmas before they were killed. He'd considered it lucky. He didn't have much to remember them by, so no way was he losing that. Still hot and sweaty, he ran out, looking around until he spotted it.

He grabbed two bottles of water. After downing one, he opened the other and poured it over his head. The cool liquid ran down his face and chest. He closed his eyes and grinned as the relief hit his skin. Repeated clicks drew his attention. He looked up to spy Francie, standing nearby, snapping pictures. He shook his head, sending water droplets flying. *Crazy girl!*

She inched closer.

"Say, can you give me a lift to Freddie's?"

"Elena not going?" he replied, drying himself with a small towel.

"She and Bobby want to spend...uh, quality time together before you guys go on the road."

"I get it," he replied. "Okay. Sure. Wait in the parking lot. You know where my car is?"

She shook her head. Skip gave her instructions and headed back to the locker room. There was something about that girl that kept interfering with his dreams about Mimi taking off her clothes. When he thought of Francie, pert was the word that came to mind. And that included more than her rack. Hell, she was only twenty-six, and he was turning thirty-one in January—much too old for a young chick like her—wasn't he?

Besides, Mimi had been married. She'd know her way around the bedroom. Skip doubted Francie had had much experience with men. She didn't have the flirtatious ways of women who'd had major sexual relationships. Francie was direct, up front—with the truth popping out of her mouth before she could censor it.

She'd made him laugh with her keen observations of situations and people. Sure, she was smart and a hugely talented artist. But she hadn't tried to seduce him, shoot him knowing glances, or run her hands seductively down his leg or chest. He'd assumed she liked being his little sister.

Skip wished he'd returned that feeling. He'd tried, but no way could he keep her in sister-mode. She had an innate sexuality that oozed out of her and called to him. So far, he'd managed to keep his hands off her, but, if things didn't pan out with Mimi, he had no idea how much longer he could pretend to be Francie's big brother.

Disappointment at Mimi's no-show act didn't dampen his expectation that she'd meet him at Freddie's afterward. She'd promised to have a bite to eat with him, so he was sure she'd show. He hoped to soften Mimi up enough to get her into his bed after the playoff series. She'd begged off so far, saying it was too soon and she didn't know him well enough. He'd respected that and hadn't pushed. If they won the playoffs, then maybe she'd celebrate with him in the bedroom.

He had another game tomorrow but then they'd hit the road. Tonight was his last night with Mimi and Francie, too. This was a best-of-five game series. They'd have two games in D. C. if a fourth was necessary. Skip doubted they could wipe out the Wolverines in three straight, but he didn't doubt they'd win overall. So, there could be two in Washington, then, if they were tied, another game back in New York.

That should give Mimi plenty of time to figure out where she stood. Tonight, Skip would get closer to her, try to reassure her he wasn't looking for a one-night stand. He'd had enough of those to last a lifetime.

At his age, settling down looked good. Being around someone he liked and could talk to coupled with steady, dependable sex had pushed him over the line from bachelor to a man looking to tie the knot. Mimi Banner, widow of a baseball star, had experience. She should be perfect for the job, right? He'd find out soon enough.

He dressed quickly, slapped on new aftershave, and headed for the parking lot. He whistled as he walked until his gaze landed on Francie. She stood, facing away from him, so he had a moment to study her, undetected. The sun on her hair made it shine. Her peachy skin was a little pinker due to the heat and the contrast with her T-shirt. Her slender body showed off her curves to perfection. He called out her name and waved.

She turned to face him, her grin lighting up her pretty face. Skip hit the unlock button, walked around to the passenger side, and opened the door for her.

"Wow. No one's done that for me, like ever. Thank you."

He slid behind the wheel. "Next stop, Freddie's."

He pulled out of the parking lot, controlling the wheel with one hand and loosening his tie with the other.

"Too damn hot for a tie today."

"You were amazing," she said.

"Thanks. I had a good day."

"I'll say. That homer was a game-winner."

"Actually, Jake's won the game."

"But without yours, there wouldn't have even been a tie. The Wolverines would have won in nine."

"True." She was his biggest fan. Even his adoptive mom didn't rave about him like Francie did. Could it be there was something more there than an admiring "sister"?

He maneuvered the vehicle into the last space in Freddie's small parking lot. There'd be plenty of teammates there, the unmarried ones.

The ones with wives would be home, having sex with their wives before they had to hit the road.

A cheer went up when he and Francie entered the bar. Skip grinned and raised his hands. Matt and Dan started a cheer, which caught on throughout the restaurant. Skip steered Francie to the Nighthawks' table with his hand on the small of her back. A quick glance around told him Mimi hadn't arrived yet. His eyebrows rose. Was she coming?

He pulled out a chair for Francie and sat next to her. They ordered drinks and steaks.

"Put hers on my bill, Tommy," Skip said, his eyes still searching for Mimi.

"Sure thing."

"You don't have to do that. It's not like I'm your date or anything."

"Don't worry about it. Let me take care of it."

She glanced at her hands. "Well, okay. If you insist."

He raised her chin with a finger and stared into her eyes. They were wide, trusting, and beautiful grays. "I do, squirt. I do."

She brushed away his hand and scowled. "Don't call me squirt. It's not like I'm your sister or anything."

"It's a damn good thing, too. Because what I'm thinkin' could get me in a lotta trouble if you were."

Next to him, Matt laughed.

"Well, well. Ten minutes late and replaced already." Mimi stood behind him with her arms crossed.

Skip turned. "There you are. I've been lookin' for you."

"I bet you have." Mimi shot a hostile glance at Francie. The younger woman's cheeks pinked.

Skip pushed to his feet. "Come on, sit down."

"Can we have our own table?"

"You don't want to celebrate the playoff victory with the 'Hawks? I get it." Skip shot a warm smile to Francie, then left the table. Tommy found them one nearby. Skip held out Mimi's chair. After sitting down, she pulled a manila envelope from under her arm.

"What's that?" he asked, taking his seat.

"The pictures."

"Pictures?"

"Did you forget posing for me?"

"No, no. I didn't forget. Keep your voice down, please."

"Why?"

"Because the guys'll pass the pictures around the restaurant. I wouldn't be surprised if they didn't snap pics and put them on the Net."

"Wanna see?" Her eyes sparkled as a smile graced her lips.

"Sure."

She drew out several and put them on the table, face up. Upon viewing his own naked butt, Skip grabbed the envelope and placed it over the photos.

"What's the matter?"

"I don't want Tommy or the guys to see."

"That's so silly. You look great."

"Yeah, yeah. They'll torture me."

She thumbed through the first few, pulling out one from the middle. "This is my favorite."

Skip studied it. She'd taken this from behind him. It was a full body shot, showing his muscles. He grinned.

"Damn. I look pretty good."

"You look damn good," she said.

Skip put the picture down. "If I look so good, are you ready to get like naked with me?"

Mimi's gaze dropped to her hands. "It's too soon. I'm sorry, Skip. I know you want more. But I'm just not ready."

He took her hand between his. "It's been a couple of weeks now."

"It's hard to explain. Things with Rowley weren't good. Especially the last six months. I know it's been over a year, but I can't seem to get past all the ghosts."

"Ghosts?"

"Stuff that went on. I don't want to talk about our sex life, if you could call it that."

"Fine with me. I don't want to know. But I'm not like him. Honest. I'm a gentle guy."

She slid her hand away. "I know. It isn't you, it's me. And what happened. I thought I could get over it fast, but I was wrong."

"I can be patient," he said, ignoring the hunger in his body.

"I want to be fair. To you. To me. I can't tell you when I'll be ready for a physical relationship."

His lips formed a tight line. If she'd have given him a date, he could wait. But open-ended, who-knows-when turned him off.

He brought her hand to his lips. "I'd never hurt you."

She sported a nervous smile but still averted her gaze.

Tommy came over. Skip flipped the photo over and ordered their food. Mimi sat quietly, then looked over at the Nighthawks' table. Skip followed her gaze. Francie was talking to some guy.

"She might be a better bet for you."

He didn't reply. She took out the other pictures and handed them to him.

"I like the first one best. I'm going to use it in a showing I'm having in Miami."

"Miami?"

"I'm going down there for a few months. See if I like it enough to move."

"You're moving to Florida?" His eyebrows shot up.

"Thinking about it."

"What about us?"

"There is no us."

"Really?"

"Don't get me wrong. I like you, Skip. It's just that I'm not in the market for another relationship. Not now, anyway."

He dropped his gaze to his hands, then busied himself taking a drink of water. She slid her hand over his.

"But I'm always open to new friends."

He looked up, a rueful grin stretching his lips. "Friends I got, Mimi. Lovers? Not so much."

Could he believe her? Would such a hot woman want to go to bed alone every night? He toyed with his French fries and tried not to stare at her chest but failed.

Chapter Four

After driving Mimi home, Skip returned to his apartment. He paced. Loneliness shivered through him in the suffocating quiet. Where was the sound of a woman's voice? Then, clear as the night sky, he heard his birth mother's voice in his head.

"Skip. Skip, darling. Would you come here?"

Of course, he'd obeyed.

"Sweetheart, would you be my little man and take out the garbage? Daddy's so tired he fell asleep on the sofa."

Skip recalled picking up the heavy bag and trudging down the stairs, under his mother's adoring eyes. His father worked two jobs to support them. Skip wondered if that had led to the car accident that killed them.

His mother had packed an egg sandwich and woken Skip up at five. Silently, they loaded their luggage into the car. His father slid behind the wheel. Skip was freezing until the heat in the car kicked in. It was dark, black as night, outside. He shuddered as his father turned over the motor.

"Next stop, the beach!" his dad had whispered with a grin.

The rhythmic movement of the car lulled him to sleep, as always. He remembered those final words. They were headed for a family vacation. Skip had closed his eyes, dreaming of building in the sand with his dad. When he opened them again, his world had been turned upside down, his parents were dead, and the peaceful happiness he had enjoyed with them was gone forever.

He rubbed his hand down his face, feeling the beginnings of stubble, yawned, and glanced at his watch. With a sigh, he thought of his birth parents as he undressed. They would have been so proud. His cell rang. It was the Quincy's.

"Oh, Skip! You were wonderful," Ellen Quincy gushed.

"Thanks, Ma."

"You did okay. Next time, hit a grand slammer."

Skip shook his head. No pleasing that man.

"What's the schedule?" Ellen asked.

"We play here tomorrow, then go to D.C. for one, maybe two games."

"And when Washington beats your ass?" Bart asked.

"One more game here."

"You'll win. I just know it."

"Thanks, Ma. Listen, I'd like to talk, but I gotta get to sleep. Game's on tomorrow."

"Okay, son. Sleep well and good luck." His mother signed off.

He sighed. Still no getting anything from the old man, even after all these years. He washed up and eased into bed. His body was a bit stiff from the running, crouching, and the tension of the game. He lay back and closed his eyes, wishing for a sexy woman with good hands to appear. But no such luck. He'd almost have traded sex for a good massage.

The alarm jolted him from an erotic dream. He rubbed his eyes and rolled over. Geez, a woody. He'd have to take care of it himself. Shit. How disappointing after his dream. As he padded to the bathroom, he remembered that the woman in the dream had been Francie Whitman, not Mimi Banner. He shook his head and laughed as he turned on the shower.

He arrived at the stadium early. After yesterday, he needed to stretch his muscles and get a quick massage from the trainer. After changing into workout clothes, he opened a brown bag and took out a bacon and egg sandwich. He wolfed it down.

"Okay, Skip, you're next." The trainer wiped his hands on a towel. Skip stretched out on the table and let Vic Steele pummel his muscles and rub a little oil into his skin.

"How's it goin'?" Vic asked him.

"Okay. We gotta win today. Gotta keep the pressure on."

"You will."

"But Dan's not pitching. Our new guy, Jason Bowers is."

"He's amazing," Vic said.

"Where'd he come from?"

"We got him from San Francisco. He'll blow those assholes out of the park," Vic replied.

Skip smiled, then closed his eyes and let Vic work his magic.

Back in the locker room, Skip stretched as Bobby Hernandez entered.

"Wanna run?" Skip asked his buddy.

"Sure. In a minute."

He stared at the second baseman. "You're looking good."

"He probably got laid last night. Unlike you," Jake put in as he passed by.

"Fuck off, Lawrence."

"No thanks. I already did. Last night," Jake snickered, backing toward the field.

"Dickwad!" Skip called. He tied his shoes and looked up. Bobby was warming up.

"Let's go," the second baseman said, grabbing Skip's arm.

"Did you get laid?"

"Engaged men never talk. Run, asshole. We've got work to do." Bobby took off, loping along the grass. Skip caught up, and the men jogged side-by-side. They saved their breath for the workout. His teammates buoyed Skip's confidence.

After running, the men did light workouts, then it was time to eat. A big buffet tempted Skip. A meat-and-potatoes man, he loaded his plate with roast beef and a baked potato.

"Don't forget the veggies," Bobby chided, elbowing his buddy.

"Okay, okay. Salad. I get it."

The men passed big pitchers of milk and juice around a long table. Skip took a seat between Bobby and Matt Jackson.

"That asshole Weeks almost got you," Matt said.

"Dickwad," Skip muttered between bites.

"Next time, I'll throw the ball at his head," Dan said.

The men laughed.

Chatter about the players on the other team continued. Matt had insights to share and then Cal Crawley addressed the men. He was a soft-spoken man who rarely busted a gut in anger. Sensible, intelligent, and experienced, he'd led the team to more than one World Series.

Skip grabbed a bunch of grapes for dessert and headed for the showers. Time to suit up and hit the field.

FRANCIE HAD BEEN UP at five, poring over her photos. One stood out to her.

"That's it," she muttered to herself, as she headed for her make-shift art studio in a corner of the small one-bedroom apartment. Francie kept the tiny space immaculate and organized.

She had uploaded the pictures on her iPad. Then she blew up the one she wanted to full screen. She picked up a brush, dabbed it in the watered down brown paint, and outlined her picture. Her cell rang. It was Elena.

"You coming to the game?"

"Of course."

"Shall I pick you up?"

"If you want. Or I can take the subway."

"It's okay. I'll swing by at one. Game starts at two. Okay?"

"Perfect."

Since it was only nine that gave her plenty of time to get started on her new work. She'd decided that this piece would be the one she'd enter in the Maya Colby Art contest. If she won, she'd be a shoo-in to get into the Paris art program. Even placing second or third would help her. She had to make this her best piece, take her time and do it right.

Francie put on an old shirt of her father's and got into the zone. She worked in layers, mapping out the space and mixing colors. Her phone buzzed.

"Oh, crap! Elena. I forgot. Give me five minutes."

"Relax, we have time. I'm a little early 'cause I knew you'd forget."

"Very funny. I'll be dressed in five."

"Take ten and look your best." Her friend chuckled.

Francie had laid out clothes the night before. She wiggled into tight stretch jeans and pulled on a deep pink T-shirt. After running a comb through her hair, she applied some makeup.

"Why am I putting on eyeliner? No one's going to see me."

She shrugged and continued adding some artful touches to her pretty face. Skip Quincy wasn't no one. Of course, he'd be boarding the bus for D.C. after the game, but maybe she could grab a soda with him before he left. She shrugged and followed Elena's advice.

"Always look your best, full makeup before you step out of the house. You never know who you'll meet."

Mascara and rose lipstick completed the task. She wrapped her paintbrush in a paper towel and headed out the door.

Once they took their seats, Francie remembered she'd forgotten to eat lunch.

"Where's the hot dog guy? I'm starving!"

Elena flagged him down. Francie ordered two hot dogs, fries, and a beer.

"You eat like a man," Elena said, munching on a frankfurter.

"Can I help it if I missed lunch?"

"Are you so into a new picture?"

"Yes, and it's just like when you're into a new book. I lose track of time, space, everything."

"I can't wait to see it."

"I think this is going to be my best yet. I'm hoping it will place in the Colby art show."

"That would be amazing! You're so talented. You deserve to win."

"Then my stepmother will have to acknowledge that I'm good."

"Who cares what she thinks? Soon, you'll be old enough to take over the trust fund and she can go to Hell."

"Yeah, but that's too late for art school."

"Maybe for the spring semester. But there's always fall."

"I suppose," Francie replied, offering her fries to her friend.

The men came out on the field and stood for the national anthem. Francie's heart fluttered when she spied the shortstop. She put her food on her chair and her hand over her heart. But her gaze was on Skip. She sang along with him. When the song finished, he glanced up and caught her eye. He smiled and doffed his cap. Heat warmed her cheeks.

"If you go to Paris, you won't be able to come to the games," Elena said.

"I know. Everything comes with a sacrifice."

Her friend chuckled. "I could feel that all the way up here," Elena whispered, staring at Skip.

"We're just friends. He treats me like his little sister."

"Think again, Francie. You two have chemistry."

"I wish." She picked up the second hot dog. Adoration didn't put a damper on her appetite.

"FRANCIE'S HERE AGAIN," Skip said to Bobby as they took their positions.

"I know. Elena told me."

"It's nice."

"Francie's got a thing for you," Bobby said.

"I don't think so. She looks at me as a big brother."

Bobby laughed. "In your dreams."

"You think so?"

"Everybody but you knows it. She's hot for you, buddy. Go for it."

"Play ball!" The umpire shouted as he threw the ball to Jason Bowers.

"Focus, Skip. Plenty of time when we get back to move in on her," Jake said, heading to third.

Skip shook his head and laughed. One minute, Bobby was threatening him if he even asked Francie out. The next, he was pushing them into bed. Guys, go figure. He took his position in a crouch, glove open, and followed the ball.

The game was close until the seventh. After Jason walked three batters in a row, Cal took him out. Spencer Larkin, their new relief pitcher, took the mound. The batter hit Larkin's first pitch out of the park, knocking in four runs.

The Nighthawks couldn't bounce back and the Wolverine's won, six to three. The atmosphere in the locker room was subdued. Skip changed then hung around outside, waiting for the bus.

"Hey, stranger," came a female voice.

He turned around and spotted Francie.

"Thanks for coming to the game. Sorry we lost."

"Me, too. But you played well."

"Almost had an error. Bobbled the damn ball. Should have been more careful."

"There's a lot of tension in these games. It's easy to make a mistake."

"No room for mistakes in pro baseball," Skip said, shaking his head. He leaned against a car, his gaze perusing her.

"It's nice you come to the games."

"Whenever I can. School is mostly at night." She rested her rump against a car door.

He nodded. "Means a lot."

"Doesn't Mimi come to watch you play?"

"Nah. She said the games make her nervous."

"You sound like you don't believe her."

"Who am I to say? But Rowley played and I'm guessing she went to some of his games. The wives always come. Not to every game, but to some."

"I wouldn't want to miss one. I mean, if I was married to a player. Not that I would be. I don't have any plans, I mean. Just sayin'." Francie stumbled over her words.

"Yeah. I get it. Some of them show up just to make sure their guy doesn't meet anyone after the game."

"Do married players do that?" She straightened up.

"Not many. But there are always a couple of assholes on the team." He shrugged.

"Would you do that? I mean if you were married?"

"Hell no. Not that I have any plans or anything. I mean, I'm not moving in that direction."

She shook her head. "Of course not. Why would you?" Francie cast her gaze to the ground.

"That's a lie. A big fat lie," Skip blurted out.

Her head snapped up. "It is?"

"Yeah. I wish I had what those guys have."

"You want to get married."

"All guys do, I think. Some sooner than others."

"I guess."

"What about you?" His gaze met hers. Her cheeks reddened.

"Haven't thought about it," she said, avoiding his eyes.

"I don't believe you. Every woman thinks about marriage."

She stiffened.

"Don't get me wrong. I don't think that's bad. Honest," he said, backpedaling.

"Some men do. Some men think women want to trick them into marriage. That marriage is all for the woman and nothing for the man. That's not true. I'm going to be a professional artist and teach to earn my living. I won't need a man to have a good life."

"Need, want. Maybe not the same thing. Don't you want to get married? Live with a man?"

"Maybe. Someday. When the right guy comes along." Again, she didn't look at him, but the color in her cheeks gave her away.

"Yeah? Well, maybe he already has."

She raised her head, their eyes met. Before she could respond, another voice rang out.

"Watson!"

Skip turned around. "Billy? Billy Holmes?" Because his last name was Holmes and Skip had been his sidekick, Billy'd always called him *Watson*, like the sidekick in the Sherlock Holmes books and movies.

"That's right, buddy. Holmes is back."

"I've got work to do and you've got a friend here, so I'll be saying goodbye. Elena's driving me home. Good luck in Washington. I'll be rooting for you," Francie said, heading for Elena's car.

"Wait, Billy," Skip said, then faced Francie. "Thanks, Francie. Means a lot, you watching." Skip said, catching up with her. "How about a good luck kiss?" She stopped short, and he lowered his mouth to hers. The kiss was short but intense. "Now we can't lose," he murmured.

"Good luck," she said, then was gone.

Billy came up behind him. "Hey, sorry if I spoiled something with your girl."

"She's not my girl. Just a friend."

"Yeah, right." Billy shot him a knowing smile.

"What are you doing here?"

"Came to see my old buddy."

The men shook hands. "Good to see you. What are you doing these days?"

"Just got out of jail."

Skip raised his eyebrows. His old pal from the orphanage had had little guidance from caring people. He had not been adopted. Skip wondered if Billy resented him for getting out of that place. If he'd known that Skip's life hadn't been exactly *Leave It to Beaver*, he wouldn't be jealous.

"Yeah. I violated parole after doing three for our car theft. You got off easy."

"I was twelve."

"Right, right. I didn't mind. Honest. It was all my idea. You only tagged along."

"I was sorry you had to do time. What are you doing now?"

"I got a chance to study auto mechanics through a mail order course in jail. I learned a lot. I want to set up my own shop."

"That's great!" Relief flooded Skip. Billy had been his first and only friend at Little Angels. He'd been grateful the teen had taken pity on him. Billy had been the big brother Skip had always wanted. After the joyride, Skip got a tongue lashing, and Billy got juvie. Obviously, he'd gotten into some bad stuff after that. Skip didn't want to know what his friend had done.

"Yeah. I found a partner. But I need to come up with fifty grand for my half of the business."

"Fifty grand?"

"Yeah. Sting has the building and the equipment, but he doesn't know shit about cars. I do. So, he said I could buy in for fifty large."

"You want me to give it to you?"

"A loan. Just a loan. I'll pay it back. Promise."

"Look the bus will be here any minute. Let me think about it while we're on the road. When do you need to know?"

"As soon as possible. Sting said he'd give me three weeks to raise it."

"Good. Fine."

"Look, I'll sign papers. And I got a certificate," Billy said, pulling out a piece of paper from his pocket and unfolding it. "See? I graduated. An eighty-five average, too."

Skip studied the paper for a second. Billy was telling the truth. Before he could ask any questions, the bus pulled into the parking lot.

"It looks good. I'll probably do it. Give me a week. Congratulations on the course. I'm proud of you."

"Proud of me? Hell, you're the star. I'm proud of you, buddy. You done real good."

Bobby came by and punched Skip in the arm, gently. "Let's go. Bus is here."

Skip and Billy hugged briefly. His friend thrust a piece of paper in Skip's hand. "That's my number. Call me when you get back."

"I will." Billy walked toward the bus with Skip.

"Good luck. I hope you win."

"Me, too." Skip nodded, then boarded. He'd been stunned to see his old friend. He had heard Billy had gotten in trouble but didn't know the details. He was relieved that the Holmes to his Watson had chosen a better path. Did he have the money to lend Billy? He sure did. After the playoffs, he'd call Verna Carruthers, his financial advisor, and see what his situation was and how fast he could get the money to Billy.

Although he felt beholden to Billy on several levels, he wondered if he could truly trust his friend. It had been years since they had been in touch. People think ballplayers are rolling in dough and fifty-thousand is nothing to them. It wasn't true. Would Billy turn out to be one of those people and take his money and run?

Chapter Five

The bus rolled into the parking lot of the D.C. hotel about midnight. Most of the players had slept in their seats on the way down. Weary and anxious to get into bed, Skip trudged off the vehicle and picked up his suitcase in the lobby.

The men checked in quickly and soon he was up in his room. Unfortunately, due to the nap on the way down, he was now wide awake. He laced his fingers behind his head as he lay in bed, naked under a sheet and two blankets. God, how he hated lying there alone. His mind drifted to the women in his life. In his life? In his dreams! He didn't have a woman in his life and it bugged him.

He went to the bathroom for water, then stopped at the window. The city was asleep. Except for a few street lamps softly twinkling in the distance, it was mostly dark. They were staying a hop-skip from the Washington stadium, on the outskirts of town. Bored, he reached into his bag for a book.

He'd bought one of Elena Delgado's romance novels. Bobby had been seen reading them and raved about how good they were. He knew Francie read them, too. He needed to know what it was all about. Climbing back in bed, he got comfortable and switched on the bedside lamp. Opening the book, he started on the first page.

At two o'clock, he tore himself away from the story and turned out the light. He knew he'd regret staying up so late, but it was a done deal. Who knew romance books could be so intriguing?

Though the game was a night game, he awoke to a loud banging on his door at ten a.m.

"We know you've got a woman in there. Open up!"

Groggy, he started, grabbing his robe and padding toward the hall. On the way, he recognized the voices of a few of his teammates and shook his head.

"What the fuck do you guys want?" Skip flung open the door. Bobby, Matt, Dan, and Jake stood there, wearing complacent grins.

"Well, it's about fucking time, Sleeping Beauty," Matt said.

"Where's the girl?" Jake pushed into the room and searched.

"There's no girl in here," Skip said.

"Look! Look what I found!" Jake held up the book.

"Gimme that," Skip said, grabbing the book and almost ripping the cover.

"You're reading one of my girl's books?" Bobby asked.

"Yeah. So, what?"

"Which one?"

"Love's Last Chance. Wanna make something of it?" Skip fisted his right hand.

"Good choice, man. I read that one. Pretty steamy."

Skip's face broke into a grin. "I know. I couldn't put it down. That's one hot chick in that book."

Matt and Dan whipped out their phones and ordered the book online on the spot.

"Get dressed or you'll miss breakfast. Cal was looking for you," Bobby said.

"Okay. Give me five."

Jake sat down in a chair in the room and opened the book. "We'll wait," he said, perusing the first page.

"Don't get your damn drool on the pages, asshole," Skip said, heading for the bathroom.

Skip joined his buddies as they walked down two flights to the private dining room in the motel. A handful of Nighthawks' players were already there. A few were finishing their coffee and others, like Skip and his crew, were just hitting the breakfast buffet. Skip sat next to Julio Suarez, one of the Nighthawks' starting pitchers.

"That fuckin' Weeks," Nat Owen said. "He just missed spiking Skip in the first game."

"I'll hit Weeks right in the sac," Suarez said.

"Don't get thrown out of the game. That'll just make the dickwad happy," Matt said, cutting up a piece of melon.

"And we'll lose. We need you, Julio," Jake said.

When the men finished eating, there was a team meeting with Cal Crawley in another room. The men listened to strategy and watched game footage for an hour. After, Skip slipped up to his room for a nap. He read Elena's book until his eyes began to close.

His alarm woke him at five and he got ready for dinner, then the game.

While he showered and shaved, he gave himself a pep talk. They needed to win this game to break the tie in their favor. He tied his tie and headed for the lobby to catch the bus to the stadium.

Mild confusion reigned in the visiting team's locker room. It always happened. Skip thought he was used to it, but today it rankled. Maybe because this was such an important game. It took him five minutes to find his locker. Pissed off, he changed into sweats, mumbling about the facilities while he waited for Vic Steele.

"Okay. Let's go. Stretching first. Then running—twenty minutes."

Someone in the back objected.

"Okay, okay, fifteen minutes. Then a light workout in the weight room."

The weight room. Fuck. Skip would have to figure out how much weight to use on each machine. Sometimes the equipment differed from what they had in the 'Hawks room. Vic kept a record, but only an idiot wouldn't know his own routine, right? He scowled at himself in the mirror.

"Bad mood?" Vic asked, checking off Skip's name as the shortstop headed for the field.

"You could say."

"Too bad. Get over it. This is an important game."

"Exactly. Fuckin' sucks," Skip muttered.

"What?" Vic asked.

"Everything." Skip put his foot on a bench and stretched his leg muscles. Bobby joined him.

"Elena here?"

Bobby shook his head.

"How come?" Skip asked, bending toward the bench.

"She had an interview with a magazine about her book. Besides, it's a short trip."

"So, you didn't get laid last night?"

"Makes it all the sweeter when I get home," the second baseman said, wiggling his eyebrows and grinning.

Skip had to laugh. Leave it to Bobby to be silly enough to cut through the tension.

He slapped Skip on the back. "Come on. Let's run it off."

The two men headed for the field, starting off at a lope and increasing their speed as they went along. After the workout, Skip waited to get to the shower. He checked his phone, disappointed there was no message from Mimi. But there was a text from someone else:

Good luck today. No class tonight. I'll be watching.

Francie

He didn't think anything could make him smile. But Francie did. She'd thought about him. His heart swelled. It had been a long time since anyone had gone out of their way to encourage him. His mother did, from time to time. His dad, never. He hadn't had a steady girl for the past three years.

It was Jackie in college. Then Rita for two years, then Susan, then Beth, then a series of one-night stands or road trip "relationships". The traveling killed everything for him. Either they cheated on him, or, worse, they'd show up on the road trying to catch him cheating. Not that he didn't want to, from time to time, but he wasn't built that way.

The minute a girl showed up at his hotel, searching for telltale signs that a woman had shared Skip's room, an argument would ensue. She'd embarrass him in front of the team. Keeping tabs on him, or as the guys would say, "putting him on a short leash", ground his guts, and fired his temper. The girl's visit would precipitate infuriating comments from his buddies it took him months to live down. Refusing to knuckle under to female domination, he'd dump the chick.

One of the many things he found attractive about Mimi was that she had been the wife of a player. She knew the score, had dealt with Rowley being on the road. He assumed he'd never have those jealousy issues with her. Rowley had a rep with the guys as a cheater. But if what Mimi said was true, he'd also had problems getting it up—stemming from his steroid use. So maybe he'd been faithful on the road and the crap was just rumor.

No relationship lasted more than two years for Skip. He had trust issues, coming from his background and from the discovery of a couple of girlfriends dating other guys while Skip was away. After the last one, Beth, he'd decided to stop trying to find the perfect woman to marry, and simply settle for available sex and a bit of companionship, whenever he could find it.

He had to admit that was like Chinese food—an hour later you were hungry again. Skip wanted, no—needed, a family, a real family. Someone he could count on to love him and be there. Every year the need grew, stabbing his heart, emphasizing his loneliness. He'd only have a few more years playing ball. If he didn't have something cooking outside of the stadium by then, he'd be in trouble. The glamour of being a pro ballplayer would be gone, and he'd simply be another horny guy in a bar, looking to get laid. The idea threw a cold shiver through him.

At four, the men chowed down in a private room at the stadium. The game was scheduled to start at six, so they needed to fuel up early. He sat with Nat Owen. From the few conversations he'd had with Nat, he'd realized the two men had much in common. Nat was looking for the same thing Skip was, a woman he could count on to build a family with. Nat had found his, through the most convoluted, obstacle-filled path possible. Still, his teammate smiled for no reason, kept his temper, and played his best games ever this season. Skip guessed Nat was doing something right.

When the national anthem finished, Skip donned his cap and headed for the dugout. They were up first. Skip was starting the lineup today. He grabbed a bat and swirled it around, loosening up his arm. He sauntered to the batter's box and narrowed his eyes at the pitcher. A quick glance at the third base coach, who was shooting signals, told him, he was free to swing or take.

Shouldering the bat, he took his stance and jumped on the first pitch. He connected, smacking it right between the shortstop and third baseman for a base hit. Skip took off for first. He arrived safely, enjoying a nod from Cal and thumbs up from his teammates. A hit on the first pitch of the game shifted things in favor of the Nighthawks.

Capitalizing on Skip's strong start, the Nighthawks went on to win the third playoff game, four to two. While the scores were close, and one run scored on a Wolverine error, the scale tipped in favor of the 'Hawks. That didn't last.

The Wolverine's pulled it together and squeaked out a win in the fourth game in Washington, three to two.

With both teams winning two games, the fifth, and last, game would decide who played in the Championship Series. Skip was grateful they would be on his home turf—Hingus Stadium, home of the Nighthawks. Each team would give everything they had for this last game. With the players so evenly matched, the outcome was anyone's guess.

After the game, the men showered and dressed quickly. Their luggage was already loaded on the bus. The guys with wives and girlfriends at home were in a big hurry to return to New York. Skip was, too. He'd asked Mimi to meet him at The Hideout, the nightclub the Nighthawks frequented.

The teams had the next day off as a travel day before the fifth, and final, game, which would be played at night. Most of the playoff games were in the evening, to reach the most fans and cash in on a huge television audience. Except the weekend games—which were all daytime games to draw fans to the stadium and the television.

Mimi had said she'd be there if she could, but she had a photo shoot that afternoon and didn't know when it would break up. Skip had invited her to join him if she could. He wondered if Francie would be tagging along with Elena and Bobby. Maybe Bobby preferred to spend the evening in the bedroom with his girl? If no one showed, up, he'd bet he could find a girl who wanted to spend the night with him. Any way he turned it, he'd be a winner.

Jake, Nat, and Matt joined Skip, sharing a cab to the club. Bobby begged off, embarrassed when they guessed what he'd be doing. Still, it didn't make him abandon Elena for the company of his teammates. They understood. Bobby was the newest man to find his woman. The others were meeting their women at The Hideout for a little dinner and dancing before they headed home for a night of vigorous exercise between the sheets.

The bouncers nodded to the players and admitted them. Loud music greeted Skip's ears. He loosened his tie and unbuttoned the top button of his shirt. His eyes adjusted to the darkness as he eased up to the bar. Even though they had a day and a half before they had to play again, he wasn't taking any chances and ordered a ginger ale. His buddies did the same.

The 'Hawks stood together, sipping their drinks and perusing the crowd. One-by-one each infielder was hailed by his girl. They disappeared into the dining area with their chicks, leaving Skip on his own. He checked his watch. Mimi was supposed to be there fifteen minutes ago.

He shook his head. She was unreliable. But that wasn't news. He wondered why he kept asking her out. The music got to him and he found himself moving to the beat. A redhead sidled over to him and matched her moves to his. She had a nice body and pretty face. Skip smiled.

"Samantha," she shouted over the music.

"Skip," he returned, then took her hand and led her out to the dance floor.

After the song finished, he put his palm on the small of her back and guided her to the bar.

"Whatcha drinkin'?" he asked.

"Gin and tonic," she replied.

Skip ordered for both of them and paid for their drinks.

"Hello, stranger," said a female voice.

He looked up, right into the cool, gray eyes of Francie Whitman.

"Hey, Francie! Ya made it!"

The redhead nudged him in the ribs.

"Oh, yeah. This is Samantha. Samantha, Francie."

The women nodded at each other but not in a friendly way. Sweat broke out on his brow. He wiped it with a cocktail napkin.

The music started up again. A dark-haired man about three inches shorter than Skip reached out for Francie's hand.

"Wanna dance?"

"Sure."

She went off with the stranger, leaving Skip's brow furrowed.

"What's the problem?" the redhead asked, downing the rest of her drink.

"Don't know that guy."

"So? That's what this place is for. Meeting people. It's just a dance. She your girl or something?"

"Just a friend."

"What do you care?" Francie looked up at Skip, then faced the stranger. "Let's dance."

The redhead dragged Skip back out on the dance floor. He kept his eye on Francie while moving to the music with Samantha.

What did she mean by that? Of course, he cared. He cared a lot about Francie and didn't want that dickwad crowding her, getting her drunk, and taking advantage of her. When the dance was over, Samantha made a face.

"You've got a thing for that girl. Why don't you dance with her? Thanks for the drink."

Before he could reply, she moved on.

Francie leaned against the bar while her dance partner bought her a drink.

"Fucking sleaze," Skip muttered before joining them.

He stood next to Francie, who was deep in conversation with Mr. Asshole, as Skip had already tagged him.

"Skip Quincy, here. And you are?"

"And how's it your business? Can't you see I'm talking to this chick?"

"She's not a chick."

"Really? And she's none of your business, either, asshole," the man said, before turning his back to Skip.

"It's okay, Percy. I know him."

"Percy? Did you say, Percy?" Skip laughed hard, slapping the man on the back.

"Okay, asshole, wanna take this outside?"

"Percy? Really? Your real name is Percy?" Skip laughed so hard tears trickled down his face. Jake and Matt, with their women in tow, joined Skip.

"This asshole's name is Percy. And he's coming on to Francie," Skip said to his teammates, trying to keep a straight face.

"Coming on to Francie?" Matt frowned, turning his gaze on the young man.

"He's not doing anything. Back off, Skip. We're just talking," Francie piped up.

"Can a guy buy a woman a drink here without you goons descending on him?"

"Goons? Did you just call us goons?" Jake asked, his hand fisting at his side.

"Percy!" Skip dissolved in laughter again, slapping his thigh.

"I call goons as I see 'em," Percy said.

"Who are you? A fuckin' umpire?" Matt asked, pushing closer.

"Get offa me! I'm gonna call security."

"Do you know who we are...Percy?" Skip asked, barely able to hold a straight face.

"Yeah. A bunch of goons who intimidate guys in bars."

"Francie is a friend of his. And we're baseball players."

"Yeah, right. And I'm the Easter Bunny," Percy replied.

"You are?" Skip said, his lips quivering as he tried to contain his merriment. "Oh my God. Can I have your autograph? I've always wanted to meet the Easter Bunny! Hey, guys, Percy, here is the Easter Bunny!"

At that, all three Nighthawks burst into loud laughter, slapping each other on the back. Even Francie cracked a smile.

"Can I have your pawprint?" Matt asked, cracking up again.

"Turn around. Show us your fluffy tail," Nat said.

"What the fuck?" Percy looked around.

"They're laughing because they *are* pro baseball players. They're New York Nighthawks," she told him.

"No shit?"

"No shit," she responded.

"Then I should ask for their autographs."

"Uh, yeah."

Percy whipped out a piece of paper and a pen. "Would you guys sign for me?"

The men were howling with laughter, crying, doubled over. They each scribbled their names down while trying to catch their breath. Percy carefully folded the paper and put it in his pocket.

"You're dating New York Nighthawks?" he asked.

"Skip and I are just friends," she said.

Pushing by Skip, Percy took her hand and said, "Come on. My place or yours?"

Skip, wiping his cheek with the back of his hand, grabbed Percy's lapel with one hand.

"She's not going anywhere with you. She's my girl. You moved in on her. Now I suggest you leave before we wipe the floor with you."

Francie's mouth hung open. She stared at him.

"You were talking to a redhead," Percy said.

"Is this guy giving you trouble, Skip?" The bouncer's burly form appeared out of nowhere.

"Nope. He was just leaving. Right, Percy?"

"Aw, fuck you all," Percy said shooting the bird, and heading for the door.

"See you at Easter," Jake called out after him. Matt was still laughing.

"Don't forget the eggs!" Matt said, shaking his head. Jake fell against the bar, howling.

"Skip Quincy, this is the lowest thing you've ever done," Francie said.

"I know a mover when I see one. Someone's gotta look out for you."

"I have been looking out for myself since I was seven. I don't need you to chase away men." She folded her arms across her chest. "Besides, I wasn't going to leave with him."

"That was a love-'em-and-leave-'em type. Believe me. I oughta know."

"Why? Because you're one yourself?"

"Used to be."

"Oh? You've reformed? I don't think so. I'm going home." She threw her purse strap over her shoulder. Skip grabbed her arm.

"Don't go. Not yet. It's only ten."

"What's the point? If any guys come over to dance with me, you'll just call them names, intimidate them, and chase them away."

"Stay and dance with me." He took her hand as a new song started.

It was a slow tune, and he pulled her into his embrace. She pushed up on tiptoe at first but finally settled in, resting her head on his chest. Oddly, although she was much shorter than he, her body fit with his. He rested his cheek on her head. The sweet scent of coconut seduced his nose. Damn, she smelled good. He extended his long fingers from her shoulder to twirl a few strands of her silky black hair.

When the song ended, Francie stepped back, took a breath, and straightened her hair.

"Where's Mimi? Why isn't she here?"

"I don't know. And I don't care."

"That was fast."

"Hey, you don't have to hit me over the head with a hammer to say you're not interested."

"Really?"

"Come on, Francie. Do you want to tell me, honestly, after that dance, that we don't have chemistry?"

He stared at her and she blushed.

"I didn't think so." He grinned, lacing his fingers with hers.

"You treat me like a little sister," she blurted.

"I thought that's what you wanted."

She shook her head.

"Let's change that right now," he said, leaning over to press his lips against hers. She melted against him, resistance gone. Her curves softened against his hard muscle. He wanted her, right then and there. Skip put the brakes on, straightened up, and stepped back. A man standing behind him piped up.

"Get a room, buddy."

"Fuck off, moron," Skip said, his stare on Francie.

"Ya don't have to get hostile."

Jake, Matt, and Nat surrounded Skip.

"We're going," Matt said.

"Yeah. Gotta make up for lost time," Nat said, grinning.

Skip slapped them on the shoulder and nodded. "Got it. See you tomorrow."

"Tomorrow?" Francie asked, watching the three couples leave.

"Practice. It never stops."

She glanced at her watch. "It's late. Class tomorrow night. Gotta go. I have a lot to do to get ready."

"I'll take you home."

"I can take the subway."

"Come on. My car's right outside."

She glanced away from him, her hand trembled once as she reached for her bag. He'd never seen her like that. It warmed his heart. With one kiss, he'd made her shiver. Damn, he hadn't lost his touch.

"Come on, sweetheart," Skip said, heading for the street.

They bid the bouncers goodnight. Skip opened the door to his Lexus for her.

"You could come home with me."

"You're kidding, right?"

"Nope."

"I thought I was your little sister," she retorted.

"So did I. Until that kiss. That was no sisterly kiss."

"And that was no brotherly kiss, either."

He laughed. "You give as good as you get, don't you?"

Before she answered, he wondered if that was true in bed, too. A twinge in his dick warned him to stop thinking like that, especially while he was driving.

Chapter Six

Francie sat back against the leather seat in Skip's car. She'd had her limit: three drinks. Warmth coursed through her. She glanced at Skip's profile as he maneuvered the car through the West Side traffic. His looks took her breath away. Handsome, nice, and protective—maybe too much so. But what a combination—so different from her old boyfriend.

The alcohol had played tricks with her mind in the past, lowering her defenses. She'd given in to her sensual nature more times than she cared to recall. Never one to ignore birth control, the only regret she'd faced in the morning was waking up next to a foul-smelling, hung over, selfish guy who couldn't even remember her name.

She'd conquered that weakness and hadn't spent the night with a loser in a long time. In fact, she hadn't made love with anyone in an age. This was Skip Quincy, baseball star, decent man, and anything but a loser. She wanted him and had almost from the first time she'd met him. This was her chance, wasn't it?

Her brow knitted. To go with him or not to go with him, that was the question. Biting her lip, she stared out the window, ignoring the desire pumping through her veins. At the stoplight on 95th Street, he turned to her.

"What'll it be? Home or with me?"

The warmth in his eyes tipped the scales.

"With you," she said before she could change her mind.

He grinned, took her hand, and kissed it. The light changed, someone honked, and Skip stepped on the gas.

"You won't regret it. Believe me. You won't."

His deep voice wrapped itself around her, making her shiver. She chewed her lip for a moment as need grew in her belly. It had been too long since she'd had sex and forever since she'd had love. Could Skip provide both? She gave her head a little shake. *Don't blow this up to be something it's not. It's a convenient night of what you hope will be mind-blowing sex, nothing more.*

She met his gaze and smiled. She'd settle for a memorable night with the shortstop. He turned his attention back to the traffic. When they reached his building, he pulled into the lot in the basement, then escorted her to the elevator. She drew comfort from the fact that he lived in the same building as Bobby and Elena. If anything bad happened, she had a place to go.

He opened the door and let her enter first. After switching on a light in the entryway, he took her jacket and hung it in the front hall closet.

"I've got your favorite wine in the fridge. Moscato, right?"

"You remembered?"

He made an exaggerated bow.

"Thanks, but I've had enough."

"Mind if I have a beer?"

"Go ahead."

"We're on the wagon until after the series, but one beer is okay." He nabbed a bottle and screwed off the cap. She leaned against the small kitchen table and looked around. This was her first time in his place.

The kitchen was beautiful. Black appliances gleamed. Black granite counter tops provided a gorgeous contrast to the white cabinets. The place was immaculate.

"I never cook. And I have a housekeeper. Otherwise, this place would be a pigsty," he said, before taking a long swallow of his beverage. "You don't want anything? Cup of tea?"

"You know how to boil water?"

He laughed. "Hell, yeah. Who do you think I am, the Easter Bunny?"

She laughed. Skip put the empty bottle on the counter and drew her close. He tilted her chin up to receive his kiss. His lips were slightly cold, and he tasted deliciously like beer. He folded her into his embrace as his tongue swiped against her mouth. She opened, and he entered, seducing her with every move.

She inched closer, pressing her chest against his. Her nipples hardened. She knew he could feel that, a signal for him to take it further. He let out a sigh, raised his hand, and combed his fingers through her hair.

"Beautiful," he muttered, before continuing his assault on her mouth.

When he kissed down her neck, Francie closed her eyes. This was going exactly the way she had imagined. His arm around her waist tightened as his hand came up to cover her breast. When he touched it, electricity shot through her, kicking up every nerve ending.

She arched against him, pushing herself farther into his hand. He squeezed, making her jump slightly.

"Did I hurt you?" He muttered.

"Uh-uh. Nope. Don't stop," she breathed into his ear.

A salacious chuckle escaped his throat. "I hear you. Let's get more comfortable."

He broke from her and took her hand, leading her out of the kitchen, down a short hallway to his bedroom in the back. He flipped the light switch at the door. Soft light came from two bedside lamps. An issue of *Playboy* hogged the nightstand. The room was simple. White walls, dark wood floor, and dresser. One easy chair and a king-size bed, with a navy and white bedspread. Pictures on the walls were of famous ballplayers and mountain scenes.

Skip ripped his T-shirt over his head and tossed it on the chair.

"Come here, baby," he said, opening his arms. Francie didn't need another invitation. She was on him, running her hands down his chest, through the light brown hair there, and over his pecs. Touching him ignited a fire in her core.

He slipped his hand under her shirt and eased it up.

"Let's get rid of this. It's in the way," he said, tugging on her skirt.

Gripped by sudden shyness, Francie stepped back.

"Me first? No problem," he said unbuttoning his pants and pushing them off—then his boxers. He tossed them on the chair. Francie stared at him.

"Okay?"

Her mouth went dry and words stuck in her throat, she nodded.

His body was magnificent. Toned muscles in his abdomen matched the strong thighs and calves of his long legs. His broad shoulders, almost hidden by his dress shirts drew her eye. Then her gaze slipped down to his biceps bulging slightly. Of course, he had to have strong arms to do all that throwing.

"Your turn," he said, stepping closer.

The pulse in her neck sped up. Her gaze traveled down his fabulous chest, following the line of hair on his belly, leading to his dick. Her eyes widened as she unbuttoned her blouse. He was bigger than she'd expected and already getting larger. She swallowed saliva and fumbled with the catch on her skirt.

"Need help?" he asked, reaching around her to unclasp her bra. She let it fall away, down to the floor. He hissed at the sight of her bare breasts.

"Sweet!" `

His eyes almost burned her skin. He inched closer. Her heart beat faster as his hands closed around her breasts. She looked up, and he lowered his mouth. Angling his head, he deepened the kiss. Slowly he slid one hand down to rest on her waistband. Deftly, he unbuttoned her skirt, then unzipped it. It pooled on the floor.

Skip wound both arms around her tight, lifting her off the floor and walking them to the bed. They fell and bounced on the mattress, laughing. She lay back, watching him devour her with his eyes.

"These have gotta go," he said, hooking his thumbs in the sides of her panties and sliding them down. He tossed them on the chair. Cool air pebbled her skin. She covered herself with her arms.

"Shy? With me?"

She nodded, her eyes searching his.

"Oh, baby. Don't be shy," he said, easing her into his embrace. He held her close, stroking her hair until she relaxed. "You're beautiful, honey. Don't hide. Let me look at you."

Slowly she backed up. He cupped her cheek, then brushed her lips with his. His warm smile soothed her jangled nerves.

"Let me touch you. Let me love you," he whispered.

She reached out to cup his cheek, her thumb rubbing against his scruff, then she moved her hand to his neck. She drew him to her and kissed him. Hooking her leg around his hip, she pressed herself against him.

A soft groan from the ballplayer encouraged her.

"Honey, when you do that," he began, then stopped. He shifted his weight, looming over her. He kissed her breast while his hand stole up her leg. Francie stroked the back of his head and shut her eyes. When his fingers hit the mark, she let out a little gasp of pleasure.

"Good?"

"Very, very good."

He chuckled and kept it up. Heat sparked in her. He slipped a finger inside. She moaned, her hips riding along with the motion. He pressed the heel of his hand right up against her most sensitive spot. As if lightning had shot through her, her hips bucked.

"Oh, God. Skip!"

"Are you protected, baby?"

Eyes closed, she shook her head. Cracking them open, she watched his long arm reach for the nightstand drawer. He plucked out a condom. She glided her hand down his abs to his shaft. Closing her hand around it, she squeezed gently. Damn! He was as hard as the granite counter in his kitchen.

"Yeah. I'm there. Just for you."

He kissed her passionately. She clung to him, her fingers clutching his muscles. He stopped to pinch her peak before ripping open the condom with his teeth. He kissed the reddened nipple.

"These are amazing."

"You're amazing," Francie choked out, need flaming inside.

He rolled the protection over his dick then knelt between her legs.

"One more thing," he said, lowering his head to taste her.

"Oh my God, Skip!" She threw her head back and gulped in air.

After a few swipes, he pushed his tongue inside her, then pulled back.

"Now the main event." He grinned.

Grabbing her hips with both hands, he repositioned her. Pushing her left leg up, he let it rest on his shoulder, then rubbed himself up and down her, wetting himself. He entered easily, giving out a loud groan when he was all the way in. Bending down he kissed both breasts before he moved his hips.

"Baby, you feel so damn good. So tight. Damn." He closed his eyes and got into a rhythm.

Francie let go, giving in to her need. Her hips followed his as they rocked together. Intense heat spiraled up and up through her. He fastened his lips to hers, preventing her from talking.

Their chests, slippery with sweat, glided together and apart effortlessly. She drank in his scent, seasoned with a touch of aftershave and soap. She ran her fingers from his cheek, down his neck to his shoulder. Digging her fingertips into his muscles she felt his strength. Need gathered inside, ratcheting up heat, hotter and hotter. He pumped in and out faster and harder. She closed her eyes.

Before long, her body reached its limit, and she burst into a strong orgasm. After months without sex, the pleasure and release of tension flooded her. She cupped his cheek and stared into his eyes. Love shone back at her, throwing her. She'd expected to see lust but not love.

Skip buried his face in her neck and ramped up his pace. A loud groan and the stilling of his hips indicated he'd reached his climax, too. He collapsed, almost crushing her until he pushed up on his arms.

Sweat dripped off his forehead onto hers. He grabbed a pillow and wiped their faces with it.

"That was amazing," he said, pulling out of her, and resting back on his haunches.

"Mind-numbing," she said, watching him.

His gaze raked her body, taking in every inch. Instead of being embarrassed, she grinned.

"You are incredibly beautiful. Though you keep it covered up, lady."

"What do you want me to do, run around naked?"

He tilted his head. "Not a bad idea."

She laughed, gripping his shoulders, and trying to shake him. But he was like a stone wall.

"Do you do this often?"

She shook her head.

"You should. You do it so well."

He stretched out next to her, and she seized the chance to snuggle into him, resting her head on his chest, drawing her legs up to his.

"Stay tonight," he said, stroking her back.

"Can't. Work to do."

"So, you start a little later in the morning? I have practice at eleven."

The offer tempted her. What would be so bad if she didn't get back to her painting until ten thirty? Not a damn thing.

"Okay." The promise of delights yet to come whirled through her brain like sugar plums on Christmas Eve.

He pulled the blanket over them and turned out the light. "Let's rest before round two."

"Round two?"

"Honey, waking up to you here with me, well, no way can I resist temptation."

Her heart swelled. Still, she refused to accept happiness. Maybe it's just sex, don't blow it up to be something it's not. She had chastised herself for doing that very thing with her ex, blaming herself for losing him. Not this time. Caution and keeping it light were the way to go.

He switched off the lights. She curled into his warmth. Snuggling with him in bed was almost as good as the lovemaking. Almost. She grinned to see how little of the king-sized bed they occupied. He rolled onto his side and slid an arm around her waist. She turned her back to him, inching back until her rump was flush against him. He patted it and kissed her neck.

"Nice. Not too big, and not too small."

"Glad you approve," she shot back.

A squeeze made her squeal. He snickered and placed a gentle bite on her neck.

"I could eat you up, baby."

"How about tomorrow? I'll put myself on the menu."

"Hell yes. For breakfast."

"You're on. Goodnight."

"'Night, honey. Sweet dreams."

"You, too."

Her eyes drifted shut. Cuddled into his embrace, peace flowed through her veins. Her muscles relaxed, her body rested against his, and she fell asleep.

AT THREE O'CLOCK, FRANCIE rolled over, bumping into Skip's tall frame. He grunted and moved away. Her eyes flew open, curious to see what could be in the bed, but the room was dark. Warmth emanated from his skin. She leaned closer and sniffed his delicious, male scent. It was Skip.

"Hmm?" He lifted his head.

"Sorry. Didn't mean to wake you."

A large palm landed on her belly. He glided it down to the juncture between her legs. Sliding a finger between her folds, it was inside her in a second.

"Still wet," he muttered. "We should do something with that."

Francie giggled, combing her fingers through his short hair. "We should?"

"Definitely."

Before she could respond, she heard him fumbling with something, then the sound of something ripping. He removed his hand.

"I've got something better for in there," he said.

He eased her onto her side, facing him. Then he put a hand under her right knee and raised her leg to her chest. She extended it, resting her calf on his shoulder.

"There," he said.

He pushed her toward the head of the bed, grabbed her hips and thrust his shaft into her.

"Oh, shit, yeah. Much better, right?"

She drew in a breath as he pushed all the way in. "Damn!"

He moved in her for a bit, then eased her over on her back. Shifting to a more comfortable position, he pushed up on his arms and pumped into her. Francie could barely catch her breath. She steadied herself with a palm down on the bed, raised her leg again, and wrapped her arm around it, holding it to her chest. In the darkness, she focused on the sensations flying through her body. Skip appeared to be unstoppable. She gave in to his energy, letting the heat from his chest warm her.

Moving her hand up to his cheek, she felt the dampness there. Francie leaned in and licked. It was salty. She made him break a sweat—a good thing, right?

Before she knew it, tension spiraled inside her and exploded into a forceful orgasm. She blurted out his name in a loud groan. Before she could speak, his mouth was on hers. She opened, and his tongue took hers. Melting inside, she clung to him, becoming one, moving with his rhythm.

His grip tightened as he pulled her so close their skin stuck. He buried his face in her neck and groaned into her as release claimed him. Her hand on his back felt gooseflesh for a second, then it was gone.

"Holy shit," he muttered.

"Yeah. Exactly."

After he returned from the bathroom, she flopped over on her stomach. He slung his leg over hers, digging his toes under her calf and fell asleep. The next thing she knew, it was eight, and the sun lit up the room. She yanked the pillow over her head and shut her eyes.

"Time to get up, honey."

Francie ignored him.

"Don't make me tickle you to get you up," Skip said.

Tickling sucked! She slid the pillow away from her head. "I hope you're not one of those nauseatingly cheerful morning people," she said, through clenched teeth.

"I'm not. But we both have to get up. We have work to do."

She didn't argue with his rationale but still gritted her teeth as she pushed up from the bed. Stark naked in the midst of lovemaking was one thing, but in the cool light of morning, it was something else, entirely.

Skip bounced out of bed, standing in all his naked glory. There wasn't a modest bone in his body. She stared without embarrassment.

"Aren't you going to return the favor?"

She shook her head, holding the sheet against her chest. Skip reached into his closet and pulled out a dress shirt. He tossed it on the bed.

"Here."

She grabbed the garment and slipped it on, then made a quick trip to the bathroom.

"You realize I've already seen everything."

"That was at night. This is different," she called out from behind the door.

"Really? Do you have something to show me you didn't have last night?"

She poked her head out. "No, but it's, well, it's, it's just different."

He laughed. "It's okay, baby. Be shy. Just don't take all day in there."

She washed up and was out in less than five minutes. His shirt hung down to her knees. She'd rolled up the sleeves.

His gaze traveled her length. "Shirt looks better on you than me."

"I like blue."

"I like you." He bent to give her a quick kiss before heading into the bathroom.

Francie dressed and combed her hair with his comb. She pulled the bedclothes up and made the bed. When he came out, she was ready to hit the road.

"Wow! Look at you, all dressed and stuff," he said. "You even made the bed. Fantastic."

"Don't your other women do that?"

"What other women?"

"You're always telling the guys..."

"What I tell the guys and what's true are two different things."

He dressed, then offered to take her out to breakfast.

"I really don't have time. My portrait is less than half finished, and I have to show it to the professor tonight."

"Okay. A portrait, huh? Anyone I know?" He opened the front door.

Heat flushed her face. "I don't think so."

"Oh, too bad. I'd like to see your work sometime."

"I'm not ready. Not good enough yet."

"I hope you'll call me when you're ready."

"Sure."

No way could she show Skip what she was working on. They got in his car and he dropped her in front of her building. After putting the car in park, he leaned over and kissed her.

"Thank you for last night."

She smiled. "Me, too."

"I mean, you were amazing. I feel great. I hope it was as good for you as me."

"It was."

"I'll call you."

She frowned. Those words were the kiss of death. Every man who'd ever said that to her had never meant it. Those were "You'll never see me again" words.

"I mean it. After the playoffs. When we win. Will you celebrate with me? Come to the victory dinner?"

"Of course."

"Great."

One more passionate kiss and a honk from a car behind and Francie got out of the car. With one wave of his hand, Skip drove away. No way would she have told him that the night before had been the most spectacular of her life.

Chapter Seven

Francie floated into her apartment. She changed into painting clothes and uncovered her

Canvas. Thoughts of Skip kept her senses on high alert. Recalling his touch, his scent hijacked her brain from work. Her cell rang. It was Elena.

"So, girl. Where were you last night? I called three times."

"Out." Francie wandered over to the couch and sat down.

"Really?"

Francie swore Elena arched an eyebrow.

"With who?"

"Skip."

"Skip? Did you spend the night with him?"

"Why the third degree?"

"Aha! So you did. I love whenever you don't want to answer you change the subject. Hey, girl, I know you too well. Was it great?"

Francie sighed. No fooling her best friend. "Awesome."

Elena giggled. "I'm so glad!"

"Me, too. Now I have to get to work. This portrait has to be at least eighty percent done for class tonight, and I'm way behind."

"Can I see it?"

"Aren't you writing?"

"I need a break. Why don't I bring lunch? Can you break for food at noon?"

"Well..."

"Corned beef on rye."

"You twisted my arm. Let me get to work."

"See you then. So glad you had fun last night."

"Me, too." Francie ended the call and returned to her work area. She stared at the painting for a bit, then got the colors out and started mixing. Energy flowed through her as she forgot her surroundings and focused on the canvas. She let go of conscious thought and tapped into her sensuous self. The brush moved as if on automatic pilot.

At noon, the buzzer sounded. Francie wiped her hands, then answered the door. Elena entered, chattering away about her new book and Bobby.

"Okay. Let me see it."

"It's not ready."

"You're a talented artist. Come on."

"I'm not."

"You're doing well in school," Elena said, putting the bag of food on a small table.

"Not really."

Elena stopped what she was doing to stare at her friend. "I thought you had a B average?"

"I do. But that's not good enough. Professor Stark said, technically, I'm the best in the class. My work is always perfect—technically. But that it lacks emotion. Passion. It's what he called *workmanlike*."

"That's bullshit. I love your landscapes."

"They're pretty, but my figure work, portraits are flat. He's right. It's what my stepmother sees, too. She said I have no talent. I'm afraid she's right."

"Oh, come on! That's crap!" Elena flopped down next to her friend.

"I think I know what Stark is talking about. I think this one is different, but I'm too close to it to know."

"Let me see it. I'll tell you. Honestly. I will."

"Okay."

Elena was always truthful. Francie's stomach knotted. Was she just a hack?

The women pushed to their feet and Francie led her friend to where she had her easel and paints. She took a deep breath, her palms sweaty.

"Here."

Elena moved out from behind Francie and stepped in front of the painting. She gasped, her hand flying to her mouth.

"Wow! Oh my God! This is...amazing. Just amazing. So lifelike."

"I can do that. But does it have life?"

"Lady, the woman who painted this is obviously in love with the man."

"You think so?"

"There's so much passion here, one could have an orgasm just looking at it," Elena said.

"Something happened this morning when I started painting."

"You're in love with him, aren't you?"

Francie looked at the picture. It was of Skip, naked to the waist, pouring a bottle of water over his head. She had painted it from the photo she took at the stadium. Trying to see the work through her friend's eyes, she admitted it had life in a way her portraits never had before. Painting it had been an act of love. Every brushstroke that defined his body reminded her of their night together.

"This is beautiful. He's so alive. Like I could reach out and touch him. I love this, Francie. You have to enter it in the school contest."

"Oh, I couldn't."

"Yes, you can, and you will! Don't believe me? I bet Professor Stark sees the same thing that I do. It's fabulous. It's alive, it's sexy, sensuous. God, just looking at it turns you on."

"I know," she said with a chuckle.

"Horny girl! You have to show this to Skip."

Francie shook her head. "No way."

Elena pursed her lips together. "Okay. But you *are* entering it in the contest."

"I don't know."

"See what Professor Stark says."

"If he says I should. Then I will."

"If you win that contest, it's automatic admission to the program in France."

Francie sighed. "That would be a dream come true."

"And stick it to your stepmother, too."

Hunger gripped Francie's gut. "Come on. Let's eat."

SKIP ENTERED THE LOCKER room, grinning.

"Someone's happy today," Matt said, opening his locker.

Skip wiped the smile off his face. He didn't need the guys ragging on him.

"Hmm. I'd say someone got laid last night," Nat added.

Shit!

"Better not have been Francie," Bobby muttered, shooting a dark look at his friend.

"None of your fuckin' business."

"I'd say our shortstop finally got some," Jake piped up.

"I'm telling you to shut the fuck up!"

Bobby shook his head. "I told you not to mess with her."

"Why are you assuming I was with Francie last night?"

"Because Elena texted me. That's why."

Skip's eyes widened. *Shit. Fuck.*

Bobby poked his finger in Skip's face. "If you break her heart, you're dead meat."

"Who said I'm going to break her heart? What if she breaks mine?"

"You're on your own, asshole. You started this."

"I didn't force her to do anything."

"Better not," Bobby muttered, slipping on his sweats.

Skip grabbed the second baseman by his T-shirt and pushed him up against the wall.

"Francie and I are none of your business. Keep your fuckin' nose out."

"Okay, okay. It's just that..."

"Just nothing. Not one fuckin' thing. I like her. Okay? Now back off." He released him.

"All right. All right." Bobby held his palms up. "I'm out of it. She's a nice girl. That's all I'm saying."

"Damn right she is. So, let her alone."

Vic Steele poked his head in. "Stretching on the field in five."

Grumbling, Skip threw on his sweats. Why did everyone make assumptions about him? He was more likely to get a broken heart than Francie. Ever since he got up, in his head, he'd replayed their time together. The smoothness of her skin, the taste of her lips, and the scent of her hair kept his body on high alert.

"Get over it. We've got a game to play and we need to win. Put this crap between you two aside and focus on the game," Matt said.

Skip pulled his shirt over his head. Bobby stepped over.

"No hard feelings," he said, putting out his hand.

Skip took it and pulled his buddy into a quick hug. The two men went out on the field, buzzing about the Wolverine's lineup.

Skip stretched his calves, then his thighs before jogging. Bobby caught up with him.

"Things good with her?"

"Fantastic."

"Great. You deserve it," Bobby said.

Skip smiled at his buddy. Now, he could concentrate on the game.

After warming up, they had a strategy session with Cal Crawley, then went to the workout room. Skip lifted weights with ease, pumped on the bicycle almost without breaking a sweat, and ran faster than usual on the treadmill. He was ready for tomorrow.

The men hit the field. Three players practiced hitting. Skip and Bobby did their usual, the long-toss.

"Work on your bounce throw," Cal said to Skip and Nat.

Nat took his position at first base and Skip bounced the ball to Nat. The first baseman fielded it and returned it to Skip who continued. Jake picked up the ball and tapped one to Skip. He ran toward it, twisting to throw a bouncer to Nat. They kept that up until Vic intervened.

"That's enough. Don't strain that arm. We need it," the trainer said, signaling for the men to come in for lunch. Skip rubbed his arm. The muscle was strong and relaxed. The men headed for the buffet.

Skip stepped away to make a call.

"Hi. Did I interrupt your work?" He leaned against the wall.

"That's okay," Francie said.

"How's it going?"

"Good. Really good. How's practice?"

"Great. Never felt better."

She laughed. "I can guess why."

"Can you meet me for dinner at Freddie's?"

"Class tonight."

"Oh, yeah. I forgot. But you gotta eat, right?"

"I grab something here. Class is six to nine."

"Oh, damn. That's too late." He thought about asking her to spend the night. The next game was a night game. With such short notice, it would sound like a booty call. He frowned. Bad enough to be misunderstood by his teammates, he didn't want to do that to Francie.

"But you're going to win, right? Then there's the victory party."

"Of course. Yes. We're on?"

"I wouldn't miss it for anything."

"No class?"

"Nope. Not on Friday."

"Wish me luck," he said.

"I do. I know you'll win."

"Thanks, babe."

He ended the call. He'd miss her at dinner, but she was a woman with a talent, a dream, and he admired that. After lunch, practice resumed. Everyone took a turn at the plate, giving the infielders plenty of hits to field. At five, Cal called it quits. Skip was tired and hungry. Before he could shower, his phone buzzed. He hoped it was Francie with a change of heart about tonight, but it was Billy Holmes, instead.

"Hey, Billy."

"Hi. So? What did you decide?"

"I've got a check for you. Fifty grand. And papers to sign. Can you meet me at Freddie's?"

"Freddie's?"

"Yeah. A restaurant near the stadium. After the game. Tomorrow."

"The game?"

"You're coming, aren't you? I left a ticket for you at the box office."

"You did?"

"Of course. Wait for me in the player's parking lot."

"Thanks, Watson. Knew I could count on you."

"Just don't waste it, Holmes."

"I won't. I'll tell you all about it when I see you. Good luck."

"Thanks."

He ended the call. A warm feeling surrounded his heart.

AT FIVE, FRANCIE STEPPED back from her canvas to put a frozen dinner in the microwave. She'd barely have time to eat it and get to class on time. While she cleaned her brushes, she gazed at the painting.

The figure came alive. He almost leaped off the canvas. She grinned. With this work, she understood what Professor Stark meant. Using her spot-on technique, she'd somehow managed to unleash her emotions.

Perhaps she could attribute it to the steamy night she'd spent with Skip. She'd let her guard down and tapped into the well of emotion swirling inside. Whatever it was, the more she looked at the painting, the more she liked it.

Of course, there were places that needed a little work. A few more touch-ups, blending, work she could easily do in a day. The microwave finished its job, and Francie sat down to eat. She tried to stop staring at her work but couldn't. This was her best, by far. Her nerves kicked up, thinking about Professor Stark's response.

"He'd better like it," she said to no one.

After finishing her meal, she threw on jeans and a sweatshirt and packed up the painting carefully as it was still wet. She was supposed to leave it in the studio at school and work on it there, but the big, cold building shut down her senses.

"Taxi time," she said to herself. No way would she risk injury to this work on the subway.

PERSPIRATION GATHERED between her breasts as she entered the room. The three-hour class was studio time. Each student had his or her own easel and kept their supplies there. Francie schlepped over to hers.

"Ms. Whitman. You were supposed to leave all that here," Professor Stark said, coming up behind her.

"I'm sorry. I was having trouble, and I needed to work on it at home."

"Please leave it here now. Let me see what you've done."

Her chest constricted, and her palms got damp. She wiped them on her jeans before she unwrapped her canvas. She slipped it on the easel, bumping into the legs and almost dumping it on the floor. Professor Stark caught it.

"Easy, easy there," he said, securing it on the supports. He stood back, his hand cupping his chin, stroking the facial hair there as he stared at her work. Francie's heart had settled in her throat. She could barely swallow.

"Hmm. Very interesting," he said, shifting his weight.

"Interesting? What's interesting?" she blurted.

"This, the way the drops fall. Very realistic, yet there's something almost impressionistic about the whole work."

"Really?" Her blood pumped faster.

The professor turned his head one way, then walked a few steps to the right and perused the painting again.

"This is magnificent, Ms. Whitman. You finally got it."

"It is? I got it?" Francie's breath came faster.

"The emotion. This painting is dripping with it. Your technique is perfect, as usual. But this time you've captured the emotion. His joy. It's there all over, even in the drops of water. They have a joyous bounce. Bravo, Ms. Whitman. Bravo!" He grinned at her.

Francie hugged her waist. Words stuck in her throat. She was barely able to choke out "Thank you."

As the students entered, the professor motioned them over. He talked about her work, pointing out places where her technique was perfect and others that communicated emotion, pure joy. Francie's head buzzed, her heart rate was still above normal, and her grin so wide it hurt.

He called on the class for comments. Everyone, except one jealous woman, loved the piece. One young man, who she'd had coffee with a few times, sidled up next to her. He'd asked her out. She'd gone once, but there was no chemistry. After all, he wasn't Skip Quincy.

"I get why you turned me down," he said.

She turned to face him. "Why?"

"This guy."

Heat flew into her cheeks. Mortified, she covered her mouth with her hand. "I don't know what you mean."

"Aw, come on. This painting screams it. Like Professor Stark said. It's a work of emotion. And that emotion is love."

She lowered her gaze to the floor. She didn't love Skip Quincy. It was simply a crush, right?

The young man laughed. "See, you're blushing. If it isn't love, then it's pretty darn close."

"You're wrong."

"Bullshit. Hey, don't knock it. You did the best work in the class. You ought to give this guy a medal for opening you up."

She looked up at him, at the painting, then back at him, again. "You may be right."

"Trust me. I am. If a girl painted a picture like that of me pouring a bottle of water over my head, I'd propose to her." He laughed. "Great job, Francie."

She got a round of applause from the other ten students, minus Miss Green Eyes. The professor discussed touch-ups she needed to do.

"You should enter this in the Maya Colby contest, Francie," Professor Stark said.

"Oh, I couldn't. I'm sure there will be a dozen pieces there better than mine."

"I don't think so. Trust me. Get your work out there. You'd be surprised."

She sighed. "I'll think about it."

She donned her smock and fished a brush and paints out of her wooden art case. She wasn't in love with Skip Quincy. How ridiculous! It was simply a crush, a temporary thing. Right? She couldn't be in love with him? He's a love-'em-and-leave-'em guy, isn't he? Would he break her heart? A dozen questions distracted her.

"Ms. Whitman, don't let your success go to your head. Get started on those changes. Forty-five minutes have already passed."

"Yes, Professor. Sorry."

Daydreaming would have to wait. So what if she loved Skip? That was her business, wasn't it? She smiled as she mixed colors. Turning her attention back to the canvas, she studied his torso. She shaded the skin slightly, blending in the color to eliminate lines.

As she worked, the smile stayed in place. Love flowed through her as she put brush to canvas. The Colby contest—could she enter? Could she possibly win? Professor Stark thought so. Maybe, for once in her life, she should listen.

Chapter Eight

C al gave the Nighthawks a pep talk in the locker room. "We need this win. This will put us into the Championship Series. It could go either way. But we have home-field advantage. They've been struggling to catch up since the beginning. We can do it. Be focused, but loose. Relax, keep your eye on the ball, and do your best. We're the better team. We should win this."

The men stood, put their hands in for a cheer, then headed to the field. It was a clear, cool night—perfect for a game. Skip had a lightweight sweatshirt on under his uniform. He sang along with the national anthem, but his gaze searched the stands until he found Francie. She raised her palm in greeting, and he nodded.

When the song finished, Skip stuffed a wad of gum in his mouth and headed for second base. He stopped to doff his cap to his girl. He punched his glove, stretched his legs, and crouched.

Dan Alexander was pitching, because he was their best pitcher. The pressure was intense. The first batter took his stance in the box. Skip glanced over to see Eddie Weeks in the on-deck circle. Anger rose in Skip's chest. He hated the weasel after Weeks tried to spike him. The first batter grounded out to second. Nat threw the ball back to Bobby, who tossed it to Skip, who rifled it to Jake at third.

Eddie Weeks came to the plate. Wearing a malicious, shit-eating grin, he glanced at the Shortstop. Bile rose in Skip's throat. Maybe Dan would rifle one right to Weeks' sac. By accident, of course. One could always hope.

"It'll be a pleasure to throw that fucker's ass out," Skip said to Bobby.

Dan went into his wind-up. Skip crouched low, his weight on the balls of his feet. He was ready. A swing and a miss sent the ball from Matt back to the pitcher. Skip stood, then got back into position, his eyes glued to the ball. Eddie let the ball pass. It just nicked the outside corner. That was two strikes.

"He's swingin' on this one," Jake called to Skip. Nodding, he narrowed his eyes and got into position. He prayed it'd be coming right at him.

Crack! The sound of wood smacking ball met Skip's ears. A powerful grounder headed his way. He ran full speed to meet the ball. It took a funny hop, but he scooped it up on the run. Eddie, known for speed, was smokin' his way down the first base line. Reaching into his glove, Skip snatched the ball out. Facing the left field stands, he twisted his body to the right and brought his arm up. Because he was off-kilter, he couldn't get his usual power into the throw. This was it, time for the bouncer he'd been practicing.

Nat moved his left foot so that the outside was flush up against the bag, but he wasn't on the bag, so Eddie couldn't spike the shit out of his foot. The ball bounced perfectly. Nat scooped it up about a second before Eddie's foot hit the bag. The umpire called, safe. Cal Crawley leaped up and came flying out of the dugout. He approached the umpire and the two men put their heads together. Skip had seen it clearly. The ball reached Nat before Weeks touched the base.

The umpire called time out to view an instant replay. Skip swiped his sleeve over his sweaty face. The players stood around while the decision was being revisited. Eddie said a few choice things to Nat. Skip watched as color rose in the first baseman's face as he scowled at the Wolverine. Then Eddie shoved Nat. Nat pushed him back. Bobby ran over to calm the first baseman down.

Even though the air was cool, sweat poured off Skip's face. The last thing they needed was for Nat to be thrown out of the game. Although Skip hated Eddie's guts, he joined Bobby and placed his arms on Nat's.

"Nat! Fuck, man. What are you doing?" Skip and Bobby pulled their teammate away from the opponent.

"That fucker called Nicki a whore."

"Forget him. Nicki's no whore. He's just trying to get you mad enough to throw a punch and get tossed. Without you at first, we'll never win. He knows that," Skip said.

Nat looked at him, then at Bobby, who had his arm around him.

"Yeah? Okay, okay. You're right." Nat's color slowly returned to normal.

"Fuck it. He's the whore," Bobby said.

Nat cracked up. Skip patted him on the butt, then he and Bobby returned to their positions. By then the timeout was over. The umpire reversed the call and Eddie Weeks was out. He stomped his foot and cussed a blue streak, his face within an inch of the umpire. The Washington manager was out of the dugout in a flash, but he was too late. The umpire tossed Eddie out of the game. Now the manager screamed at Eddie, and the Nighthawks' infield laughed behind their gloves.

The next batter hit a bloop single that dropped behind Skip but in front of the left fielder. Then Dan struck out the next batter to end the inning.

The Nighthawk's hit the dugout. Skip grabbed a bottle of water and twisted off the cap. Back to his old slot, he'd be batting third. Nat was up first, and Bobby warmed up in the on-deck circle. Skip stood next to Cal and guzzled his beverage.

"Watch this new guy," Cal said, pointing to the Wolverine's pitcher. "He's just up from the minors."

"Aren't they taking a big chance putting him in this game?"

"They have two pitchers on the DL. They had no choice. Their pitching was spotty this year. So this guy is their new hope. We have to knock him out." Cal chewed gum.

Skip watched as pitch after pitch zoomed past the batter. Nat struck out and returned to the dugout, swearing. Bobby took his stance.

Pointing, Cal said, "He's a righty and favors the inside corners."

Skip headed to the on-deck circle. The pitcher was nicking the corners, just getting the ball in the strike zone, making it hard to hit.

"Come on, Bob. Slam it," Cal called to the second baseman.

Skip warmed up with his favorite bat. It was balanced just right for his large frame. Bobby hit a line drive above the shortstop's head and took off. The left fielder ran in, but not in time to catch the ball. Bobby beat out the Wolverine's off-balance throw.

Skip stepped up to the plate. He backed up a bit farther than usual, expecting low, inside pitches, just as Cal said.

The pitcher changed it up and threw high and outside on the first pitch. It was a ball. Next up was also outside, but it touched the lower corner and was called a strike. Skip glanced at the third base coach. His signs gave Skip the green light to swing. The hit-and-run was on.

He shifted his weight from foot to foot, widened his stance a bit, wiped one hand on his pants, and gripped the bat. This was it. This would be his low and inside ball to be strike two.

Skip swung and popped it into the stands, foul. The next pitch was the same. This guy didn't give up. Skip narrowed his eyes and shouldered his bat. Another one popped foul, and another, and another. Skip set his mind to breaking this pitcher down. How many could he throw low and inside? Eventually, he had to get one down the middle.

Skip stepped back, out of the batter's box. He needed to throw the guy off his rhythm. The pitcher knew, with two strikes, Skip had to swing. He'd be pitching shit until Skip struck out. He had to continue to get a piece of the ball. The pressure tightened. No way was he striking out. Skip kept his face an expressionless mask. Once again, he took his stance, this time closer to the plate. The pitcher wiped the sweat from his forehead. The guy was getting tired. He couldn't afford to throw so many pitches to each player or he'd never make it past the fourth inning.

Skip had to hang in until the pitcher's control slipped. And there it was. His gift from God—right smack dab down the middle, waist high. The ball sailed into Skip's comfort zone and he swung with everything he had. Thwack! He felt the hit in his hands and looked up as the ball sailed toward the outfield but veering left.

He took off for first, keeping his eye on the left fielder who was running his ass off. That was Weeks' position. It was obvious the guy was new. Being such a fast dickwad, Weeks might've caught the ball. But the substitute didn't stand a chance. Skip had to smile. Weeks' hot temper might have cost his team the game, if not at least these two runs.

By the time the Wolverine got to it, the ball had floated high enough to be out of reach. It landed in the stands. Home run! A two-run homer, in fact. The crowd rose to their feet, cheering. Bobby waited for him at the plate. The two friends high-fived before returning to the dugout. His teammates mobbed him.

"Well done, Skip," Cal said, tossing a half-grin at him.

That was high praise from the taciturn manager. Pride washed through him. The next two men struck out.

As Skip grabbed his glove, Cal shook his head. "This guy's going to be tough to beat."

Sure enough, the rest of the game turned into a pitchers' duel. The final score was two-zero, Nighthawks won the game and the playoffs. Now they'd be heading for a best-of-seven Championship Series.

There was only one more game left to play between the Texas Bulls and the Montana Rangers before the League Championship Series would begin. The 'Hawks had four days of rest coming.

Champagne corks popped in the locker room. Men wearing only towels toasted each other, chest-bumped, and cheered as loud as they could.

"We still have another series to play before the World Series. Don't get out of shape," Cal admonished.

"They worked hard. Let 'em enjoy it," Vic said, raising a plastic cup.

"To Cal! And Vic," said Skip vaulting his cup high in the air.

His teammates joined him in a cheer for each manager and coach. A security guard tapped on the door.

"Gentlemen. There are ladies out here, waiting for you."

"Oh, shit! Francie!" Skip downed the rest of his drink, then shoved his boxers on and his suit. He was tying his tie as he walked out to the parking lot.

"Watson!"

Billy Holmes leaned up against a car. Skip waved to Francie and approached his buddy.

"Got the cash?"

"A check. First, you gotta sign this," Skip said, fishing a pen out of his breast pocket.

"What's that?"

"Just a paper that says you agree to pay me back."

"Sure, sure. Anything," Billy said, taking the pen and scribbling his name.

"Here you go. Good luck. Let me know how you're doing."

"I will."

"Did you like the game?"

"Sorry, Watson. Didn't have time to catch it. I gotta go now. My, uh, partner is waiting."

"That's too bad. Okay. Good luck," Skip said.

Billy threaded his way through the parked cars and jumped in a black vehicle waiting outside the lot. Skip pushed doubt out of his mind. No time now to worry about Billy. He was a man and would have to take care of himself. He loped over to his girl, who had been watching and waiting.

"I'm sorry, honey, he said kissing Francie's cheek. That was an old friend I had some business with. And the guys got crazy. You know how it is."

"I get it."

"You ready?"

"Can you drive?"

"Am I sober enough?"

"Uh huh."

"Of course. Besides, it's only a few blocks."

He opened the car door for her, then slid behind the wheel. Aware that he'd had two glasses of champagne, Skip reduced his speed and focused on the road. They were the first to arrive at Freddie's.

A victory banner stretched across the front door of the bar. The Nighthawks' table sported a few noisemakers and bottles of champagne on ice. Skip held out a chair for Francie.

"Maybe I should drive you home," she said, eyeing the bottles on the table.

"Maybe you should come home with me. I'll even let you drive." He took her hand and raised it to his lips.

A SHIVER SNAKED DOWN Francie's spine. Whenever Skip touched her, her skin jumped with electrical current. She stared up into his blue eyes, innocent and lustful at the same time. His stare alone weakened her knees.

"We'll see," she replied, not willing to commit.

He leaned over to whisper in her ear. "That night was the most wonderful of my life."

Her breath caught. Before she could answer, his teammates and their women streamed through the door. Elena took the seat Francie had saved for her. The table filled rapidly, and another one was added on.

The men ordered food and passed around beer.

"Hey, guys!" Tommy clapped his hands. "My friends have volunteered to drive you guys home tonight. So drink up. Next round is on the house!"

The men cheered, clapping, and refilling their glasses. Francie watched, like a fly on the wall. Her gray eyes grew large as she listened to conversations between the men and their women. The team trashed Eddie Weeks. Skip leaned over.

"Eddie practically handed us the game. He's their fastest guy, best scorer and can catch almost anything hit to the outfield. With him out of the game, winning wasn't so hard."

"Really? Then why did he do what he did?"

"Because he's an asshole, in addition to being a great ball player."

Bobby faced her. "Just because a guy can play ball, doesn't mean he's not an idiot. Weeks did exactly what we wanted him to do."

"You wanted him to start a fight with Nat?"

"Not exactly," Nat piped up. "But once Weeks started it, and we saw what he was trying to do, we turned the tables on him."

"Of course, getting the right call from the ump didn't hurt," Skip said, laughing.

As the evening progressed, he rested his arm over her shoulders. The women asked her questions. Elena, her best friend, had had one beer too many and boasted about Francie's talents, much to Francie's discomfort.

"You should see her work. She's the best."

"I'm not, really." Francie said.

"Oh, yes she is. And the one she's just finished? Her professor said she should enter it in the school contest."

"Really?"

"He said that, but I'm not going to."

"Why not?" Skip asked.

"Because it's not that good. And it's kind of private," she explained.

"Private? A private painting? Now I gotta see it."

"Oh, no, no. I don't think so." She shook her head.

"I think so. I've wanted to see your work. Tonight's the night."

"The painting is at school. We leave our work in the studio and work on it there."

"Damn. Really? Damn. A shame."

"You will when she wins first prize," Elena said.

"And what is first prize?"

Francie tried to signal her friend not to answer, but Elena ignored her.

"First prize is automatic admission to the Paris art program. It's run by New York Arts and Letters. Affiliated with Manhattan University."

Francie covered her face with her hands.

"Can't you get into the program on your own?"

"I might be able to. My grades. Well, I have 'B's, but not many 'A's."

"This picture will get you an 'A' for sure."

"Elena, you're my best friend. You're prejudiced."

"It has passion."

"Elena!"

"I'm just quoting your teacher. He said she lacked passion, but this new one, well, it has a ton of passion."

"Passion?" Skip looked at her. "And what is this Paris Art thing?"

"It's a one-semester art class in Paris. They don't accept many students. You have to be in graduate school and display a special talent. Which I don't have."

"Yes, you do!" Elena pounded her fist on the table.

"Guess your best friend knows better than you do," Skip said. "You want to go to Paris for six months?"

"Five. It's been my dream since I started grad school."

Skip raised his glass. "I hope you get it."

"Thanks." She clinked hers with his.

If she left for five months, Skip would surely find someone else before she returned. Maybe Mimi Banner would cave and take him to her bed. Francie sighed. The one night with Skip had been a dream come true but not a regular thing. Maybe she'd go home with him tonight, but soon he'd be in the league playoffs, then, maybe, the World Series, and she'd be forgotten.

But what memorable nights she'd have with him. Food began arriving. Skip grabbed her hand and squeezed once before digging into his steak. Francie had ordered scallops. The men were hungry. Conversation halted while people turned their attention to their meals.

Shy Francie watched Skip attack the meat with enthusiasm. He appeared confident and in charge, surrounded by his buddies. She admired him. Her self-esteem had died with her mother when Francie was twelve. Not close to his daughter, her father didn't know what to do, so he quickly found another wife. Francie hadn't received this new woman with open arms. There were two strangers living with her, her father, and her stepmother.

Eventually, she got closer to her dad. He admired Francie's painting—said it reminded him of her mother, who had been an artist, too. They had bonded through her artwork. Then he died of a sudden heart attack, and she was left with a stepmother, who was her legal guardian and in charge of her inheritance, but not her friend.

When she moved into the same building as Elena, the young women became friends. Sharing their family issues, they leaned on each other for support. Content with her best friend and her art, Francie hadn't been looking for more. Disappointed in love, she hadn't expected to find it when she tagged along to a baseball game with Elena, where she met the shortstop.

Skip's friendship had opened up a whole new world. He complimented her, and teased her, like a big brother. While she had been attracted to him from the start, he didn't appear to feel the same—until recently. She had kept her feelings private until Elena guessed.

That night, at The Hideout, liquor had loosened the couple's reserve. After months of hands-off friendship, they had taken things to the next level. But did that mean they were dating? Maybe it did, since they were together for the victory dinner, too. Accustomed to disappointment, Francie didn't expect anything from him, but she couldn't control her dreams.

EVEN THOUGH HE HAD four days off, Skip halted his drinking at two beers. He didn't need to spend the entire time recovering before the League Championship Series began. He'd planned to spend more time with Francie.

Their night together had surprised him. Who knew such a quiet, awkward girl could have such passion? Hell, not him, that's for sure. He'd pegged her as *friend* material and had treated her like the little sister he'd never had. When the guy at The Hideout moved in on her, something inside Skip went berserk.

He'd never thought of himself as protective until he met Francie. Feelings new to him made him uncomfortable. Still, he'd not desert her and leave her to the wolves. After their night together, he realized she wasn't quite as innocent as he had once believed. He couldn't suppress a lusty grin as he glanced at her before returning his attention to his plate. She knew her way around the bedroom. And wasn't he the lucky one?

When he finished his steak, he wiped his mouth with a napkin. Leaning over, he whispered in her ear. "Come home with me tonight. I want to show you something."

She chuckled. "I've already seen it and it's mighty fine." Her eyes danced.

He laughed. "That, too. Something else."

"Okay."

Everyone ordered dessert. The party broke up after they'd divided the check. Food had sobered Skip. Francie bid Elena farewell and slid into the front seat of Skip's car. When they got to his apartment, he hung up her coat, offered her a drink—which she declined—then pulled a colorful folder from his dresser drawer.

"Come here," he said, motioning for her to join him on the bed. Francie crawled up next to him. He put his arm around her.

"What's that?" she asked, pointing to the brochure.

"It's a place called 'Cottage on the Lake.' It's in Pine Grove, about two hours from here."

"And?"

"Every year, I rent it out for a weekend. Between play-offs and stuff. Cal gives us a couple of days to get our heads straight and rest before the next series. And I go here. I usually go by myself. But I'd like you to come with me. We'd leave early tomorrow and come back early Monday. I have practice on Monday."

"Me?"

"Yes, you. Is there someone else in the room?" He grinned.

"Tell me about it."

"It's a small place. Two bedrooms on Cedar Lake. Right on the lake. It's got a fireplace and a boat tied up to its own dock. It's cute. I think quaint would be a word you might use."

"Running water?"

He laughed. "Of course. A bathroom. Nice kitchen, too. But you wouldn't have to cook. The lady who rents it to me leaves some cool stuff in the fridge. Casseroles. Stuff like that."

"It sounds charming."

"So you'll come?"

She nodded.

He drew her into his arms. "Great!"

"I bet the leaves are changing about now up there."

"Yeah. It's beautiful. The colors around the lake will knock you out."

"We can make love in front of the fire."

"Oh, baby, you read my mind."

"Let me see," she said, plucking the worn paper from his hand. Inside were pictures of the living room, kitchen, and bedrooms. There was a small fireplace in one of the bedrooms, too. Warm colors on the walls gave the place a cozy feel. One shot from the living room sofa showed the view of the lake through picture windows.

"This looks great! You go every year?"

"I forget about baseball for a while. I'll take you on a drive."

"I'd love that. I don't have a car, and I miss it."

Skip leaned over, his lips sought hers. "With you there, it'll be even better."

Francie eased down on her back. He looked into her eyes. They were cool and hot at the same time. Looming over her, he lowered himself and allowed his mouth to ravish hers. His hand came up to close over her breast.

A small moan escaped her. She squirmed underneath him.

"Want me, babe?" he asked.

She nodded.

"Good answer," he said, before ripping his shirt off and tossing it to the chair.

Francie sat up and did the same. She continued to disrobe. After shedding his clothes, Skip pulled down the comforter and sheet.

"After you," he said, gesturing to the bed.

She jumped in, bouncing and giggling. He watched her breasts jiggle, joined her, and clicked off one light.

"Francie, honey. Over here. Let me take you around the world," he said.

After turning off the other lamp, she moved into his embrace.

Chapter Nine

Sunlight woke Francie. She stretched her arms, bashing into Skip. He groaned and rolled over. Her body hummed, and her smile wouldn't quit.

"Go back to sleep. It's not time," he mumbled, his voice heavy.

She snuggled closer to him. He flopped one arm over her middle and was snoring quietly before she could blink. She took a deep breath, loving the scent of him while he slept. Rolling on her side with her back to him, she cuddled closer, her backside squished against his hips.

"Grrr. If you're gonna do that, then I'm up. All of me."

She laughed as his fingers pinched her nipple. "So, you're serious? Do we have time?"

"Baby, there's always time for lovin' you."

She rolled on her back and gave in to her desires.

By eight-thirty, the couple was zooming down Broadway, heading for Francie's place.

"I'll wait outside, okay?"

"I won't be long."

Once inside, she threw a few garments in a suitcase. Stopping on her way to the door, she pulled out her chalks and a pad. Might be colorful foliage for a picture. She was due to hand in a chalk drawing before the end of the semester anyway. This might be the perfect setting.

Skip maneuvered the car across the George Washington Bridge and onto the Palisades Parkway. Francie watched the bright yellow, orange, and red-leafed trees whiz by the window. The colors captivated her.

"This is beautiful," she said.

He grunted his agreement.

She leaned back against the leather seat, letting her eyes drift shut. The sound of Vivaldi's Four Seasons drew her attention. She faced him.

"Classical music?"

"Figured it wouldn't wake you up. Guess I was wrong."

"I love classical music."

"I do listen sometimes. Like when I'm in the car. It helps when there's a shitload of traffic. Keeps me calm."

She snuggled into the seat and shut her eyes again. The soothing music coupled with the gentle rhythm of the vehicle put her to sleep. When she awoke, they were at a gas station. Skip filled up the car. She yawned.

"Hey, Sleeping Beauty." He raised his palm to her window. "We're almost there."

"Great!"

She got out and headed for the ladies' room. Stretching her legs brought her fully awake. Skip threw the car in gear and they ambled back to the highway. He turned off the music, and they chatted about the scenery for a few minutes. Skip filled her in on the little town. Her heart beat faster when she saw a sign that said, *Pine Grove, 2 miles.*

Skip slowed to a crawl as they approached a little white house with teal blue trim. He pulled ahead and backed into the tiny driveway just off the main route. He retrieved their bags from the trunk and followed her to the front door. It wasn't locked, so they went right in.

The entryway was tiny, the couple could barely fit. She stepped into the living room. Skip eased by her and carried the luggage into another room. Francie looked around. There was a navy-blue velveteen sectional sofa going along two pale yellow walls. It faced a large picture window overlooking the lake. On the wall on the left, about six feet from the end of the sofa was a small fireplace. An oak coffee table, big enough to hold a jigsaw puzzle, and a rocking chair pulled the room together.

She flopped down on the sofa. "This is charming. I love it."

Skip leaned against the archway, standing within a few feet of the ceiling.

"I thought you would."

"I do. Very much."

He held out his hand. "Come on."

The kitchen was quaint but big enough to house a small table. Perfect for an intimate breakfast for two. The bedroom had a queen-sized bed, another tiny fireplace a small dresser, and a black-and-gold rocking chair. The coverlet was a handmade quilt in a blue, green, and white calico prints. The walls were white. Photos of local scenery were framed and hung over the bed and dresser.

"Let's go outside," he said. There were three steps leading down to a small deck and more ending at the little dock. A motorboat was tied up.

Her stomach rumbled. She checked her watch. It had been a long time since breakfast.

"I'm starved," she said.

"Let's see what Lorraine left us," Skip said, heading for the kitchen. The note, held to the fridge by a magnet, listed two lunches and one dinner.

"Quiche is pussy food," Skip said.

"What?"

"You heard me. Girl stuff."

"Have you ever eaten a quiche?"

He shook his head.

"Then you must try it. Let's see. It's in the fridge." She took out the quiche Lorraine, his landlady, had prepared and shoved it in the microwave.

"Nice she made it in a glass dish," Francie said, setting the proper time. Then she got down plates. Skip put up a pot of coffee.

"If I'm still hungry, we're going out for a burger, okay?"

"Deal."

After they ate, Skip took her hand and led her outside. They sat, holding their mugs, on the deck and gazed at the lake. A heron swooped down, fishing for his lunch. Francie almost pinched herself. Being in this little house with Skip, she could pretend they were married and living on the lake. Of course, he couldn't live there and play baseball. Well, maybe for the winter. She wondered how harsh the cold was upstate. Still, snuggling together by the fire with the lake at their door would be romantic.

She reminded herself that while that might be a dream come true, it was light years away from reality. Before they had to leave, she'd enjoy the closeness and passion of this man every single second. Wishing beyond that would only lead to heartache.

He eased his arm around her shoulders as she scooted up close.

"This is so beautiful."

"Yeah. I never get tired of this view."

I'd never get tired of you, she thought.

"I'm glad you're here," he said.

"Me, too." Francie smiled, happiness flowing through her. She sighed and leaned closer, resting her head against his shoulder. Was this the ultimate bliss? She laughed to herself. The ultimate bliss was making love with Skip Quincy—there was no doubt about that.

Skip stretched out on the bench and put his head in her lap. She stroked his hair as he dozed. He had good reason to be tired. As she watched the sun shift, she gently extricated herself, substituting a cushion for her thighs, and moseyed down to the dock. Pleasantly cool air caressed her. Ducking inside for a moment, she retrieved her chalks and pad. The light was at a perfect angle to highlight the blazing autumn colors of the trees hugging the shore.

Angling her chair to get the best view, she opened the box and began her drawing. Knowing the sun would shift soon, she worked quickly. Drawing while Skip snoozed gave her privacy. She wasn't ready for him to see her work. Criticism cut to the bone when it was someone whose opinion she valued. She'd never attain the level of star he had mastered on the baseball diamond, but she'd try her damnedest.

Francie captured the beauty before her with a perfect blend of colors, dappled with sunlight. She expressed her passion in the piece like she had in her painting. Perhaps her love affair with Skip stoked her fires enough to push her work to the next level. The drawing came to life, the oranges like fire, the golds so warm, and the fading green staking its claim.

"Wow. That's great," said a deep, masculine voice.

Startled, Francie jumped.

"Sorry. Didn't mean to scare you." He placed a large, warm hand on her shoulder.

"Do you like it?

"It's amazing. You've got it. Captured how it looks, only better."

Her heart swelled. "Really?"

"I never lie."

"Never?" She cocked an eyebrow.

"Well, okay. Maybe I bend the truth a little from time to time."

"Who doesn't?"

"Oh?" Now it was his turn to direct a penetrating stare.

"Not often. Not often. Just like when a friend is wearing a new dress and I think it's hideous, I never say that. I always find something nice to say, even if it isn't totally true."

"You're really talented."

"Thank you."

"Can I have this?"

"This?"

He nodded.

"I'd give it to you, but I need it for class. We have a chalk drawing due at the end of the month. I can use this."

"Okay. Got it."

"But afterward, if you still want it…"

"I do."

"Okay, then. It's yours."

"Want a drink?"

"Hot tea?"

"Coming up."

"I hope you don't mind if I keep working while the light is just right."

"Not at all."

He went inside. Francie chuckled to herself. Imagine, a star baseball player was getting little ole Francie Whitman a cup of tea!

She turned her attention back to the foliage. Her fingers flew, drawing, shading, blending. By the time Skip returned with her cup of tea, she'd finished. She blew the chalk dust off, then faced him.

"The way you like it. Milk and sugar, right?"

"What a memory!" She took the mug.

Skip had coffee. He put it down on the table and bent over to examine her work.

"This is truly amazing. I mean it's like a photograph, only it isn't. There's more. Like life or something. The picture is like it's moving. I can't explain."

"You mean it has passion?" she prompted.

"Bingo! Exactly! That's it. Passion. It has passion. Just like you." He turned hot eyes to her.

Her heart sang. She'd done it, crossed over, added feeling and emotion to her work.

"Thank you. Thank you so much. That's what Professor Stark said. He wanted to see that in my work. And only recently—it happened. And now again."

"I'm proud of you. I bet you're the star pupil."

"Far from it. But I'm moving up."

He bent to kiss her.

"I know just where I'll hang this when you're done with it."

The couple went to a local hangout for dinner. They ate burgers with a medley of farm-fresh fall veggies on the side instead of fries.

When they got back, they cuddled up and watched a movie. At ten, it was bedtime. Skip yawned.

"How can you be tired after that nap?"

"Who said anything about being tired?" He reached for her, sliding her onto his lap.

While his mouth worked hers, he removed her shirt and bra. Francie returned the favor, then pushed against his warm skin. The hair on his chest tickled her nipples, making them hard. She wanted him. Pressure increased, making her squirm.

"Want it?" he mumbled, his breath hot on her ear.

"Yes."

He set her on her feet, pushed up, and grabbed her, slinging her over his shoulder. Francie gasped, then giggled as he trudged off toward the bedroom.

"Cave man?"

"Yep. Cave man wants his woman."

He flipped her, gently, down on the bed and was on top of her in a second. She closed her eyes, giving in to the passion coursing through her. She spread her legs, and he rested between them.

"Let's see who can get naked fastest."

"What's the prize?"

He shrugged. "I'll think of something."

The contest ended in a tie. They fell into the bed, locked in an embrace. Francie closed her eyes and let her lover take her to the moon.

THE LOUD HOOT OF AN owl woke Francie. She started, gazing out the window at the full moon shining down on the lake. The moonlight made a silvery path right to their cabin. She pushed up on one elbow in time to see a large-winged bird soar across their window.

She shook Skip.

"There's an owl out there."

"Hmm? Wha...?"

"An owl."

"Good for him. Go back to sleep."

"He's like right here. On our deck."

"Yeah, yeah." Skip slipped back into slumber.

Francie slid out of bed and shrugged Skip's shirt over her shoulders. She rolled up the sleeves as she padded to the back door. Standing still, she watched the big bird who sat perched on the deck railing. He hooted again, jarring her for a moment.

She guessed he was looking for food.

Glancing at the clock, she saw it was way past midnight. Two in the morning, to be exact. She yawned and remained at her post. The bird turned his head. Without notice, he spread his wings and took off. She watched him skim across the surface of the lake. He ascended and landed in a tree to the left of the water. She couldn't see him but heard one more hoot. She couldn't see if he had scooped up a fish or was still looking.

"YOU WANT ME TO KILL an owl? A big rat, okay, but an owl?" Skip, totally naked, joined her.

"Not kill him. Look at him. He was beautiful."

"Not as pretty as you."

"I'm no owl." His body drew her eye.

"Prettier," he said, combing his fingers through her locks.

She opened the back door and stepped out on the deck. Shivering in the cold night air, she folded her arms across her chest.

"Look at the moon. It's full," she said.

He joined her. "All the crazies are out."

He slipped his arm around her. She snuggled closer.

"I'm a heat machine. That's what I've been told," he said.

"By the hundreds of women you've slept with?"

"You mean the thousands, don't you?" His eyes danced, and a smile played at his lips.

She gave him a soft slap. "Stop kidding."

"And hundreds wasn't kidding?" He raised his eyebrows.

"Wanted to see how many there've been."

"Honestly? I don't know. Never kept track."

"Liar, liar, pants on fire. Every man keeps track."

"Not me."

"Really?"

"Yep. I can't count that high," he said with a straight face.

Francie burst out laughing. Skip joined her.

"Listen, babe. No one before you matters. Okay? I wasn't married, didn't cheat on anyone. I just took what was offered. Let it go."

"I guess everyone has a past."

"How about your past?"

"I don't have much of one."

"Tell me."

"Nope. It's off limits."

"Anyone ever break your heart?"

"Once."

"Want to talk about it?"

She shook her head. He hugged her.

"Do you feel sleepy, 'cause I don't," she said.

"Not now," he replied. "We make love or have a glass of wine."

"Why can't we do both?"

He chuckled. "Smart girl. Sure. Let's see what we have." He headed for the kitchen while Francie got comfy on the sofa. She spread out a small afghan she found folded over the rocker.

Skip returned with an open bottle of Cabernet Sauvignon and two glasses. He plopped down next to her. She went to the back door and opened it.

"Let's get the night air," she said.

"It's cold out there."

"Here," she offered him the blanket. They hunkered down under the soft wool and sipped. With his long arms, he drew her against him. She rested her head on his chest.

"You're so confident. You believe in yourself. I wish I could be like that."

She felt his laugh ring in his chest before she heard it.

"That's what you think."

"Really?" She sat up to meet his gaze.

"I get butterflies before every game. I remember what my father, my adoptive father, used to say before every Little League game. 'You'll never be a pro ball player but do your best anyway.'"

"Did he really?"

"Yep. It had the opposite effect on me. Made me try harder to prove him wrong."

"Is he still alive?"

"Yeah. We don't get on much. I like my adoptive mom okay, but Dad, well, he's a waste of time."

"How so?"

"He never wanted me."

She raised her eyebrows. He continued.

"Yeah. I think their infertility thing was him, not her. I think he was embarrassed and pissed off. He'd rather not have had kids than get me."

"Are you sure?"

"I don't have any proof. But he used to say things, like, 'See that moving van down the street? We don't have to keep you. Nothing's final. We could move away like that and leave you here anytime we want.

So, you'd better behave. Or else.'" Skip's stomach clenched, his eyes watered briefly. Francie took his hand in both of hers.

"That's terrible," she said.

"It worked. I was scared shitless I'd be left homeless or have to go back to the orphanage."

"Orphanage?"

"Didn't you know? Yeah. I was riding in the car with my real parents one minute and in the hospital the next. They were killed. No next of kin. I was shipped off to Little Angels."

"Oh my God. How horrible!" She hugged his chest. "You must have been terrified."

"No kidding. When the Quincy's came along, it was a lucky break for me."

"Was it terrible at Little Angels?"

"It wasn't terrible. I mean if you'd never had parents, what the hell? Ya know? But I did. I had great parents. I cried for them every day for months."

Francie's eyes watered. Skip brushed a tear off her cheek with his thumb.

"Don't cry, baby. It worked out."

"That must have been so hard."

"You never know about stuff. Life. Shit happens. Sometimes fast, too."

"You're a great player. You never make an error," she said, stroking the back of his hand.

"I do. Just not a lot. But I do. Shortstop is the hardest position. My dad told me I'd never make the high school team. Too hard, he said."

"And did you?"

"You bet I did. Coach Guardino made sure I was ready. That bastard worked me into the ground. We practiced and practiced. Every day before and after school. Lifted weights, too. Until I had the strongest throwing arm in school."

"So, you got the job?"

"It wasn't like that," Skip said, his face lighting up. "It was an accident. The guy who was supposed to try out for shortstop got sick. He couldn't come. They asked me. My dad said 'no', but the coach grabbed my arm and offered me up. I pleaded with him not to. If I didn't make shortstop, I'd have been eliminated from the team."

"Oh my God!" Francie's eyes connected with his. "What happened?"

Skip blinked back tears. "I said I couldn't do it. But Coach said I could. He took me aside, away from my father and talked to me."

"Wow," she said softly.

"Yeah. He said I'd been doing it all along. He said he'd been grooming me for the position, and I was ready. I didn't believe him. I remember his words. 'You gotta have faith, Skip. I know you can do it. Now you gotta know it, too' and he shoved me out there. I didn't look at my father because I knew what he was thinkin'. And I just did it. I fielded everything hit to me. I beat every runner to the bag. I did it. Just like Coach Guardino said."

Tears were running down Francie's cheeks. Skip hugged her tight.

"Don't cry, honey. It's okay. It came out great. Look at me. Where am I? Everywhere my dad said I'd never be."

"I'm so proud of you."

Her declaration hit Skip between the eyes. After his parents died, he'd never heard those words, except from the coach. His heart squeezed, and his breath caught in his lungs. He leaned over, grabbed the tissue box, and handed it to her. She wiped her eyes and blew her nose.

"Thanks," he choked out, barely able to breathe. His heart swelled as he leaned over to kiss her.

"You're amazing. Best in the league."

"I do okay. Cal's gonna keep me a while longer."

"I'd say so."

"And what about you? Look at that picture. I couldn't do anything like that. And I don't know anyone else who can. You have so much talent."

"Not really," she said, shaking her head. "My stepmother doesn't think so. And she controls the purse strings. At least until June."

"What happens in June?"

"My birthday. I'll be twenty-seven. It's in the trust I get control of when I turn twenty-seven."

"Trust?"

She nodded. "My dad left money for me in trust. My stepmother is in charge of it now."

"Wow. I never had any money. Nothing from my real parents and my adoptive father never gave me a nickel. I went to college for two years on part baseball scholarship and loans, which I paid off myself."

"That's motivation."

"Damn right. Baseball saved me. I don't know where I'd be without it."

She nodded, bringing the back of his hand to her lips.

"My buddy, Billy. Billy Holmes. I'd be where he is without the Quincy's and baseball."

"Billy?"

"My best buddy from Little Angels. He got into crime. Just got out of jail. I'm helping him out a little. He's starting his own garage."

"That's awesome. You're a good friend."

"He kept me sane. He's still my friend, even though I was adopted, and he wasn't. That says a lot to me. He aged out of Little Angels at eighteen. I hope he can find his way now. What about you?"

"Nothing much to tell. You've heard it all already. I'll never be as good at art as you are at baseball."

"There's no pro league for art. You're so damn good. You're already a major leaguer."

"Hah! That's funny."

"I mean every word."

She cupped his cheek. "You're so sweet sometimes."

"Only sometimes?"

"When you're not being hotter than hell."

He chuckled. "Feeling sleepy now?"

She nodded.

"How about round two? I guarantee you a good night's sleep after."

"I thought you'd never ask," she said, smiling.

He scooped her up as if she was cotton candy and carried her into the bedroom, shutting the door with the heel of his foot.

Chapter Ten

A gentle breeze from the window woke Francie. It was seven and the sun was rising. Rolling over on her side, she watched Skip sleep. Cuddling closer, she breathed in his warm scent. The way he smelled, tasted, and the feel of his skin kept her senses on high alert. Not yet awake, he turned his back to her.

After staring at his muscles, she ran her palm along his spine. His body was perfectly formed. Touching him sent a shiver up her arm. She followed the trail of her hand with her lips. He jumped a little, then groaned.

"Are you starting something?" He rolled over to face her.

"Who me?" She batted her eyes.

He laughed. "Come here, you," he said, sliding her up, crushing her breasts to his pecs. "You feel good."

"So do you." His body created more heat than a wood stove. He slipped his leg between her thighs and his hand over her breast.

"Morning wood," he whispered, nibbling on her earlobe.

She shivered. He was ready to rock and roll, but she wasn't.

"I think I have the key to your ignition."

With that, he pushed back the covers and knelt between her legs. When his tongue touched her flesh, she arched her back.

"Oh, God, Skip!"

He chuckled, then he got back to work.

Tension grew inside her. Her eyes drifted shut as she gave in to desire. As if he was a mind-reader, Skip knew exactly when to stop. Francie groaned.

"Don't stop."

"Don't intend to," he said, covering himself, then mounting her. He slipped his dick inside her. She folded one leg at the knee and drew it to her chest. Skip pushed in farther. Bracing himself on his forearms, he moved his hips. His mouth hovered over hers while his fingers played with the ends of her hair.

"You're beautiful," he said, his eyes staring straight into hers.

Francie didn't believe him, but it didn't matter. He'd said it, and, at the moment, he believed it. She cupped his cheek, drew his head down, and kissed him. He stopped moving for a minute to ravage her mouth, taking her with his tongue and lips. Passion coursed through her, winding down to her core. She moved her hips. He got the message, picked his head up, and thrust into her hard.

"You want it, baby?"

She nodded.

"You got it."

He buried his face in her neck while he got his rhythm. Her senses tightened, heading for overload at breakneck speed. She clutched him with her thighs and wound her arms around his shoulders. Francie closed her lips on the soft tissue at the base of his neck as the intensity of feeling burst into a strong orgasm, shaking her body, and bucking her hips up.

She felt his breathing change. His chest expanded and contracted quickly beneath her embrace. Her fingernails scraped through a light sheen of sweat on his back.

"Oh, shit," he moaned.

Under her fingertips, his muscles tensed. His body shivered for a second as his release hit him. Francie kissed his neck. He relaxed, easing down on her, droplets of sweat from his forehead wet her hair.

The warmth of love surrounded her heart. How could she love him? She barely knew him. Of course, that wasn't true. They had been hanging around together for months. She'd become part of the Nighthawks' group through her friendship with Elena.

Love wasn't in Francie's plans. Nope, no way, no siree, no time for love—she had work to do, a degree to get, and a course in France to attend, if she got lucky. There was no time for Skip or any other man. But there he was, and she couldn't pull away. She needed him, whether she wanted to or not. He filled an emptiness in her heart. His love was like a drug, and she had become addicted.

He kissed her locks while she combed his unruly mop back with her fingers. How could she ever give him up if she couldn't stop touching him? Every time they were together, she'd put a hand on his forearm, push his shoulder, bump hips, or take his hand.

Drawn to him like a planet to the sun, Francie thrived on his attention. She blossomed under the warmth of his smile. Besides, he liked her chalk. That did it. She was his for the taking. And take he did, with gusto, style, and passion to spare.

"BABY, THAT WAS FANTASTIC."

Skip stroked her hair. The silkiness of the strands as they slipped through his fingers enticed him. She smelled great, too. Some perfume or body wash or whatever—he had no clue. But he liked it. He brushed his lips against her forehead.

Easing out of her, he padded to the bathroom. When he returned, she had put on underwear. A simple camisole and bikini panties in pink caught his eye.

"You have a great butt," he said, reaching around her to give it a squeeze.

"Thanks. You, too."

"Class today?"

She shook her head. "Not until five."

"Let's go out to breakfast."

"Okay."

"Shower first," he said, grabbing a towel out of the closet. "Join me?"

"We'll never get out of the house."

"I could have breakfast delivered." He cocked an eyebrow.

She laughed. "I need to come up for air."

"Okay, okay."

She slipped her arms around his waist. "Save it for me."

"It'll always be there for you, baby," he said, bending down to kiss her.

"Always is a long time," she muttered and pushed up out of bed.

He looked away, then stole a sideways glance at her. Always? What made him say something so stupid? He promised her forever even though they'd only known each other a couple of months. Could she hold him to it?

Francie appeared to be ignoring him, except for the two small spots of red in her cheeks. His foolish words embarrassed her. Maybe she didn't feel the same. Whoa. Wait a minute. How, exactly, did he feel about her? Thoughts positive and negative tumbled through his brain at breakneck speed. He shook his head slightly.

"Don't worry. I'm not holding you to that." She turned her back to him.

He smiled in relief. "I think I need food."

"Me, too." Facing him again, she eased close and put her arms around his waist. "Last night was great."

"You're, you're, well, something special," he said, bending down to kiss her.

"You, too. Take your shower. I'll get dressed." She stepped back and moved about the room, gathering her clothes. Skip headed for the bathroom. He took the world's fastest shower and grabbed clean boxers, jeans, and a shirt from the closet before entering the room.

Francie stood at the dresser, combing her hair. He'd always thought he preferred long hair. Every girl he'd dated had had it. But Francie's almost-black short locks bounced with an energy that drew him. His hands had a mind of their own. They wanted to get lost among the soft strands. The desire to touch her, here, there, and everywhere grew.

He gripped his pants and shoved his legs in.

Zipping up his fly, Skip turned to her. "Let's go. I know a little mom-and-pop diner. Great breakfast."

"I'm starving."

"They serve huge portions."

He took her hand and headed for the car. The warm scent of bacon mixed with that of fresh coffee in the cozy little eatery.

"Well, howdy."

"Hey, Margie," Skip replied, doing a quick read of the nameplate on her chest.

"This your girl?"

"Yep."

"Pretty. Whatcha having this morning?"

Service was quick. Food arrived before they even finished their first cup of java. Skip ate an omelet, two pancakes, bacon, and home fries. Francie downed two poached eggs and toast. Her eyes widened as he chowed down.

He watched as she twirled her hair around a finger and lowered her gaze when she spoke about herself. How could a girl so pretty and talented be so bashful? He didn't get it. She should be on top of the world. She had a God-given ability that few could equal, yet she seemed so tentative.

He stopped shoveling in eggs to take a drink of juice. He reached out and covered her hand with his. She looked up and smiled. Something about that, like she cranked up the wattage in the room, everything seemed brighter.

Hell, what did he know about being a husband or a father? What did he know about how a healthy family functioned? Nothing. He'd be the last guy he'd trust with one kid, let alone two. And with a woman, the same woman, day in and day out? Mr. "if it's Tuesday, you must be Sarah"? Could he be faithful forever?

A sharp pain shot through his chest. It was quick, too fast to be important, right? He was no family man. Yet that's all he'd ever wanted, next to being a baseball star, was to have a warm, loving, close family –like the one he'd lost. After a road trip, he'd envied the married guys. Wives waited in SUVs in the stadium parking lot for their men. He'd watched the passionate kisses they got, the cheers from their kids.

And he had no one. No one cheered when he got off the bus from the airport. No one waited behind the wheel of the family car for Skip Quincy. Nope. He could screw a different woman every week, every night, if he wanted. No one would object. Was that what he wanted? Would he trade sexual freedom for true love? In a heartbeat. He returned his attention to Francie.

"I met my ex freshman year," she said. "Four years later, he broke my heart. There's nothing more to tell."

"Asshole gave up the greatest chick he'll ever have," Skip said, reaching for the check.

He paid, and they returned to the cabin. It didn't take long to pack. He got behind the wheel and headed for the Palisades Parkway. The sun was out, warming the chilly fall day. Traffic was light. No reason to rush. He settled back and slid his hand over hers while Vivaldi played. A new feeling washed over him. One he'd never had before—contentment. Or at least it was what he thought contentment would feel like. A sense of calm, nothing frantic, not worried, stomach relaxed and happy, mind at ease—no worries.

"I had a wonderful time. Thank you for bringing me."

"You're welcome." He'd never shared his secret spot with a girl. Francie fit in perfectly. She liked it as much as he did, and it scared the shit out of him.

"Do you bring all your girlfriends there?"

"You're the first."

She didn't respond but turned her gaze to the window. He enjoyed the music for a few minutes. What did it mean to her, to him, that she was the first at the cabin? He pushed the question out of his mind. Why ruin a beautiful day with stupid, tension-building ideas?

"You should draw this stuff. The trees here are awesome."

"You're right. Just hard to do while we're whizzing by," she said, trying to hide a smile.

He laughed. "Guess I'm no artist."

"Maybe not, but you're a great lover and ballplayer."

"Two out of three ain't bad."

He dropped Francie off at her apartment, then drove home. He snarfed down two burgers he'd picked up and got to bed early. Hell, with the amount of sex he'd had over the weekend, you'd think he'd be asleep in two seconds. Didn't happen. He tossed, flinging his arm out, only to have it land on the mattress, instead of warm, soft flesh. He was minus one person. How could the absence of such a small woman make the bed seem so empty?

This wasn't good. He pushed up and padded to the window, his go-to place when he couldn't sleep. How many people in those lit up apartments were in love, happy, married? Why did it seem like everyone in New York was happily married, getting it regularly, and living a normal life except him?

He had practice tomorrow, then they started their seven-game series with the Texas Bulls. The series didn't worry him. His confidence was solid. The Nighthawks were on a roll, playing the best ball they'd played all season.

But this missing Francie crap had to stop. Wandering into the living room, he looked for a distraction. On his bookshelf was the latest book by Bobby's fiancée. He plucked it from the shelf and headed back to bed. Nothing like a steamy novel to relax him. Sure enough. By page fifty, Skip's eyelids drooped. He switched off the light and fell into a dreamless sleep.

UP AT SEVEN, SKIP DRESSED quickly and headed right for the stadium. Hunger gnawed at his innards. He made it in time for the breakfast buffet. Grabbing a plate, he piled it high with eggs, bacon, sausage, and home fries. Bobby had saved him a seat. He manned his fork like a shovel.

"Where were you? Elena and I thought we'd hang out with you and Francie," Bobby said, between bites of bacon.

"Upstate," Skip managed to get out before he took another mouthful of eggs.

"Huh?"

Skip chewed, swallowed and faced his friend. "You know, that little dump I go to."

"Oh, yeah. That cabin on the lake?"

"Yeah." He attacked a sausage link.

"Alone?"

Skip shook his head.

"With Francie?" Bobby asked.

Skip nodded.

"I thought you had a rule about not taking women there."

"It's not a rule. Just never dated anyone when we had the hiatus before."

Bobby nodded. "Sure, sure. Keep telling yourself that."

"What do you mean?"

"You're falling for Francie. Admit it."

"Nope. She's nice, talented, cute, but I travel solo."

"Yeah, right. I don't think so. Not anymore."

"Not everyone is looking for marriage, just because you are, Bobby."

"Getting laid regular is nice."

Skip glanced at his friend. "I do okay."

"But just okay. I do great."

"Come on, guys. Finish up. Let's get out there," Vic Steele said, clapping his hands.

The men wolfed down their food and headed outside. They spent half an hour stretching and letting their food settle before jogging. Skip and Bobby ran alongside Matt Jackson.

"When we're done, come to home plate, Skip. I want to show you something," Matt said.

Skip nodded. When he got there, the catcher had his glove on and was throwing a ball in the pocket, then taking it out.

"A guy I know, a coach, gave me this tip. I'm throwing to Jake. Watch, Skip." Matt cocked his arm and released the ball.

"Yeah? So?"

Grinning wide, Matt opened his glove.

"What the hell?"

"See? You thought I threw it to Jake, but I dropped it in my glove instead."

"That's amazing."

"Yeah. Imagine how many guys you could pick off?"

"Hell, yeah! Brilliant."

"Gotta practice. If you do it and the glove isn't lined up just right, you'll drop the ball on the ground and it's over, the asshole will steal. But if you do it, then wait for the sucker to step off the bag. You tag him and, blam! He's out."

"Fantastic!"

"Practice with Nat and Bobby. They need to learn it, too."

Skip had worried about Austin Sales, second biggest base stealer in the league. And he was on the Texas Bulls. But with this trick, Skip would be prepared to spring the surprise of a lifetime on Sales.

Since the Bulls had a better season than the Nighthawks, the first two games were happening in Dallas. By late afternoon, practice was over. The men showered and dressed in suits before boarding the bus to the airport. Once settled in his seat, he called Francie.

"How's the painting going?"

"That chalk?"

"Yeah. Whatever. The one you did at the lake?"

"It's finished."

"Can't wait to see it."

"Where are you?"

"On the bus. First two games in Dallas. Then we come home."

"I'll be watching tonight."

"You will?"

"Of course."

"What about your classes?"

"I'll watch after class."

"Okay. I don't want to interfere with your career."

She laughed. "You're not."

"Good."

"Good luck tomorrow."

"Thanks. We'll need it."

"You'll be fine."

He closed his mouth before words he wasn't ready to say popped out. He didn't have any substitutes, so he simply shut up.

"Skip? You still there?"

"Yeah. Hey, take care of yourself. I'll see you when I get back. Okay?"

"Okay."

He clicked off his phone. Before guilt could grab him by the neck, the phone rang. Assuming it was Francie, he responded quickly.

"Hey, look. I know I should have said something, but..."

"Skip?"

He stopped and blinked. "Mimi?"

"Who did you think it was?"

"Not you."

She laughed. "I can see that. I just wanted to call and wish you luck tomorrow. I hope you beat the crap out of the Bulls."

"Thanks. You got a thing about them?"

"Rowley hated them. That guy Sales was always beating out Rowley's throw."

"I know exactly how he felt."

"You get 'em. Hear me? Grind 'em into the ground."

Skip laughed. He'd never heard her use that tone before. "We got this. No worries."

"Good. Take care."

"You, too."

She hung up first. Skip sat back.

"Two at a time?" Bobby cocked an eyebrow.

"Now wait a minute. Don't you go sayin' anything to Francie."

Bobby simply stared at him.

"I didn't call Mimi. She called me."

"It had better stop there."

"Stay out of this, Bobby. There's nothing going on. She called to wish me good luck."

"I bet. Can't keep it in your pants for five seconds, can you?"

"You should talk. You used to leave tons of women in the dust."

"Well, that was then. I've got a permanent woman now, and I'm happy with her."

"Good for fuckin' you." Skip glared at his friend.

The two men fell silent for the rest of the trip. On the plane, Skip sat with Matt, read, and slept for most of the trip. Bobby sat on the other side. They buddied up again on the bus to the hotel.

"Why didn't Elena come with you?"

"She's finishing a book. Claims I distract her. At home, the second bedroom is her office."

Skip shot his friend a look. "I bet you do distract her."

Bobby colored. "It's not like that. We're not screwing every minute of the day. Geez. Sometimes I go in there when she's typing and start talking. She gets pissed. Says I'm interrupting her concentration."

"Just can't keep it in your pants, huh?" Skip snickered.

Bobby laughed and punched him in the shoulder.

They arrived late, but the time difference gave them an extra hour. Skip went right to his room, undressed and got into bed. He opened Elena's book but couldn't concentrate. What was Francie doing? Was she with someone else? He hadn't asked her about that. They hadn't talked about being exclusive, either. He turned out the light, shoving thoughts about Mimi and Francie out of his mind. He had to focus on baseball and not women. This was no time to think about love.

Chapter Eleven

Francie packed up her portfolio case, shrugged on a denim jacket and headed for class. Even though the case was unwieldy, she'd save cab fare and take the bus. While she appreciated Skip's feedback on her chalk drawing, she wasn't sure Professor Stark would agree. After propping it up against the wall, Francie had examined it from every angle. Being totally honest, she couldn't disagree with Skip. In addition to the oil painting of him dousing himself, this was her best work.

As she traipsed up the steps into the building and headed for the art room, her breath came faster. She stopped outside the studio door. Two deep inhalations calmed her. She straightened her blouse, combed her fingers through her hair, then entered.

While the other students unpacked their masterpieces, Francie's gaze scanned the room. Another student, Tony, raised his palm to her in greeting. He'd been buzzing around her on and off since the year began. She had fended him off. It was obvious what he had on his mind and Francie refused to jump into a booty-call relationship.

That's not what she had with Skip, right? Sure, they'd spent many steamy nights together, but there was more there than that. At least on her part. Skip boosted her confidence, which had taken a beating between the criticism from her stepmother and Professor Stark. Her teacher pushed her to excel, but her stepmother? Not so much.

She unzipped the case and gingerly took the chalk drawing out. She hadn't sprayed it with fixative yet because Professor Stark would want changes. After placing her case against the wall, she stepped back to look at her work from a distance.

The more she looked at it, the more she liked it, though she'd be too embarrassed to admit it. Her father had taught her the importance of humility. She must never brag or boast. Still a small smile curved her lips.

The murmur of voices interrupted her thoughts. The teacher entered. Even though he was a short man, Professor Stark commanded attention by his presence alone. Francie clasped her hands together and wished to be first, something she didn't do often. He ambled toward her but turned to critique a pencil drawing first.

Then he came to her.

"Ready, Ms. Whitman?"

Her throat as dry as day-old toast, she nodded. He peered at the piece from one angle, then another, then head on. He tugged on his goatee.

"Hmm. Nice work, Ms. Whitman."

He went on to explain what he liked, gesturing to spots he said were brilliant.

"It seems as if you've finally captured something. Tapped into your own emotions. Just like you did on that torso. That has life. Passion. So does this. Well done."

"What do I need to fix?"

"Nothing. It stands as is. You can submit it after class."

Francie couldn't speak. That had never happened before. He'd always pointed out something that needed attention. Her smile broad, she gave the work a quick, light coating of fixative, then waited for it to dry. Tony sauntered over. After gazing at her picture for five minutes, he shot her a thumb's up sign.

"You did good," he said.

"Thanks."

In her head, she heard Skip's voice saying, "I told you so." She smiled.

"Stark loved it. Wanna go out for a beer and celebrate?" He leaned against the wall and shoved his hands in his pockets.

Celebration sounded so good. Francie had made a breakthrough, and no one could be more surprised than she. She wanted to share it with Skip, not Tony, but Skip was in Dallas. She reminded herself that ballplayers traveled, a lot. He might not be around when she needed him, like now. Today was about her. Skip may be in Texas, but Tony was here. And a beer didn't mean bed.

"Yeah. Sure. Why not?"

They closed their portfolios and exited the building together. Tony talked a mile a minute as they made their way to The Blue Book, a bar and grill across from the campus.

She ordered a beer and a piece of cake. Tony did the same. His stare almost burned a hole in her shirt.

"My eyes are up here," she said, gesturing to her face.

He blushed and grinned. "I'd love to sketch you."

"What?"

"Will you pose for me?"

"Is that why you're staring at my chest?"

The waitress arrived with their drinks. Tony took a long swallow and licked his lips.

"Have you ever modeled?"

"Only fully dressed."

His smile melted into a frown. "Oh. Too bad."

"You want me to pose naked?"

"That's kinda the idea."

"Yeah, right. And all you want to do is draw me, right?" She cocked an eyebrow.

Color seeped into his face. "Well, if something else came up..."

"Came up?" She cracked up, laughing so hard she could hardly breathe.

"No, no, you know what I mean..."

"I know exactly what you mean," she responded, meeting his gaze.

"Okay, okay. Forget it. It's just that you're so beautiful and rounded, in all the right places. I'd get an 'A' with a charcoal of you."

Francie took a bite of her chocolate cake to give her mouth something to do.

"I mean. If you want to deprive a fellow artist of an 'A', I mean..."

"Shut up, Tony."

"Is that final?" he asked.

She couldn't take her clothes off in front of Tony, even for art. She'd feel his stare. Of course, it's childish to be that modest and self-conscious, but she couldn't help it. Besides, what would Skip say? How could she explain that it was art? She imagined he'd go ballistic and break up with her. Two good reasons not to do it. She sighed and smiled.

"Nope, no way. Not doing it."

"For art?"

She shook her head.

"You'd deprive a fellow artist?"

"You got it."

He frowned, paid the bill, and huffed out of the tavern with Francie following.

"I don't suppose you'd want to come up to my place, then?"

"I'm seeing someone, Tony," she said, a smile gracing her lips.

He made a face. "Call me when you get over this guy and want to be with a true artist."

"I'll keep that in mind."

They parted ways. On the bus home, Francie looked out the window, wondering if Skip was up at bat. Once in the apartment, she opened the pizza she'd picked up and turned on the television. Sure enough, the commentator announced Skip in the on-deck circle.

SKIP PLUNKED HIS BUTT on the bench. He'd walked last time at bat and struck out this time. He watched the third baseman shoulder the bat and stare at the pitcher. This was only game two, but they'd lost game one and needed a win before heading home.

Jake hit a long fly ball to center field. Austin Sales, the fastest man in the league ran it down and plucked it out of the air like it was simply a hard-boiled egg being tossed at him. That was it, three up, three down.

Skip picked up his glove and climbed the dugout stairs, heading for his position between second and third base. As Sales passed him he muttered loud enough for Skip to hear.

"Can't hit the broad side of a barn." Sales shook his head and snickered behind his hand. Skip picked up on it. Anger boiled up inside until he remembered the trick. He'd almost forgotten it. He grinned. Having the last laugh was always best.

Bobby gave Skip a quick pat on the butt as they took their positions in the field. Skip crouched down, narrowed his eyes, and opened his glove. Austin Sales was the third batter. With any luck, that could be the third out.

Dan Alexander, Nighthawks' ace, warmed up on the mound. It might be dangerous using him now. If they won, then they'd have to use him again on only two or three day's rest. Cal Crawley didn't want to do that, but hell, these were the playoffs and there was no room for caution. The point was to win the Championship and get to the World Series, no matter what.

Dan struck out the first batter. The second one, a broad-shouldered slugger, with a rep for having a nasty attitude, stepped up to the plate. Every Nighthawk had been the butt of one of his snide comments. The whole team hated him. Skip sensed a wave of hostility as the jerk shouldered the bat.

The wind-up and the pitch—a loud crack met Skip's ears as the ball soared high and far. He watched, holding his breath. The new guy on the team, rookie Will Grant, took off. Heading straight for the wall, he leapt into the air, glove raised, arm fully extended. Skip's eyes followed the ball right into Will's glove. The outfielder raised his palm, managing to cushion the blow when he hit.

The young man bounced off, fell backward, but kept his glove, gripping the ball, high in the air. He landed on his butt but never lost the ball. Skip jumped into the air, yelling. The nasty dickwad was out! The Nighthawks cheered. Will got a round of hoots, hollers, and applause from the Nighthawks' fans who braved the Bulls' stadium to root for their team.

Austin Sales marched from the on-deck circle to the batter's box. Dan went into his wind-up. Sales jumped on the first pitch. He hit a little blooper between Bobby and the right fielder for a base hit. Hugging first base, he scowled at Skip. As the next man took his stance at the plate, Austin took a lead.

He kept increasing it, pressing the pitcher. Dan fired to first, but Sales dove back in time. Skip grinned to see the hated player eat dirt. It didn't stop Sales. He brushed himself off and sidestepped his way toward second, stopping closer to the bag this time.

Dancing a bit, shifting his weight from foot to foot, Sales did whatever he could to rattle the pitcher. Dan wiped sweat from his forehead before going into his wind-up. Skip frowned. Excess sweat meant the pitcher was worried, stressed, and it was from Sales putting on the pressure. The Bulls' player increased his lead, inching closer to Skip. He tried to keep one eye on the ball and one on Austin but couldn't. He stuck with the ball.

When Dan threw his pitch, Austin Sales took off, running full speed. He came barreling in, sliding head first, creating incredible dust, and temporarily interfering with Skip's vision. Fortunately, with his eye on the ball, he caught it, preventing it from going into centerfield and giving Sales more bases. But the throw was a little high, and he couldn't catch it and crouch down in time to tag the runner.

Sales, grinning like a chimp, shot a triumphant glance at Skip. Brushing himself off, he didn't pay much attention to the shortstop.

"Bobby!" Skip called, pulling his arm back to throw. Bobby nodded and put up his glove. Skip cocked his arm and let fly. Bobby put his hand over his glove and smiled.

"Fuck you, Quincy," Sales muttered, out of earshot of the umpire.

Skip simply smiled back. Sales took his foot off the bag and side-stepped a decent lead, looking up to watch the pitcher. But he was too late. Skip stepped over and tagged him with the ball.

"What the fuck?" Sales yelled.

Skip laughed as the umpire called, "Yer out!" The field was in an uproar. The Bulls' manager came flying out of the dugout, screaming at the umpire that it was a trick and Skip had an extra ball. The ump loped over to Skip, who was heading for the dugout. The man examined the ball and shook his head.

"Ruling stands. He's out."

Austin Sales kicked dirt, swore, and punched the air before his fellow players forced him to take his position in centerfield. Skip high-fived Matt and laughed all the way to the dugout.

"You know, that last laugh shit is true," he said to Matt.

"Yeah. Now if we could just get a fuckin' hit," the catcher said, shaking his head and heading to the batter's box.

FRANCIE MADE A POT of coffee and turned on her computer. She pulled up the pictures she had transferred from her camera. Totally unaware she was photographing him, Skip had provided many natural poses. She took her time, examining each one. Longing for him grew as she gazed at the photos, creating memories of their weekend at the lake.

The school was sponsoring a judged art show in a few weeks. Students were allowed to enter as many as five works. Francie had to get going if she was going to finish in time for the show and do her school-work, too.

She'd snapped over one hundred pictures. Selecting the right ones to use for paintings or chalks would take time. She put on some Mozart and poured another mug of coffee. The phone rang.

"What are you doing?" It was Elena.

"Working."

"On what?"

"I have to start on the pieces for the art show."

"Can you come out to lunch with me? I'm buying."

"What's the occasion?"

"Nothing. Just miss you, that's all."

"Not buyin' it. Come clean."

"Okay, I'm curious how you and Skip are doing," Elena confessed.

"There's nothing to tell. He's in Dallas, playing ball, and I'm here doing my art."

"There must be more than that."

"Nope. How's Bobby?"

"Okay."

"Just okay?"

"Better than okay since they won last night."

"Wasn't that an amazing game? I couldn't believe Skip faked out that guy."

"I got the blow-by-blow last night from Bobby."

"Too bad you couldn't get that in person," Francie snickered.

The women laughed.

"You're bad. Can you do lunch, anyway?"

"Lonely?"

"It's hard when they go on the road."

"Okay. But it has to be on the late side."

"Got it. One thirty?"

"See you then."

Francie went back to her task. After she had narrowed the pictures down to twenty, she took a break. Sipping the last of the coffee, she curled up on the window seat and watched people pass by. She had been so excited and proud when Skip had pulled that surprise play yesterday. She had no right to be proud. After all, he didn't belong to her, did he?

She'd bring along her pictures and ask Elena's opinion. Her friend had a good eye. Discussing her project would keep the conversation focused on her work and away from any mention of her relationship with Skip Quincy. If you could call it that.

The last thing she needed was advice about love. She knew how she felt, but what about him? She had no clue where she stood—girlfriend or convenient bed partner? Yet the more time she spent with him, the more hollow and empty time without him seemed. Skip filled up space, a room, a cabin, with his size and personality. He swept her away on a tide of love and positivity. He'd proved to be the first seriously cheerful force in her life, and she had become addicted. Because she needed her fix of Skip, and no matter what the cost, she'd be his as long as he wanted her.

Francie showered, changed, and tucked the pictures into an envelope. The autumn breeze and bright sunshine set a cheerful mood. She smiled as she headed for the subway and Café Bonjour, a little French pastry place where she'd meet Elena. What better locale to enjoy being in love than a French eatery?

As she walked from the train, she dialed Skip.

"Congratulations on last night."

"Thanks. Did you watch?"

"I did. And your fake-out move was awesome!"

He laughed. "The dickwad had it coming."

"Is he a bad guy?"

"Yeah. A real tool. Thinks he's hot."

"Not anymore. You brought him down."

"Guess I did. How you doing?"

"Good. Missing you."

"Yeah?"

"Yeah."

"Me, too."

She smiled. "No groupies there?"

"Plenty. So what? Wish you were here."

"Aw, thanks."

"What are you wearing?"

"I'm on the street, fully dressed. Meeting Elena for lunch."

"Don't tell her anything. Bobby's like a fucking bloodhound."

"She is, too!"

"They should leave us alone."

"I agree."

"Gotta go. Bus is leaving for the airport."

"See you soon?"

"Yeah. We're back tonight and play game three tomorrow. Dinner tonight?"

"Great. Freddie's at six?"

"If we land on time, I'll be there."

"Uh, okay. See you."

"Yeah."

Francie frowned at the phone before she tucked it into her purse. Why wouldn't he say the word "love?" Why wouldn't she? Her brows knitted. Did that mean they didn't love each other? She'd see him tonight. Time to get stuff sorted out. Were they committed or an affair of convenience?

Chapter Twelve

Most of the Nighthawks slept on the plane. Squeaking out a victory by one run added a ton of stress to the physical workout. They had split the first two games. Next three would be played in New York. It was make-or-break time and the pressure escalated.

Skip awoke during the landing. His stomach growled. He checked his watch. Yep, dinnertime was almost here. He smiled because that meant he'd be seeing Francie.

"You coming to Freddie's?" Bobby asked.

"Yeah. Francie's meeting me."

"Elena's coming, too."

"I thought you'd be running home to get laid," Skip teased.

"Tonight. I need a steak first."

"Me, too. Shit, these women wear us out," Skip said, grinning at his buddy.

Bobby and Skip talked about the game, sharing their observations. The ride was short. Skip got into his car and headed for the bar and grill, his favorite hangout. The big table on the side was ready. Tommy had it set up with utensils and pitchers of iced tea.

Skip planned to invite Francie to go home with him. He needed her, physically and mentally. Getting stuck in his head didn't help his performance on the field. He needed downtime, and listening to her talk about school and watching her create art de-stressed him.

Fortunately, Mimi Banner had hightailed it down to Florida already. She told him she'd bought a place on her last trip. She went down to get it ready for the winter and planned to stay there until May. She couldn't have arranged her schedule better for Skip.

He'd could see her when he went to Florida, after the World Series. If she'd gotten over her issues about sex, she might become his winter chick. Francie would probably be going to Paris. Would Mimi take Francie's place in his bed? How could he explain that to the young artist? Did he even want Mimi anymore? Things were getting complicated.

He took a seat at the long table and poured tea while he watched his teammates and their women file in. After ten minutes, Francie entered. She looked good. Her smile widened when she saw him. He watched the slight bounce of her breasts as she approached. She wore a black skirt and a pink sweater. A colorful scarf almost hid her cleavage. His palms itched to close over those soft mounds. Even with her high heels, she was still short. His gaze paused for a moment at the roundness of her hips before it slid down to examine her legs. She had great legs. His mouth went dry, then saliva flowed. Crap, if he wasn't careful he'd be drooling by the time she got to the table. Damn, Francie heated the room the moment she entered.

He had to hand it to her, she knew how to dress. She looked as good as a juicy steak. He rose, pulled out her chair, and brushed his lips against hers.

"Hi. Sorry I'm late," she said.

"You're not late."

He held her jacket as she shucked it. He seized the opportunity to stare at her chest while she wasn't looking. Blood pumped between his legs. *Down boy. Your time will come.*

Elena stopped over, staring from one to the other, grinning. She patted Skip on the cheek before joining Bobby.

"She's a pain in the ass," Skip mumbled, picking up his glass.

"She's my friend. She just wants us to be happy."

"Then she should butt out. She's not helping. Making me feel stupid."

Francie patted his hand. "She's okay. Once you get to know her, you'll understand. She's so happy with Bobby, she wants the same thing for everyone in the whole world"

"Like that's gonna happen?"

"Where's your positive attitude?"

He shrugged.

"Play-off tension?" she asked.

"Guess so."

"And no alcohol, right?"

He nodded. "But nobody said we couldn't have sex." He wiggled his eyebrows.

Francie threw a flirtatious look at him. "Well, then, we'd better order and eat fast."

Skip sat up straight and raised his hand. "Waiter!"

THE NIGHT AFTER GAME five – New York City

The Nighthawks had won the first game in New York. Home field advantage helped. But their luck ran out with game four, which the Bulls won by four to one and game five when the Texans squeaked out a win—three to two.

Skip and his teammates grumbled as they showered and headed home to pack for the trip back to Texas the next day. The Nighthawks were behind, two games to three, and in Texas, they wouldn't have home field advantage. Anything could happen.

Skip made plans to spend his last night in New York with Francie. They dined with the team at Freddie's, then headed home. Driven by stress and almost unbearable pressure, he made love to his girl until he was spent.

Francie lay back on the bed, fanning herself with her hand.

"Do you want me to turn on the A.C.?" he asked.

She placed a hand on his arm. "I'm fine."

Folding his arms behind his head, he grinned. "Broke my record."

"What?"

He glanced at her. "Yeah. My sex record."

"And that is?"

"How many times I've done it in one night."

She nodded.

"You're my inspiration."

"I may never walk again," she quipped.

He rolled onto his side, facing her. "Did I hurt you? Are you okay?"

"Just kidding," she said, propping up on her side. But a slight grimace gave her away.

"Bullshit. I did hurt you. I'm sorry. Can I rub it and make it feel better?"

She pushed his hand away. "I don't think so. Rubbing it *created* the problem."

He kissed her hair. "Are you sure you're okay?"

"A day's rest and I'll be like new."

"You can still paint, can't you?"

"I don't use my vagina to hold a brush. I'll be fine."

He laughed. "You were amazing. Best ever."

"You, too," she said, snuggling closer to him.

Truth be told, his dick was a bit sore. Until then, he'd had no idea that there could be such a thing as too much sex. He didn't mind. He was totally relaxed and ready to face the next game with the Bulls.

Skip pulled her into his embrace and closed his eyes. No amount of pressure could keep him awake.

"'Night," Francie whispered.

"'Night, sweetheart." The endearment rolled easily off his tongue. Aware he'd almost declared his love, he ignored it. Sleep called. He zonked out quickly.

He woke up early and eased out of the bed without waking Francie. On his way to the kitchen, he stopped to gaze at her. She resembled a well-loved woman, beautiful and satisfied. He grinned. No matter what else he might do in the world, he knew how to please a female.

Skip placed a steaming mug of java on the night table. Francie sat up.

"For me?"

"Who else?" He plopped down on the bed. "You look good even just getting up. Unusual for a girl."

"Is that a compliment?"

"Yep." He reached over and tousled her hair. "Let's go. I need food." She pushed out of bed and gathered her clothes.

He leaned over to check the time. "Quickie shower, then let's eat. Gotta be on the bus in two hours."

After swearing hands off, the lovers took a fast shower together. Skip soaped up Francie's chest, even though he'd vowed to leave her alone. She kissed him, then rinsed off.

"Do I get a raincheck?"

"How about a do-over?"

"That works."

He packed up and drove them to a little diner ten blocks from the stadium. Skip had eaten there many times and became friendly with the owner. They ordered food. The waitress filled cups with coffee.

"I don't want to talk about the game. Let's talk about you. What are you working on?"

"Professor Stark wants me to submit my work to the school art show. Due soon."

"Will you be ready?"

"I have one piece. Then he wants a series of paintings for a special exhibit."

"A series, huh? That's a lot of work, isn't it?"

She nodded. "I've got the idea and the pictures. I think I can do it. I hope I can use those for my projects next semester."

The waitress brought their orders. Skip had a Swiss cheese omelet, sausage, bacon, and home fries. Francie had only bacon and eggs.

"When are the shows? Can I come?"

"The first one is October fifteenth."

"What about the thing in Paris?" he asked, then shoveled in a forkful of sausage.

"Paris? Oh, that's a class. It's very small. You have to be chosen for it. I'll never get in."

"But what if you do? When would you go?"

"Right after Christmas."

He nodded. "I'll be in Florida."

"You're going to Florida?"

"Didn't I tell you? I go down there for a couple of weeks with the guys."

She stopped eating and stared.

"You're gonna be busy with school. Hell, you might even be in Paris."

"And if I'm not?"

He shrugged. "Let's cross that bridge when we come to it."

"Is Mimi going to be there?"

He sensed color rising to his face. He focused on his omelet and didn't answer.

"I assume she is then," Francie said.

"I think she bought a house somewhere down there."

"She told you that?"

He nodded

"Lovely. I'm your on-season girlfriend and she's your off-season one?"

"It's not like that."

"Then what is it like?"

Two spots of red colored her cheeks. Skip panicked. He took her hand, but she pulled away.

"Tell me," she insisted.

"Okay, okay. I might see her when I'm down there. We're not committed. I mean, not exclusive. You never said anything."

"Me?" She pointed to her chest. "I'm not the only one here."

"We never discussed it."

"I'm not dating anyone else and don't intend to."

"Okay, then."

"What about you?"

Skip's mouth got dry. He picked up his water glass, hoping the answer would come to him.

"Well?"

The red spots grew brighter, her brows arched, her eyes grew cold.

"I don't know. What can I say? I've never thought about settling down. I haven't been in a happy family since my birth parents died. I don't think I could do it. Be a husband and a father? What do I know about being a good father? Nothing. I'd planned to stay single."

"You might have told me about your *plan*."

"Subject never came up."

"It's up now."

"What about you?"

"Of course, I want to get married. I want to be faithful to one man and trust that he feels the same way."

"And kids?"

"I think I know enough of bad mothering to be a really good one." She blinked rapidly a few times and cast her gaze to her fork.

He took her hand. "You'd be a great mom."

"Thanks."

When the waitress refreshed their coffee, Skip sat back. He frowned. His plan to have two women wasn't going the way he'd intended. Losing Francie wasn't supposed to happen. His chest tightened. He'd never find another like her—one who'd put up with him. Maybe when snow falls in August. He doubted Mimi would take his shit. Maybe he was wasting his time with Mimi, anyway.

The waitress left. Skip changed the subject.

"When do you find out about Paris?"

"I don't know. So, you're telling me we aren't committed?"

He sipped the hot brew, his mind whirling.

"Then, if I go to Paris, I'm free to date, and sleep with whoever I want?"

He gulped too fast and burned his tongue. Reaching for the water glass, he grimaced.

"You want to sleep with other men? After last night?"

"I never said I wanted to, just that I'm free to—if I feel like it."

Instantly, he knew how a fox feels when it steps in a trap. Pain seared through him. Simply the idea of her sleeping with someone else kicked him in the gut.

"Well? I'm waiting."

The smirk on her face was like a dagger to his heart. She was torturing him and enjoying it! He watched her pick up her fork and resume eating. Meanwhile, his appetite had evaporated.

"Do we have to talk about this before the last two games in the playoffs?" He'd stall as long as he could.

"I'm so sorry! How insensitive of me. No, we don't have to discuss this now. I don't want to stress you out before the game."

He breathed deeply. Relief flooded his system. Now he'd have time to figure out the mess he'd made.

"Thanks. I appreciate it. You're special to me, Francie. I hope you know that."

"Special? Damning with faint praise."

"What?"

"That's practically an insult."

"I don't mean it to be."

They finished eating. Skip paid the bill.

"I'll drive you home."

"I'll take the subway," she said, extending her hand.

"Aw, come on. Don't be like that." He stepped closer, hugging her to him. "Come on, baby. Give me a kiss for good luck."

He tipped her chin up. Her eyes were full. She pushed away and blinked rapidly.

"I'm not feeling it."

"Please?"

A tear escaped down her cheek. He wiped it away with his thumb.

"Don't cry, honey. Don't cry. I'm sorry. I didn't mean to upset you."

She rummaged through her bag until she found a tissue. Blotting her cheek, she stepped back.

"Please, sugar. I care for you, Francie. I really do. Can't we go back to being what we were?"

"You want me to forget that you'll be dating, and I use the term loosely, Mimi in Florida? That you can't or won't commit to me? How can I just turn the page on that?"

His gaze studied her face. Her gray eyes looked troubled. Her nose had reddened a bit and there were two tear tracks down her cheeks.

"Get in the car. I'm taking you home."

Were things going to get worse in the car? Would there be a flood of tears? Most likely. Could he leave her like that? No way.

Skip opened the door, and Francie got in. He started the car and let it idle.

"I guess we need to talk."

Francie nodded before dissolving into tears. She sobbed into a tissue. He reached for her, but she pushed him away.

"I'm in love with you, Skip."

His eyebrows rose.

She faced him. "That's right. I finally have the courage to tell you the truth. I love you."

"Francie, honey. That's great." Again, he reached for her and was rebuffed.

"It's not so great for me, is it? You don't love me back. In fact, you're making plans to sleep with someone else. So, it's not great for me at all," she said before a fresh round of tears started.

He wanted to disagree with her, but she was right. He'd been hoping to get Mimi in bed for a while. But now, he couldn't remember why. What could she possibly give him that he wasn't getting major big time from Francie? Nothing. He'd been playing all ends against the middle for too long now. Did he even *know* how to be faithful to one woman?

"Look, the Mimi thing. Hell, I was just curious. I met her before you and I got together."

"So? So what? You still want to sleep with her." Her voice rose.

"Maybe not. I mean, she can't hold a candle to you."

"Oh, great! Now you're comparing me to her?" More tears.

Skip opened his mouth then closed it. Perhaps it wasn't safe for him to say anything.

"Look, you can have your freedom. All the freedom you want. I think we should stop seeing each other," Francie said.

"What? No!" Panic grabbed his throat.

She faced him. He'd never seen a more pathetic, lovesick expression in his life. His heart lurched. He took her face in his hands and kissed her and kissed her.

"Don't do that, baby. You'll kill me. Don't leave me," he whispered between lip-locks.

"I don't want to share you."

"Okay. Forget Mimi. It's only you for me. All the way, honey. All the way." He stroked the back of her head.

"Are you sure?"

"I'm sure. I don't want to be separated from you. Mimi is out."

"I probably won't go to Paris."

"Then you can come to Florida with me?"

"Maybe. I'll have final projects to work on. I'll see how it goes."

A twinge of shock shot through him. He'd never made a promise like that before, never before felt love grip his heart.

"I hope you can."

Running on automatic pilot, he put the car in gear. New feelings swept through him. What had just happened? Could Skip Quincy, cocksman extraordinaire, have committed himself to one woman? He laughed quietly at himself. Maybe domesticity wasn't so bad, after all?

"What's so funny?" Francie asked, refreshing her makeup.

"I've been a bigger asshole than Austen Sales."

Chapter Thirteen

Francie kissed Skip again, then got out of the car.

"Good luck tomorrow."

"We've got this."

"Don't let Austen Sales rile you."

"Don't worry, baby. I can handle that dickwad."

He kissed her again, put the car in drive, and headed uptown. Francie took a deep breath. She'd finally gotten a commitment, of sorts, from Skip Quincy. Her smile was tentative. Through a blur of tears and sobs, she'd heard him say he'd drop Mimi. Or that's what she thought she'd heard.

Trekking up the stairs, she unlocked her door, then plopped down on the sofa. Her head ached. Skip would be in Dallas for four days, finishing up the playoffs. She refused to think about their relationship anymore. Two half-finished canvases stared at her. Their reproach was as loud as if they had voices.

She got up and donned a smock. After tapping the classical playlist on her phone, she grabbed a palette, brushes, and tubes of oil paint, secured the photo on the wall with tape, and began work.

As she worked through the lunch hour and late into the afternoon, the pictures took on life. It wasn't unusual for her to forget time when she painted. Professor Snark said all good artists got wound up in their work and forgot about the outside world. He said it was cathartic, cured whatever was bugging them. She had to agree.

Taking a deep breath, she stood back about six feet and studied the results. As she perused the piece, additions and changes popped into her head. She picked up her brush and finished the job. After a bathroom break, she popped open a bottle of wine, heated up frozen leftovers, and turned the game on the television. Her phone rang.

"Hi, girlfriend. Whatcha doing?" It was Elena.

"Painting. You at the game."

"Yep. Family seats. How's it coming?"

"I've just about finished one. It looks pretty good. For me, that is."

"Stop that. You're a talented artist."

"Yeah, yeah. Bobby nervous?"

"Of course."

"You calm him down last night?"

She heard a low snigger. "I did my best."

"Wish I could be there, too," Francie said, staring at the screen, looking for her friend.

"Someday."

"Maybe. Besides, I have work to do. Good luck. I'll be watching."

She hung up, took off her smock, and sat cross-legged on the sofa. When the camera zoomed in for a close-up of Skip in the on-deck circle, Francie's heartbeat quickened. God, he was so handsome. His short brown hair was combed perfectly, and his blue eyes were intense.

The phone rang again.

"Keep it on. Let's talk about the game," Elena said.

"Aren't you with other wives and girlfriends?"

"Nobody here I know. Too many Texas Bulls' fans, too. It's creeping me out."

"Okay," Francie agreed.

The women talked about each pitch. Skip hit a bloop single to shallow left field. Francie almost came out of her chair, cheering.

While she ate and chatted with Elena, the Nighthawks strained to compete. They were down two games to three. This was a make-it-or-break-it game. They had to win. It was the top of the ninth the next time Skip came up to bat, Bobby was on first and Nat on second. She chewed a nail as he took the first pitch. It was a strike. She booed at the screen.

As he shouldered the bat, she held her breath. That must have been his pitch because Skip swung and connected. She could hear the crack through the TV. Jumping up and down, she watched it sail high and long, right into the stands for a three-run homer! Francie pranced and danced around. Elena screamed into the phone.

They laughed and cried tears of relief together. That was Skip, a hero in the eleventh hour. The score was five to four, Nighthawks. Francie chewed a nail as the Bulls made quick work of the rest of the batting order.

Now the Texas team came to bat. This was it. They had to score two runs or lose. Francie sat on the edge of the sofa. Her heart was in Dallas with her lover as she held her breath. Dan Alexander, usually a starting pitcher, was brought in to relieve in what the Nighthawks hoped was the last inning. Cal Crawley counted on Dan to pull off the win. As he warmed up, Francie watched Skip and Bobby put their heads together.

Dan made quick work of the first batter, striking him out. Next one walked. Matt, Skip, and Bobby conferred with Dan on the mound before Austen Sales shouldered the bat. They nodded and then each returned to his position. She saw Skip glance at Bobby.

Tension coiled inside Francie. She wanted her man to win. She paced with the phone to her ear to keep contact with Elena. Sales took the first pitch for a ball. The next was a strike. Francie couldn't believe how cool Austen Sales looked, standing in the batter's box, taking pitch after pitch.

Then the count was three/two – three balls and two strikes. She figured he'd be swinging. Did Dan have what it took at the eleventh hour to retire the side and win the game? The wind-up, the pitch, the swing. Francie held her breath.

THE CLOSE GAME GAVE the Nighthawks confidence. Dan striking out Austen Sales buoyed the team. They came into game seven hungry for a win. Skip could taste victory and see himself loping into the stadium to play the World Series.

He'd spent an hour on the phone with Francie, talking about the game before he hit the sack. The next day, energy flowed through him. He bounded down to breakfast, his huge appetite barely contained. The men chowed down with little chatter, fueling their bodies for a long, challenging contest. The Bulls were going to pull out all the stops to win this final playoff game.

Both teams lusted for the title. Some of the players had been to the World Series before, others had not. With only one game standing in the way of going down that road, Skip and his buddies set their sights on winning. Skip, his appetite voracious, returned to the buffet table three times. His teammates followed suit. Who could play all out for nine innings without food?

Cal Crawley stood up and addressed his team.

"The only strategy here is to focus. Take care. Don't make any mistakes. No errors. Errors lose games. Do your best at the plate. Watch the pitcher. This will be the second time you've faced him, so you oughta know him. Anticipate. And whatever you do, don't let any Bulls get under your skin. A fight on the field is sure to get you thrown out. The results? We lose. We can't afford to have any of our starters tossed out for some dumbass feud or remark. Don't let them get to you. Keep a cool head. Think. Observe. And play your best. You've got the stuff to win. That's all."

The men applauded. Skip finished up, then headed for the locker room. The men dressed in silence. Bobby waited for Skip to tie his shoes, then the two infielders walked out to the field together. Even though the game was in Dallas, there were New York fans there. A cheer roared in their ears as they loped onto the field. The men stood with their caps over their hearts for the national anthem. This was it, the final shot to get to the World Series.

The Nighthawks, the visiting team, were up to bat first. Nat headed for home plate. Bobby warmed up in the on-deck circle. Skip stood near the stairs, silently praying his teammates would get on base, but it was three up, and three down.

Julio Suarez was the starting pitcher for the Nighthawks. Moose Macafee was around for clean-up and closing. Since he pitched only one inning the day before, Dan Alexander might have the stuff to close, if they needed him. Cal didn't normally use top pitchers like Dan to close, but it had worked the day before. He'd do whatever he needed to get to the World Series. If they won without using Dan, then he'd have enough rest time to start in the first game. That was Cal's plan.

The way things were going, that looked doubtful. It was a pitcher's duel with few hits. Skip thanked God for keeping Austen Sales off the bases. Wound so tight with the pressure to win, Skip didn't think he could have kept his temper if Sales goaded him.

In the dugout, the men chewed gum, paced, or did both. They guzzled a ton of water to quench a big thirst born of the hot Texas sun and tension. Batter after batter flied out, grounded out, or struck out. The Nighthawks couldn't get any traction.

The Bulls weren't any more successful. When Jake Lawrence came to bat, it was the top of the eighth and the score was zero-zero. He was the clean-up man for the 'Hawks, their best hitter. But he was no more successful than the rest. The inning proved to be the same scoreless disaster as the previous ones.

This was one for the books. A double no-hitter was unheard of in a playoff series. In the top of the ninth, Matt Jackson was first up. He grounded out to second. Chet Candeleria, playing left field came to bat next. By some miracle, the third baseman bobbled Chet's routine grounder, and he made it to first base.

Next was Will Grant, the rookie on the team. Brought up to cover center field after one of the starting outfielders was injured, he'd not played long with the Nighthawks. Skip's hopes sank. With a man on base, how could he count on this kid to move Chet home? Skip shook his head—no way. It looked like the game was heading for extra innings.

The kid shouldered the bat and took his stance, holding the wood high behind him. Skip held his breath. First pitch was a ball. The kid waited, and the second pitch was a ball, the third a strike. The kid narrowed his eyes. Skip saw the third base coach give Will the signal to swing.

After popping gum in his mouth, Skip chewed double time. The pitch was a fastball, a little high and outside, the kid swung and connected.

"Holy fucking shit!" Skip said, climbing the dugout steps to get a closer look. He shaded his eyes with his hand and watched the ball sail into the stands.

Chet waited for Will at home plate. The 'Hawks were going wild in the dugout, hugging and leaping into the air. When Will got to home plate, the whole team piled out onto the field to greet him. The score was two-zero, with the bottom of the ninth the only chance for the Bulls to get even. The next batter walked, then the designated hitter picked up the bat. He hit into a double play and the inning was over.

The Nighthawks took the field. Skip set his jaw and pounded his fist into his glove. They had to get the Bulls out before they scored. Dan had done his job, retiring the side in the eighth, so Cal brought in Moose Macafee to close. The manager didn't want to wear out Dan Alexander, in case they won.

Matt had a brief conference with Moose, who warmed up then let loose his first pitch. At the plate, Austen Sales jumped on the first ball and got a single. Sweat broke out on Skip's forehead. It was his job to throw the son of a bitch out when he tried to steal second. And Skip would bet every cent he had that the speedy Bull would do just that. The little trick of not throwing the ball and tagging Sales out wouldn't work again. The Bull would be wise to the scheme—but not with the second baseman. Skip had taught Bobby the trick and they intended to use it on Sales if the situation came up. Skip kept his eye on the ball, with a glance at Sales from time to time.

Moose looked over at first base, then back at Matt. The catcher gave the signal for a pitch-out. Skip and Bobby saw it. Sure enough, Sales broke for second base. Moose fired the ball to Matt who leapt up and threw a shot right at Skip. In one fluid movement, the ball changed direction, coming hard at him.

Skip opened his glove as Austen dove into a head-first slide. Bobby was right behind. Sales managed to slide in just under the tag. Swearing to himself, Skip tossed the ball to Bobby. Austen stood up and brushed off his uniform.

"You're not gonna fool me a second time, asshole," he said to Skip.

Skip simply smiled. "I don't even have the ball."

Austen turned to glance at Bobby throwing to first. Skip crouched down, looking at Moose, as if play was ready to resume.

"I'm gonna steal all the way home on you assholes," Austen said, side-stepping into a healthy lead at second. He put his hands on his thighs and bent over. Skip put his glove out behind him. Bobby ran over and dropped the ball into it.

"I don't think so," Skip said, running up behind Sales and tagging him with his glove.

"Yer out!" The umpire called.

Sales turned around again. His face reddened. Skip swore he saw steam coming from the outfielder's ears. Every swear word he knew came flying out of Austen Sales' mouth. Then he took a swing at Skip, who ducked. The umpire threw Sales out of the game. Bobby and Skip couldn't stop laughing.

Moose struck out the next batter and Will Grant caught a long fly ball from the last one, giving the game to the Nighthawks, two to zip. The New York Nighthawks were going to the World Series!

The Nighthawks' locker room rained champagne. The players danced, bumped chests, hugged, hollered, and drank. Skip dialed Francie.

"We won! We won!"

"I saw. I saw. Congratulations! Awesome!"

"We're coming home tomorrow. Let's celebrate."

"I'll be there."

"Love you," he said, then hung up before she could respond.

"I'm gonna get shit-faced. You with me?" Matt asked.

Skip laughed and refilled their glasses from the never-ending flow of bubbly.

FRANCIE SPENT THE DAY painting. Now that Skip was due back, she hoped they'd be together. Still not sure she'd heard him right, a small part of her filled with joy. Did he say he loved her? She sighed.

Skip would arrive at the stadium about five, and Francie planned to meet him at Freddie's for a team celebration. Then they'd go back to his place for their own private one. She put away her painting supplies and ran a bubble bath. Anticipation of his presence kick started her nerves. She couldn't wipe the smile off her face. Her thoughts drifted to being with Skip. She'd missed his hugs, his lovemaking, and his sense of humor.

After a thorough soaking, and a long phone conversation with Elena about what to wear, she slipped on black velour pants, commando, and a matching tunic top. No reason to add extra clothing she'd simply wiggle out of later, anyway.

A bright pink, long chiffon scarf, and rose earrings topped off the outfit. After applying light makeup, a dab of perfume behind each ear and between her breasts, she slipped a toothbrush into her purse, grabbed a white fleece jacket and made her way to the subway.

Humming a favorite tune, she boarded the train. Her lover filled her thoughts. Annoyed by a stare from a man sitting across from her, Francie cast her gaze to her phone. She pulled up pictures of Skip. His warm smile seemed to leap from the device and surround her. It wouldn't be long now. The man got up at the next stop. He tipped his hat to her.

"Beautiful," he said, before exiting.

She grinned. His compliment boosted her confidence. *Guess I picked the right clothes.* At her stop, Francie got out and fairly skipped up the stairs to the street. She continued singing softly, to herself as she made her way to the restaurant.

A huge banner in red and white hung over Freddie's door. *Congratulations 'Hawks!* She entered and scanned the room for Skip. The place was mobbed. The scent of grilling beef surrounded her. Her mouth watered. A familiar laugh drew her attention. When she spotted Skip, her heart fluttered. He looked up, his eyes locked with hers, his smile widened.

"There she is. My girl," he said, waving as he picked his way through the thick crowd. Francie rushed forward to meet him. Within seconds he'd scooped her into his embrace. She closed her eyes as he hugged her tight, her face rested on his hard chest. The smell of the fresh shirt mixed with his scent. Did she detect a touch of aftershave, too? Warmth from his body permeated her clothing. Happiness filled her.

"Baby, baby, baby," he muttered into her hair while his hands gripped her hips.

Stepping back, she tilted her chin up to gaze into his eyes. Before she could utter a word, his mouth came down on hers for a lingering kiss. She melted into him, returning his passion.

"I've missed you," she said, after catching her breath.

"Me too, honey, me too." He slid his arm around her shoulders. "Over here. I've got a spot for you. Elena's here." He guided her to their seats. Elena sat next to Bobby who was talking to a teammate on his right. Her friend looked up.

"Francie!" Elena rose from her seat and hugged her across the table.

"Sit down, baby. What're you havin'?" Skip handed her the menu.

"I have to have a burger. God, you can practically smell them in the street," she said.

Skip signaled for a waiter who wove his way through the crush of players, wives, girlfriends, and fans. Francie glanced down the table. Most of the players were eating steak. The pitchers that used to be filled with iced tea and soda now held beer. Skip filled her glass and refilled his. The noise level made intimate conversation impossible. Skip's food was half eaten.

"Eat," she said, gesturing at his plate.

He picked up his knife and fork and sliced off a piece of meat. He offered it to her, but she shook her head, and picked up her glass. The cool beer went down smooth. With her man next to her, the upbeat din in the restaurant, people milling about, and all the smiling faces, Francie swore she had come to the best party in the city. Her burger arrived. She watched the way people moved, how they leaned closer to friends and back from strangers. All the observations would come in handy for her art.

"You're quiet," Skip said between bites.

She nodded, chewing. After she swallowed. "I'm hungry."

He laughed. "So am I. And not for steak." Lust gleamed in his eyes as they raked over her, stopping at her chest.

A zing shot through her. Emboldened by her feelings, she returned his sexy look. Anticipation of passionate time alone with the shortstop made her nipples tingle. Oh, yes, heat between the sheets with Skip would send her temperature into the tropic zone.

She rushed through her meal.

"Dessert?" the waiter asked.

Francie shook her head. One glance at Skip and she sensed warmth filling her cheeks. The waiter laughed and cleared her dishes. Skip downed the rest of his beer and took her hand.

"Ready?" Skip tossed some bills on the table.

"Yep."

They pushed to their feet, and threaded through the crowd, stopping to greet the newcomers and say goodbye at the same time. Many hands slapped Skip on the back or did high-fives. She got hugs from players and their wives.

"Sort of like a gauntlet," Skip said, shaking his head.

"Exactly."

He held the door and took her hand. Within a few minutes, they were heading for his apartment. Once they parked, her libido kicked into high gear. Easing up closer she snaked her arm around his waist. In the elevator he faced her. His heat was intense as he crushed her against his chest. She wanted him, his kiss, his touch, his arms.

While kissing, he backed them out of the elevator to his place and fumbled with the key. She stood back so he could open the door. Attempting to slow down the rise of passion in her blood, she pressed her thighs together. But that only ramped up her need.

Once the door opened, they raced to the bedroom. Skip tore off his clothes, then approached her. She pulled at her top, so he placed his hands on the waistband of her pants and shoved them down.

"Wow! Oh, man. Like, wow. Yeah. Commando."

"You like?" she asked, tossing her sweater on a chair.

"Hell, yeah. Nice surprise. Saves time," he said, practically drooling.

He flipped open her bra and sent it to keep the other garments company. Skip picked her up and brought her to the bed.

"Baby. I want you," he whispered in her ear as he put her down. Within seconds he had joined her, lying on his side giving his erection room.

"I can see that. Me, too," she said, flattening her hand on his pecs. Touching him anywhere, everywhere boosted her desire.

"Let's see," he said, sliding his palm up her leg.

She opened. Before he kissed her, he chuckled. "Yeah." He slid two fingers into her, sending her heat higher. She wrapped her fingers around him. Bending over, she took him into her mouth. He groaned, running his fingers through her hair. Francie slid her tongue and lips up and down the velvety skin, creating suction. He grew even harder.

"Oh, God. Honey. Geez, shit, man," he muttered. After a minute or two, she sat up.

He opened the nightstand. She put her hand on his arm.

"I'm on the pill now," she said.

"Really?"

"Yes."

"Great. I don't think I can hold out," he said, pushing up on his knees. With a hand on each knee, he spread her legs. He bent down, touching her with the tip of his tongue. Francie held his head between her hands. Tension coiled up inside her.

"Do it. Skip. Do it."

"You can't wait, either?" He looked up, his eyes searching hers.

"No way."

His grin widened. "You got it." He laced his fingers with hers and pushed one hand back on the bed. Directing himself with the other, he was inside her in a heartbeat. The groans were mutual. Francie raised her chin and closed her eyes, giving in to the sensations filling her. Need built as her heat level rose. He thrust in hard, then withdrew, then back in again, slowly, oh so slowly.

"You're killing me," she muttered.

"Hurting you?" He stopped, his brows knitted.

"No, no, killing me. Faster, faster. I want to get there."

"Aye, aye, Captain," he said, picking up the pace.

She gripped his shoulders, pumping her hips to match his rhythm. It didn't take long before a powerful orgasm overwhelmed her. She moaned his name as her muscles clenched around him. Skip sped up and within seconds reached his release, too. He pushed up, balanced on his arms, as a drop of sweat fell from his forehead to hers. He wiped the wetness away with his thumb, then shifted, pulling out of her. Raising her chin, she kissed his wet forehead, then his lips.

"That was just the appetizer. The main course is coming later," he said, rolling on his back and pulling her against him.

AFTER MAKING LOVE SLOWER a second, then a third time, Skip secured Francie under his arm with her cheek on his chest. Sated beyond his dreams, he lay, twirling her hair between his fingers. Peace and contentment flowed through him.

"How was it?" She asked.

"What? How was what?"

"The playoffs. Must have been really intense."

He smiled. "You wouldn't believe."

"Try me."

Not one to confide much in chicks, he didn't elaborate. "The usual," he said, kissing her hair.

She sat up. "Bullshit. Tell me. I want to know."

He tapped his shoulder, and she returned to her former position. After years of shoving his feelings aside or stuffing them so far down they seemed to disappear, he didn't know where to begin.

"Were you scared?" she whispered.

Tears stung at the backs of his eyes. Scared? She had no idea—terrified was more like it. Fear of fucking up and being the goat, the reason the team lost, haunted him

"Tell me," she urged.

"Scared? Terrified," he said, quietly.

"Really?" She tried to sit up, but he held her still. He didn't want her to see his eyes fill.

"I was brought up not to be the guy who makes the last out. The guy who loses the game."

"But it's a team sport. No one guy is responsible. Right?"

"In theory, that's correct. But my father, my adoptive father, never saw it that way. And if I was responsible for the loss. I'd pay."

"Pay? What do you mean?"

"If I was guilty there was no dinner. I'd be sent to my room after the game."

Silence. He took a breath as a shudder shot through him. "Then my father would come upstairs with his belt. I'd get a lash for every run the other team scored."

She gasped. "He hit you?"

"Only when I was little. By high school, I was too big. He tried it once when I was fourteen, but I ripped the belt out of his hand and shoved him against the wall."

"What did he do then?"

"He'd humiliate me, instead. Call me names in front of my friends. Ground me. Take away my allowance. That shit."

"Oh, Skip!" Her voice trembled.

"Don't cry, Francie. He can't do that anymore."

"What did you do?"

"I stopped bringing friends around. Thank God, the coach fixed it for me. He was a great guy."

"What did he do?"

"Once he saw how I froze in the ninth inning, he pried it out of me. The stuff with my father. So, he banned my dad from the games." A smile stretched Skip's lips. "When I got home, my dad would ask me what the score was. And I'd lie, tell him it was a tie, zero-zero." Skip laughed. "That burned his tail."

"What about your mom?"

"She tried to reason with him, but he'd shout her down, stomp off to the bedroom, and slam the door."

"How did you get over it?"

"I didn't completely. But Coach worked with me. Eventually, I loosened up. The guys were great. After I fucked up, they'd take me out for a burger or something. Got to be a running joke. They'd accuse me of messing up to get a free meal."

"That was wonderful."

"It saved me."

"How about now?"

"I don't clutch in the ninth anymore. But I get tense before big games."

"Doesn't everyone?"

"Not like me. I work it through with exercise," he said, glancing down at her, "or sex."

"That helps?"

"That helps everything." He chuckled.

"What about now? With your dad, I mean."

"We don't talk much. Things got pretty distant between us in high school. Never straightened out. He didn't want to adopt me in the first place. Mom did."

"Do you still talk to her?"

"Yeah. About once a month, I call. Talk maybe ten minutes. They're banned from family seats at the game, too."

"Oh, boy. Guess that's necessary."

"It is." His eyes filled. "My real dad would have been so proud."

He reached for a tissue. Francie pushed up and planted a kiss on his cheek.

"I'm proud of you. You're incredible."

"You're just in love with my dick," he said, only half joking.

"It's more than that. Much more. Don't you know that?"

"Let's change the subject. You've got the best pair of tits on the East Coast."

Chapter Fourteen

In the morning, the couple lounged in bed until ten. They made love, sipped coffee and discussed plans for the day. After visiting a museum and taking a long walk, they ended up at Freddie's to meet their friends for dinner.

By the time Skip and Francie arrived at the restaurant, the crowd had dissipated. Only Matt, Bobby and Dan were there with their women. Listening to his teammates, he didn't see who came in the front door.

"Hello, son," said a deep voice.

Skip looked up. His parents stood at the end of the table. His heart dropped to his stomach. *Oh, shit!*

"Dad. Mom. What are you doing here?"

"Can't we come and wish our son well before he goes to the World Series?"

"I guess." Skip turned away. Sweat broke out on his forehead. Francie took his hand.

"Can we join you?" his mother asked.

He sure couldn't inflict them on his teammates. He pushed to his feet.

"Why don't we go over here? Tommy? Can we take this table?"

"Sure, sure," the barkeep said. He picked up their glasses and utensils and transferred them to a table for four.

As they sat down the waiter delivered their food.

"What do you guys want? It's on me," Skip said as Tommy handed his parents menus.

"That's very generous," his mom said.

His father ordered filet mignon, the most expensive item. His mom selected fish and chips. Francie dug into her shrimp Caesar salad, keeping her eyes open and her mouth shut.

"Go ahead and eat, son," his mother said, "your girlfriend is."

Francie's face colored. She mumbled, "I'm sorry." She dropped her fork.

Skip's father ordered a martini. "Aren't you drinking?" He looked at Skip.

"I have beer."

"That's not a man's drink."

"It's enough. I don't drink much. Especially during the season," Skip explained.

"Some men can hold their liquor," his father replied.

Anger crept up Skip's chest. He knew his face would turn red. He took a drink and kept quiet. Same old, same old, just like high school—his father humiliating him. This time, Skip refused to give him the satisfaction.

He couldn't win with Bart Quincy. If he put him down, his father called him a disrespectful, ungrateful child. If he apologized, Skip hated himself. He simply shut up and focused on his food.

"I hope you'll excuse me if I start before your food arrives. If I don't eat now, my steak'll get cold. I hate to eat alone. Francie, please join me."

"Would you introduce us, Skip?" His mother asked, staring at Francie, then at him.

"Oh, of course. Sorry, sorry. This is Francie Whitman. My mom and dad," Skip said and then dug into his meal.

"Nice to meet you," Francie said.

"Likewise," his mom said. His father eyed the girl in silence.

Skip stole a glance at Francie. Her face had turned from flushed to pale. She ate her salad slowly, her gaze riveted to her food. Skip's appetite flew out the window, but he continued to put steak in his mouth, chew, and swallow it. He'd be damned if he'd let his father rob him of a good meal.

The martini arrived shortly before his parents' food. His father took a healthy swig. Skip wasn't much of a drinker, but he knew that martinis should be sipped. He started to sweat. Would his father get drunk? Skip wiped his forehead with his napkin.

"Are you prepared, son?" Bart Quincy asked?

"Yep."

"Don't let your father rattle you, dear. I'm sure you're ready for anything. And if you mess up, it's okay," Ellen Quincy said.

He gave his head a shake. His mother had a knack for saying the wrong thing. He glanced up and made eye contact with Francie. She looked like a deer in the headlights. *Shit, shit, shit!* Were they scaring her off? That was the last thing he needed.

She pushed back and stood up. "Excuse me. I'm going to the ladies' room."

Skip rose to a crouch, then returned to his seat. He prayed she'd return. There was a back door out of Freddie's, and Skip wouldn't blame her if she hightailed it out of there.

"I hope you remember what I taught you," Bart said.

Anger boiled up inside Skip. "You mean what you beat into me?"

"I didn't beat you."

"What do you call what you did with that belt?"

"Just teaching you a lesson. Look how well you've done. You should thank me!"

Skip took a deep breath. If he blew, he'd embarrass himself, Francie, and his teammates. He trained his gaze on his food.

"Cat got your tongue?"

Skip remained silent.

"Okay. I can understand you being ungrateful. I know what I did. And now you're going to the World Series. The least you could do is thank me."

That was it. Anger heated to the boiling point inside him, melting his control.

"Thank you? Thank you? I should have called children's services and reported you for child abuse! I thank my coach, who rid me of all the stupid shit you put in my head!" Skip's voice rose with each sentence.

"Stupid shit? Training you not to screw up?"

"That's not what you did, you sadistic bastard! That's not what you did at all!"

"You shouldn't call your father names," Ellen said.

"You should talk. Where the hell were you when he was hitting me, huh? Nowhere. Why didn't *you* call children's services?"

He watched his mother blush. Instantly, he regretted his attack on her. She was weak. He knew that. But not Bart, he didn't regret one word to Bart. He should have told him off long ago.

"Everything I've achieved is in spite of you! Not because of you. My coach, my teammates, my manager...they are responsible for my success. And me. I've done it on my own. I worked my ass off to be the best. And I am. And you had *nothing* to do with it."

Skip pushed his steak away. He couldn't swallow anything anymore. His father picked up his knife and fork. His mother shoved a French fry in her mouth.

"Are you serious about that little girl?" she asked.

"No way. She's just a friend." He finished his beer.

"Like I believe that. You're making it with her," Bart said.

"It's not serious," Skip insisted.

"Didn't you tell me she's a student? An artist? She'll never make a dime. She's probably after your money. I'm glad you're not serious about her. You should be dating a model or an actress. Someone with looks and money. After all, you can't play baseball forever," Ellen said.

"Don't worry, Mom. She's temporary." There was no way he'd discuss his feelings for Francie with his parents. The minute he revealed he was serious about Francie, she'd come under attack, too. The least he could do was spare her.

"She's hot," Bart said.

Skip's stomach lurched. He prayed he didn't blow dinner at the table.

The footfall of boots caught his attention. Francie returned to the table. She was paler than when she left. He hoped she hadn't heard his mother's remarks. She picked at her food.

"You leave tomorrow?" his mother asked.

"Yep." Skip signaled for the check. "You done?" He turned to Francie. She nodded but kept her gaze on her plate.

"Hey..." He reached over and tipped her chin up. Her eyes were bright. Too bright. *Damn! She heard. I'll never dig my way out of this.*

"I'm done. Yes. I'll go on home now. You have to leave tomorrow. You need a good night's sleep." Then she flushed, turning a bright red as if she'd revealed a secret.

"Let me settle up, and I'll take you home."

"You live here?" Bart asked.

Francie nodded, avoiding his stare.

"I'm sure she can find her way home. We're not finished. It's rude to leave us here," Skip's father said.

"He's right. I can find my way home," Francie said, her voice small. She leaned over, planting a kiss on his cheek as she pushed away from the table. "Good luck."

"Wait! No, Francie. Just hang for a minute."

"I have work to do."

Ellen reached out and wrapped her fingers around her son's arm. "Don't stop her. I'm sure she has things to do."

"We need to talk," he said.

"I don't think so. Goodnight. Nice to meet you," Francie said, grabbing her jacket from the back of the chair and scooting out the door.

"Damn! You did it now. She heard you."

"Oh, I doubt that. She just knew when to leave," Ellen said.

The waiter brought the check. Skip rose, but his father stopped him.

"I said it's rude to leave when we're still eating."

"We have nothing to talk about. I need to speak to Francie."

"So, she means more than us?"

"We're done here. I have nothing more to say to you."

"Of course not. Well, don't screw it up. Like you usually do," Bart said, finishing his drink.

"If you were younger, I'd take you outside and beat the crap out of you for a remark like that."

His father stared at him.

"Cat got your tongue?" Skip said, pushing to his feet and heading for the door.

Francie was too frugal to take a taxi. She'd be on the subway. Skip started his car and headed downtown. He figured he'd beat her by at least five minutes unless there was a train waiting for her at the station. Anger, frustration, and humiliation bubbled up inside him. Food rattled around in his stomach. He had to get things straight with her.

A car in front of her building pulled out as he turned the corner. *A good omen.* He rang the bell and there was no answer. Peeking around the side of the building, he saw her lights were out. With a sigh of relief, he leaned against the building.

He didn't wait long before he spied Francie, heading down the avenue. He moved forward to greet her.

"Baby!" He opened his arms only to be met by a stony stare.

"Baby? 'She's only temporary. It's not serious.' Really? Don't 'baby' me." She folded her arms across her chest.

"That was just to get them off your trail."

"Really? Sounded pretty convincing to me."

"Sweetheart. Would I be here if that was true? Can we talk inside?"

She shot him a skeptical look but nodded, then fished her keys out of her bag. She aimed for the lock, but her hand shook too much to connect. Skip took the key from her and opened the door. He followed her inside and sat on the sofa.

"You want something to drink?"

He shook his head. The last thing he needed to do was put anything else in his stomach. She sat at the other end of the couch.

"What do you want?"

"You. I care about you. It's real. What we have. Real for me. I just said that to get them to shut up. If I told them the truth, I'd never hear the end of it. They'd criticize the shit out of you, put you down. I don't want that."

"You're pretty convincing. Still. You did say I meant nothing to you."

"I repeat, would I be here if that was true?"

She shrugged. "I don't know. Maybe. Maybe it's all about the sex?"

He laughed. "Yeah? Really? Dragging my ass to an art museum to get laid? I don't think so. I could go to The Hideout and get laid."

"Oh? And are you?"

"What? Am I going to The Hideout? No. How could you ask that?"

She sighed and collapsed back into the cushions. "I don't know. Yesterday I felt really good about us. But they, actually your mother, wiped it all away with a few words. Or maybe you did? Or maybe you both did? I don't know. I'm confused. Maybe we're not such a good idea."

"Don't say that. We are."

"I'm tired. I'm going to bed."

"Can I stay?"

She stopped at her bedroom door, faced him, and nodded. Skip said a quick thank-you prayer to God as he crossed the threshold. Old wounds had resurfaced at Freddie's. The arrows his father shot had met their mark, though Skip would never admit it. A night with Francie would fix that. Cure it enough for him to get through the first two games of the World Series. There was no time to waste, no margin for error. He needed her.

They undressed in silence. For the first time, sex wasn't the primary thing on his mind. He wanted more. They slid between the sheets. She pulled up her comforter and turned her back to him. Skip lay staring at the ceiling. His heart squeezed at the distance his words had caused. How could he break the silence and ease the strain between them?

His heartbeat quickened. "I'm going to L.A. to play in the World Series tomorrow. Might hit a home run, if I got a good luck hug or something," he said, crossing his fingers in the darkness.

"You're counting on me to boost your confidence for the series?"

"Well...sort of. Not really. Maybe?"

She laughed. "You're not a word guy, are you?"

"You're asking now?"

"I get it."

She rolled over and cupped his cheek. He leaned in and brushed her lips with his, then pulled her up against him. Her warmth soothed him.

"Do you really love me, Francie?" Terror filled him, as he whispered.

She replied, "I do. Scares the crap out of me. But I do."

"Why? I'm a jackass sometimes?"

"All men are."

He laughed. "Guess that's true."

She kissed him.

"So why?" he persisted.

"You're a good man. You're nice. Kind. Smart in ways I'm not. You're good to me. And you're funny."

"Funny. Yeah. I am. The other stuff? I don't know."

"You have a good heart. You're loyal."

He stroked her hair. "You're too good for me. I don't deserve you."

"Yes, you do."

He drew her to him. She snuggled into his embrace. Exhaustion swept over him.

"Is it okay if we don't make love tonight?" he whispered, barely able to keep his eyes open?

"Sure."

He thought maybe she said something else, too. But if she did, he didn't hear it because he was sound asleep.

BAD DREAMS PREVENTED Francie from getting a solid night's sleep. She awoke early. Throwing a robe on, she padded into the kitchen where her painting stood. She draped an old sheet over it. Skip shouldn't be seeing that now.

She filled the coffeemaker then sat at the window while it brewed. The aroma filled her small place, making her stomach rumble. Gazing at a handful of people bustling down the street, she fought with herself over whether or not to believe Skip. She'd heard him with her own ears, say she didn't mean anything to him, then he said it wasn't true. What should she think?

While she waited for him to get up, she called the deli and ordered egg sandwiches. Then she poured coffee and studied the snapshots she intended to use for paintings. Her mind wandered back to the upcoming art competition. The few coveted spots in the Paris art program would be awarded to the best artists. She'd decided to take Stark's advice and enter the painting of Skip pouring the water over his head.

She bit her lip. Did she want to go to Paris? She didn't want to leave Skip, but, yes, she wanted the education and attention to her work she'd receive there. With a short laugh, she decided not to worry because she didn't have a chance anyway. But Professor Stark seemed certain she'd win, at least third place. She respected his opinion, but fear of getting her hopes up, only to lose, kept her enthusiasm in check.

She whipped the sheet off and took another look at the picture.

"Can I see it, too?" A deep voice startled her.

She hurled the covering over it before facing him. "No."

"Why not?"

"No one sees it before it's exhibited."

"It's going to be shown somewhere?"

"The school has a fall art competition. The prize is a seat in the Paris art program."

"You're entering?"

She nodded, studying his face for a reaction.

"You're so talented, I'm sure you'll win."

"I'm not."

"Then you'll go to Paris, won't you?" His grin drooped into a tiny smile.

"I don't know."

"Would you stay here with me? Go to Florida?"

"I don't know."

"It's the chance of a lifetime. Paris, I mean. Florida will be here next year. And so will I. But not Paris. Right?"

He had a point. "Maybe," she hedged.

"You're pretty cagey this morning," he said, pouring a cup of coffee.

The doorbell rang. Skip slipped on his jeans and answered it. He paid the delivery man and carried the paper bag to the table.

"Hey! I was supposed to pay for that," Francie said.

"What difference does it make?"

"Just that you're at my house."

"So, what? Let me take care of you a little."

"So your mom can call me a gold digger?"

He took her in his arms. "Hey! Forget her. Forget that. She doesn't know you. I do. That's bullshit."

"You don't feel that way?"

He laughed. "Honestly, do you really think I do? Would I be hanging with you this long if I did? Come on, Francie. Lighten up. I thought you knew how I feel about you?"

"How? By osmosis? You never talk about it."

"I'm not big on fancy words and stuff."

"You can say that again."

"Who said 'actions speak louder than words'?"

She shrugged.

"He had the right idea. You're my girl. That's it. Okay?"

She pulled away and refreshed their coffee. "Tell me what you expect to find in L.A," she said.

While she ate, Francie listened to Skip relate what he knew about the pitchers and players on the Lions, which wasn't much since he hadn't faced that team before. He explained where the Nighthawks' weak spots were. Watching his eyes light up, the animation in his face as he spoke about baseball, warmed her heart. Skip loved the game, his team, and even his opponents.

Francie hoped he wouldn't be mad when he saw the painting at the show. Using him as a model, she'd made him a part of her life, too.

"Do you really want to see the painting?"

"I do."

"You can come to the gallery. The show opens next week."

"During the series?"

"You can see it afterward. It's going to be up for two weeks."

"I'll be there. I'm going to Florida right after Thanksgiving Day. The guys are doing a big meal thing at Matt's house, like they do every year. Then we head south. Can you come, too?"

"My semester doesn't finish until like December fifteen."

"Can't you fly down for the weekend?"

She shook her head. "I'll be working on final projects then. It's the busiest time of the year."

"But isn't this your final project. I mean the picture you can't show me?"

"That's for the show. He's giving out the final assignments tonight."

Skip nodded. "Guess we'll have to do it next year."

"Maybe for Christmas?" She hated the note of hope in her voice.

"Of course! Christmas! Perfect." He gave her a big smooch, then gathered up the paper and dishes, and padded into the kitchen. "I've got to pack and get to the bus."

She nodded. "Okay. Wish I could be there. I know you're gonna do great!"

"Yeah?"

She came up behind him and snaked her arms around his middle. "You're a star, Skip. Don't ever forget it."

"I think we have time for one more thing," he said, leading her to the bedroom.

"You read my mind," she replied, shutting the door.

Chapter Fifteen

In his luxurious room at the Palm Resort hotel, Skip unpacked and set up the room the way he liked it. The clock read two o'clock, but to him it was five, Eastern Time. His stomach rumbled. Dinner time approached. A knock, then a voice.

"You in there, Quincy?"

"Yeah." Skip opened the door. It was Bobby.

"Get your suit on. We're going swimming before dinner."

Skip slipped on his trunks and joined the team. The men clowned around in the pool, then showered and dressed for dinner.

They went to bed early because Cal had scheduled practice at eight the next day. The first game would take place the day after. Skip fell asleep before he could dial Francie.

The front desk called him at six. He was down to breakfast at seven and on the bus for the stadium at quarter to eight. The team practiced all day. Stretches, running, agility, catching, batting, fielding—it was nonstop.

They broke for lunch, then convened for a strategy session with Cal. Returning to practice after the break, the Nighthawks worked until five. After a quick dip in the pool and some shenanigans by the younger team members, it was shower, dress up, and dinner. Exhaustion drove him to his room by eight. A movie then lights out. His cell rang.

"Baby!"

"Skip. You haven't called. Is everything okay?"

"Things have been crazy here. We practiced our balls off."

"I want to wish you good luck tomorrow." Her tone was cool.

"I'm sorry, Francie. It wasn't that I wasn't thinking about you."

"I know. The game is on your mind. I get it."

"There just wasn't time."

"You ready for tomorrow?" She changed the subject.

"Ready as I'll ever be. Wish you could be here."

"Me, too." Her voice softened.

"And right now, too. I've got a king-size bed and it's too damn big without you."

She laughed.

"Lights out. Hope you're painting a lot," he said.

"I am. Goodnight. Love you."

"Love you, too."

After he switched off the light, his thoughts turned to his girl. Naked images of her danced through his mind, and his body responded. He relieved himself because he'd never do well tomorrow if he wasn't rested. He finished with a groan, cleaned himself up, and then stretched out on the bed.

Something about Francie turned him on more than other women. He'd wondered about it but had come to no conclusion. Sure, she was hot with a great body, but there was something more. Could it be love? He'd never been in love before, so how would he know?

Lying there, the truth hit him. It was just as Bobby had described—faster heartbeat, sweating, smiling, touching her at every opportunity. Skip had all the signs. It was love smacking him between the eyes, making his heart squeeze, and sending cold fear through his veins.

Love meant being vulnerable, getting hurt, someone stomping on your heart with work boots. He'd managed to stay safe, keep love at arms' length so far, how did it creep in? It had to be Francie, a one-of-a-kind girl. She took him by surprise by becoming his friend first. With his guard down, Francie simply marched in and took over his heart.

There was nothing he could do about it. He couldn't talk himself out of love, so he might as well enjoy it. Would he get as goofy as Bobby when he talked about Elena? Probably. He grinned. Relaxed and content, sleep washed over him.

In the morning, he awoke, refreshed, at six. After a brief shower, he put on his white shirt, suit, and tied his tie before going down to breakfast. Skip piled a plate high with scrambled eggs, bacon, sausage, home fries, and toast. He poured a big glass of orange juice from the pitcher on the table and listened to the team.

"It's gonna be fuckin' hot today," Matt Jackson said.

"Have you heard this one? A dick walks into a bar," Jake Lawrence said.

"My mother's having the whole family over to watch the game on TV," Chet Candelaria said.

"Yeah, I have! And he sits next to a pussy," Nat pipes up.

Jake laughed. "Right. And the dick says, 'hi, gorgeous.' And the pussy doesn't say anything."

"Wait, wait! I got it," Nat said. "So the dick says, 'what's the matter, cat got your tongue?'" Jake almost choked on his food. Dan and Matt cracked up.

Same old, same old—Nighthawks conversation never changed. Dirty jokes, the weather, and family. Skip smiled to himself. He counted on them being predictable. At least there was something in his life that didn't change.

On the bus, the men quieted down. Winning this game mattered. It would start things off in their corner. But the Lions had the home field advantage. That would make it tougher. After they arrived, the men warmed up, then donned their uniforms.

They loped out onto the field and held their hats over their hearts while a Marine quartet sang the national anthem. Scanning the stands, Skip's confidence rose when he saw red and white banners, the Nighthawks' colors. Whew, there were fans in the bleachers to cheer them on. When the song was over, they put on their caps and headed for the visiting team dugout. Bobby patted him on the shoulder.

"It's gonna be okay," he said.

Skip nodded. "Right." It was. As long as he didn't make the game-losing mistake.

FRANCIE COULDN'T GET Skip off her mind. She dressed and gathered her paints, ready to give finishing touches to the picture for the competition. The game didn't start until eight. Elena had opted to stay in New York. She'd be coming over to watch and bringing home-made guacamole and dulce de leche ice cream.

Francie flipped on her classical playlist. As she mixed colors, tension built. Nerves about her portrait of Skip mixed with concerns about his game. Both had to win. Forcing the anxiety-producing thoughts from her mind, she focused on what she needed to do. She'd analyzed her work last night and made notes.

Opening her notebook, she scanned the list, stopping to make each revision. That was her dad. He'd taught her to be organized and it had paid off.

Stepping back, she cast a critical eye at her work. Damn, it was good. The picture had captured the hills and valleys of his body, muscle development, sweat, and the sinewy strength and sexiness of him. For the first time, she considered herself a real artist.

It took an hour to clean her brushes, put away the paint tubes, and clear up the mess. She took a shower and placed an order for pizza before Elena arrived. When the doorbell rang, Francie greeted her friend with a smile.

"Here." Elena handed her the food and made herself at home. "Where's the painting?"

"It's drying. This way." Francie put the dishes down in the kitchen.

Francie led her friend to the kitchen. Elena gasped. "Oh my God! Francie! This is the best." Elena stretched her hand out toward the picture. "I can practically touch his body. He looks so real. I can feel the sweat, the water, and how refreshing it is."

"Thank you."

"This is so professional. Stark is gonna love it. I love it. Has Skip seen it yet?"

Francie shook her head. "I told him I never show stuff to people before it's finished."

"You show me everything."

"You're different."

"He's gotta see this. He's gonna flip. Seriously."

The sound of the national anthem coming from the television in the living room drew their attention.

"Time for the game. I'm a nervous wreck," Elena said. "I hope Bobby doesn't screw up. He's gotta hit a home run."

"At least one. One from Bobby and one from Skip," Francie said.

The women high-fived and sat down in front of the tube. By the third inning, they had the coffee table covered with dishes, including a half-eaten pizza. The score was tied, three to three. Skip's moves on the field were smooth, his throws right on target. He was a master. She took pride in her lover.

The game ended with the Nighthawks winning five to four.

"Come back tomorrow."

"You come to my house."

"Look at all this food. Come here and we can finish it up."

"Okay. But I have to write first."

"And I have to paint."

"Weren't our boys amazing?"

"Awesome."

They hugged goodnight, and Elena left to flag down a cab.

The next night, she brought homemade brownies, and they finished off the food from the night before while yelling at the screen. The Nighthawks, who could do no wrong the night before, were the strikeout kings today. Skip had fanned twice, Bobby bounced a short hopper into a double play. The men bumped into each other in the outfield, causing an easy fly ball to fall between them, putting a Lions player, who would have been an easy out, on base.

Francie and Elena booed calls against the Nighthawks and stuffed themselves with rich food. The score was four to two, Lions favor, when they opened a bottle of wine.

"I can't take this on soda alone," Elena said, yanking on the corkscrew.

"This is horrible. What happened?"

"Some days they have it together, and some days they don't."

Francie blew a raspberry at the screen. Her heart ached for Skip. Each game meant the world to him. He wouldn't take a loss well. The Nighthawks rallied in the seventh, but the Lions came back stronger and won, seven to four.

"Our men will need attention when they get back tomorrow," Elena said.

Francie nodded.

"Every cloud has a silver lining," Elena added, a twinkle in her eye.

THE NIGHTHAWKS HEADED for a plane back to New York immediately after the game. Getting home was top of mind for the team. Finding the coach alone for a moment on the plane, Skip slid into the seat next to him and apologized.

"Forget about it, Skip," Cal said. "What's done is done. Everyone makes mistakes." The manager patted the shortstop on the shoulder.

Could he believe Cal?

"No one gets through a season without making errors. We'll all human. Let it go."

"Okay." Skip nodded, still uneasy about making what he considered the game-losing error in Los Angeles.

"I mean it. Christ, son! If you can't let it go, it's gonna fuck with your head. I need you out there one-hundred percent."

"I'll be there, I promise." Cal shook Skip's hand. Skip returned to his seat next to Bobby.

"See? What the fuck did I tell you? Forget it, man. Geez. We've all fucked up in important games this year," Bobby said.

Skip closed his eyes. Exhaustion claimed him. The plane was quiet with most of the players asleep. They landed in New York late. The bus was waiting. It was the middle of the night by the time Skip got home. He flopped into bed and slept until eleven.

After wolfing down a big breakfast at the diner, he headed to the stadium for practice. Tension grew in the locker room. Skip couldn't wait to hit the track. Running worked out his nerves. He paired up with Matt, and the two ran in silence. Hitting an easy stride, the teammates stayed abreast for the entire two laps. Afterward, they sucked down water at the cooler. Bobby, Nat, and Jake joined them.

Cal gathered everyone around for a strategy session, then dismissed the team.

"Go to sleep early tonight. We need to win tomorrow."

Skip pushed through the door at Freddie's. Elena was there already.

"Where's Francie?"

"She had to finish up some work."

He cocked an eyebrow at Elena.

"I don't know. You'll have to ask her," Elena said, not meeting his eyes. Something was going on, he could feel it.

"What's up, Elena?" The last thing he needed was tension with his girl.

"Nothing. She has her work, too. I know the Series is important, but it's not the only thing happening in the world. I don't have all the details. You'll have to ask her."

That was enough to tell him he didn't want to know. His brain could only focus on the Series right now. Everything else would have to wait.

"Okay, okay. Thanks." Skip buried his nose in the menu, even though he knew it by heart. "Lemme have the Philly cheesesteak tonight, Tommy."

The owner raised his eyebrows. "Breaking with tradition?"

"Yeah. Guy's gotta do something different sometimes."

He ate quietly, watching and listening to his teammates and their women. He missed Francie. Secretly, he wondered if she'd stayed away because he'd screwed up so badly the last game. Maybe she was ashamed of him. If she was, he could hardly blame her. He cringed at the thought of what his father had said. He'd probably cursed up a storm at the TV during the game.

Checking his watch, he finished up and left. He needed a good night's sleep. Once in his apartment, he dialed Francie.

"Everything okay?"

"Yeah. I am just overloaded right now. I didn't realize the contest rules included three back-up pieces. They do that, so you can't cheat and get someone to do a really good painting and pawn it off as yours. They want to see a body of work."

"I'd like to see a body, too. Your body. And I don't mean pictures." He chuckled.

She laughed. "Tonight is tough. I'm wiped out."

"You're not mad at me for screwing up?"

"What? Of course not! Where did you get that idea?"

"I messed up."

"So did other people. You're human, Skip. Everyone makes mistakes sometimes."

He let out a breath. "Yeah. That's what Cal said."

"Believe him. Besides, I'm in this with you, regardless of what you do on the field."

"Really?"

"Don't you know that? It's late. Get a good night's sleep. Maybe I can spend the night with you tomorrow."

"I hope so."

"Good luck tomorrow."

"I've got a ticket for you at the box office."

"Great, thank you. I'll be there."

"Goodnight, baby."

"'Night, Skip."

He put down his phone and headed for bed. Maybe having no distractions would be better. He doused the light and sank into a deep sleep.

THE NEXT MORNING, GUILT invaded Francie's heart. Should she have put her work aside to spend the night with Skip? She chewed on the back of a brush as she contemplated a blank canvas.

Pulling out a picture of Skip, naked, she propped it up next to the easel. Mixing a dab of burnt sienna with enough turpentine turned it to the consistency of watercolors, so drawing with it was easy. The color was light enough that she could easily paint over it.

Professor Stark wanted to see the beginnings of a picture by noon. She had dragged herself out of bed at six. By eight, inspiration had struck. Something about staring at a picture of Skip motivated her. This shot was of him from behind. She vowed she'd never paint his private parts, even though it was tempting.

Focusing on sketching the shape of his butt, she licked her lips. The desire to touch him grew until it interrupted her work. Since the day was going to be a waste anyway, with her at the game, then dinner with Skip, she might as well spend the night.

Memories of their nights together made her pulse leap in anticipation. She'd learned much from Skip, who was a master in the bedroom, the perfect lover.

Closing her eyes, she could feel his hot, sweaty back against her fingertips as she gripped him, her hips gliding up and down with his. The feathery-light touch of his lips on private places, his hands slipping into her blouse or under her skirt made her pulse race.

Skip's support, encouragement, and refusal to accept her negative view of her work spiked love in her heart. There was something about him, something she couldn't put into words. When she was with him, the world glowed in brighter colors, and she was safe.

Her love scared her. She'd never been so totally immersed in a man. The fact that he fulfilled her dreams so completely frightened her. Every week she'd been torn between the desire to run and the desire to stay. Fortunately, the latter had won. Happiness she hadn't known since childhood flowed steadily through her.

Returning to her task, she worked quickly, finishing up the rough outline by eleven thirty. She snapped several pictures of the new piece, donned a jacket and headed for the art building and Professor Stark's office. She waited while he finished with another student. Her pulse jumped as the minutes ticked by. Would he like it, or would he say it was trite? Would she have to start over or could she continue? Doubt stressed her, pulsing in her brain like a headache.

Finally, the door opened. The departing student frowned at Francie and made a beeline for the elevator. Could she see a few tears in her eyes? Francie swallowed.

"Miss Whitman. Come in," he said, standing aside.

Francie wondered if the walk to the guillotine felt like this. She shrugged off her jacket and pulled up the pictures on her phone.

"Let's see what you've got," the teacher said, stepping closer.

She handed him the phone.

"I have more pictures of this model that I can use. This isn't the only one. If you don't like it—"

He held up his hand. "Shh. Let me take a look."

The ticking clock got louder with each minute that passed. She studied his face, looking for a clue to his reaction but found none.

"Good. Very good," he mumbled, switching to the next picture.

When he'd finished, he went to his desk and eased down into his chair.

"You say you have more shots of this model?"

She nodded, her mouth dry.

"How many?"

"Maybe a dozen, maybe more?"

The professor chuckled. "I see. He's a personal, um, friend?" He raised his eyebrows.

"Uh huh," she mumbled, feeling her face color.

"Excellent. You've turned a corner, Miss Whitman. This is a great beginning. And since you have all those other photos, I have an idea. Sit down."

Relieved, she could hardly believe her ears. She opened the notebook app on her phone and took notes as he talked. His idea was amazing, spectacular, something she'd never imagined.

"This is just what the judges are looking for. It will show versatility, the ability to create different attitudes from the same model. If you're successful with this plan, I'm sure the judges will award you a full scholarship to Paris."

"A full scholarship?"

"That's right." He nodded. "You deserve it. Now get to work on these. I expect you to have seven more completed before the plane leaves."

"But, I..."

"Get going. I hope you don't have anything planned for the next month?"

She shook her head.

"Good. I expect this to be your best work. Focus. If anyone can do this, you can, my dear. Don't let me down, I'm counting on you."

"Seven? Seven canvases?"

"More if you can manage. But they must be top quality."

"I understand. I'll do my best."

"Excellent. Good luck," he said, rising and extending his hand.

Francie took it and left. She didn't remember getting home. She floated like a hovercraft, just above the ground. When she got to her place, she turned off her phone, put on her smock, and went to work. Professor Stark had faith in her. Skip believed in her. Now it was time for her to know in her bones that she could produce outstanding work.

She set the alarm for six. That would give her enough time to eat something and get to the stadium by eight. It was a four-leaf clover day for her, and she hoped it would be for Skip, too.

Chapter Sixteen

The team sat with Cal before the game.

"Their ace, Hank McKensey is pitching today," Cal said, unwrapping two pieces of gum.

"His fuckin' change-up is impossible to hit," Matt Jackson added. "He likes to go low, so if you do connect it's just a bouncer, not a home run."

"Bastard," Skip muttered, shaking his head.

"Skip, Jake, Bobby, watch out for Boots McGuffin. He's their best stealer. Number four in the league. But he always comes in feet first, cleats up. He's done damage, too. Be careful. We can't afford to lose any of you, even for one inning." Cal made eye contact with each player.

Vic poked his head in the door. "Time."

The players filed down the chute to the field. They held their hats over their hearts while Emerald, famous singer and wife of star Connecticut King Wide Receiver, Buddy Carruthers, sang the national anthem.

When the song was over, Skip made eye contact with Francie. He doffed his cap to her before jamming it on his head and loping to second base. He pulled his glove out of his back pocket and took his position between second and third. Dan Alexander was pitching. Boots McGuffin came up to bat.

Sure. They're starting off with their fastest guy. Figures. Skip crouched down and kept his eye on the ball. McGuffin had stolen bases in each of the first two games. One of those steals was Skip's fault. His toss to Bobby at second was too high. Skip gritted his teeth. Determination to get the dickwad out coursed through his veins. The point was to keep Boots off first, then he couldn't steal shit. Boots, what the hell kind of name was that? Maybe they'd been expecting a dog or cat and got a kid instead. Skip chuckled to himself, keeping his eyes on the ball.

The Nighthawks were caught off guard when McGuffin started off with a perfect bunt that dribbled down the third base line. There was no question of him beating it out. Shit! That's exactly what the Lions wanted, get the fucker on base so he could steal his way across and home.

Skip was pissed, and the first inning wasn't even half over. This was going to be a long game. He took a deep breath and stared at McGuffin. The idiot was wearing a shit-eating grin as if to say *Bet you didn't see that coming!* And, hell, no, they didn't see that coming. What tricks were the Lions going to pull out of their bag next?

When the next batter shouldered his bat, McGuffin was almost halfway between first and second. Skip sidestepped toward second and the runner moved back to first. This time, it was a bloop single to short right field. Ordinarily, this hit could be fielded by either the second baseman or the right fielder and the guy going to second could be thrown out—easily. But not Boots. As soon as the batter swung, he took off, rounding second. The ball hung in the air just long enough for him to get halfway to third. He roared in, sliding head first, knocking Jake Lawrence off-balance. The ball bounced before the base and hopped over Jake's glove into foul territory. Boots leapt to his feet and smoked his way to home.

The crowd screamed. The Nighthawks ran around looking like Keystone Kops while Boots McGuffin scored the first run. If this was the way things were going to go, it was going to be a long game, and New York would be scrambling to catch up. Skip gritted his teeth. He didn't know if Jake or the right fielder got credited with the error. It didn't matter. L.A. had one run and the Nighthawks had yet to come to bat. And there were no outs.

Dan struck out the next two batters. Skip fielded a bouncer and threw the batter out at first. The 'Hawks went to the dugout. With the Lions ahead by one, the pressure was on. Each Nighthawk batter got a cheer from the hometown crowd, but it didn't help. Something was off. They couldn't get a man on base.

Boots McGuffin blew a raspberry behind his hand at Skip as the Lion rounded second on a ground rule double that bounced into the stands. Barely keeping his temper in check, Skip counted to twenty, as his coach had advised, when anger threatened to take control. Dan struck out the next batter and got the one following to foul out. A bouncer to Nat at first made for an easy third out.

Skip managed to draw a walk. When Lion first baseman, Eduardo Lopez, turned his back, Skip made a dash for second. He slid in, safely, and Jake Lawrence knocked him home with a line drive into the hole between right and center field.

That was the Nighthawks' only run. They lost, four to one. From time to time, a low sound of swearing and grumbling disrupted the silence in the locker room. Discouraged, Skip took his shower and dressed without breaking a smile. Nelson Hingus, the team owner, accompanied Cal Crawley as they entered the locker room.

Embarrassment swept through the room. The men were uneasy facing the owner after a loss. Especially one that involved three errors. Skip thanked God that he hadn't committed any of the errors but felt bad for his fellow teammates who had.

There was meaningless rah-rah crap meant to cheer up the team, but it failed miserably. It was one thing to lose when they were outgunned, but to lose because they fucked up was hard to swallow. The air in the locker room grew heavy, and Skip couldn't wait to leave. He shook Mr. Hingus' hand, nodded to Cal, slapped Jake on the back and beat it out the door. Bobby wasn't far behind him.

"Freddie's?" Skip asked. A late supper after a night game tempted Skip.

"Nope. Home."

Skip nodded.

Francie and Elena were waiting outside. He got why Bobby wouldn't want to face fans and teammates after such a crushing loss. They were down in the series, two games to one. And Bobby's error had resulted in a run scoring. His bad throw home drew Matt Jackson just far enough off the plate to let the runner score.

Skip didn't blame Bobby. The ball took a bad hop, causing the second baseman to bobble it for a second. Then he was off-balance when he threw. It could happen to anyone. Skip was grateful it didn't happen to him. Bobby kissed his fiancée, and they got in his car. Skip slid his arm around Francie's shoulders.

"Come on, baby. Quick dinner then my place?"

Francie nodded. He opened the car door for her.

"I'm sorry you lost," she said, sliding into the front seat.

"Me, too," he said, putting the vehicle in gear and pulling out of the lot.

FRANCIE DIDN'T KNOW quite what to do to help Skip through his loss. She knew how he felt because she'd had a few people make disparaging remarks when they walked by her work, not knowing she was the artist. It hurt, probably not nearly as much as losing two out of the first three games of the World Series, but pain is pain.

When they got home, she headed to the kitchen.

"Coffee?"

"Nah. It'll keep me up. We have another game tomorrow."

"Glass of wine?" she asked.

"Maybe half. To help me sleep."

"Or there's something else we could do to help you sleep," she said, ratcheting up her flirty.

"Yeah?" He sidled up to her, snaking his arms around her shoulders.

"Come on," she said, taking his hand and leading him into the bedroom.

He took her in his arms for a passionate kiss. His mouth was hungry, devouring hers. His fingers splayed across her back, holding her close. His heat melted her body. She felt boneless, weightless as she conformed to the contours of his frame. He drew her up, off the floor.

Time stood still as Francie lost herself in the feel and taste of her lover. The rasp of his beard on her cheek, the smell of soap and man, plus the feel of soft T-shirt over hard muscle shot her pulse up. Closing her mind, she lost herself in her senses. Her fingers gripped his shoulders as her legs twined around his. He lowered one hand to her rear, boosting her higher and closer, and walked her to the bed.

Breaking their embrace, he tossed her on the mattress. Francie landed, laughing.

"Don't go anywhere," he said, raising his hand. Skip headed to the bathroom. When he returned he was clad only in boxers.

"My turn?"

"Let me do it," he said, kneeling between her legs. He slid his hands up her ribs and over her breasts to rest on her collarbone. "You're beautiful."

"No way," she said, before he stilled her, placing his fingers on her lips.

"If I say you're beautiful, you're beautiful."

"Yes, sir."

He cracked a smile. He combed her hair off her forehead and kissed from there down her nose to her lips. A light brush against hers, and he continued to her neck. The scoop of her blouse got in the way, so he removed it, also her bra. He closed his fingers around her shoulders with his thumbs resting against her chest.

"Fantastic!" He kissed his way down her chest, stopping at her breasts.

The minute his lips touched the tender flesh, desire rocketed through her. She wanted him. Francie combed her fingers through his hair and down over the back of his neck.

"When you do that..." he began, but his lips closed over her nipple and he stopped speaking. A moan escaped her lips as he tugged gently. She pressed her fingers into the muscles below his neck and raised her hips.

He slid his hands down to the waistband of her jeans, inching toward the button, but tickling her in the process. She jerked, laughed, and quickly unbuttoned her pants and unzipped them.

"You make it so easy," he said, easing them over her hips and off. His gaze burned her body.

He glided his finger down the satiny smoothness of her panties, teasing, tantalizing. Pressing the flat of his hand against her, he massaged, gently, in circles until she thought she'd lose her mind.

"Oh, God. You're torturing me."

"Am I? Good," he snickered.

She reached down, finding him easily as his erection poked through his boxers. Soon he'd be using it to bring her pleasure. His hardness gave her chills. She leaned over and took him in her mouth. He stopped moving.

"Damn," he muttered softly.

Francie held him firmly while she slid her mouth up and down his shaft. Adding gentle suction she kept it up, listening to his groans. He sat still, giving her total control. She'd wondered how he'd react if she took over. Hearing no objection, she continued, sliding down, then up, adding a touch of pressure from her lips to the tip.

"Oh God! That's it. That's it. Stop. Stop," he said, grabbing her upper arms and easing her away. "If you don't, I'm gonna blow."

He slid the side of his hand over her slit. Like a match to gasoline, she caught fire. Squirming, she shoved the panties off and fell back.

"You want it, baby?"

"God, yes."

His eyes captured hers, his look intense, the blue brighter than ever. Lust mixed with love in his gaze.

"You're not ready."

"I am."

"Not yet. Patience."

She wriggled her hips. "No patience. Want you now!"

He ignored her words, closing his big hands around her thighs. He gave a gentle squeeze and parted them.

"That's it," he murmured, lowering himself to her body. He swiped his tongue over her, sending her heat level up to white hot. As he stroked her, she bucked her hips.

"Please, Skip. Please." She grabbed his arm and yanked.

"Take it easy."

"Sorry, sorry."

"I guess you're ready, huh?" He laughed.

"Do it. Do it!"

He separated her knees. Holding himself, he rubbed up and down her slit. Once he was well lubricated, he poised over her. Giving her a quick kiss, he lowered his hips and pushed in.

"Ahhhhh," Francie moaned, her eyes drifting shut. He lowered his chest until it rested lightly on hers. Rumbling laughter vibrated through his body, tickling her.

Opening her eyes, she connected with him. She reached up, tenderly cupping his cheek, running her thumb over his scruff. She arched her back, pressing her breasts against his chest. The contact thrilled her, sending signals south.

The touch of skin upon skin sparked fires deep inside. Thigh to thigh, hip to hip, breast to breast, they lay glued together by their love. Ruled by her senses, she succumbed to the richness of his presence. His scent, aftershave mixed with a dab of sweat, and a whole lot of Skip, entranced her. She licked his shoulder, tasting the shortstop seasoned with a touch of salt.

He thrust in and pulled out, muttering sweet words here and there, amid his grunts. Sweat broke out on his forehead and chest. She met his rhythm as they moved in sync. Then he changed, speeding up, pumping into her faster and faster.

Tension coiled within her, spiraling up and up. All thought flew from her mind as an orgasm took her, clenching every muscle, and then releasing pleasure to every inch of her.

She cried out his name. He curled his back, pressing his forehead against her shoulder.

"Baby," he muttered, then let out a loud groan. He collapsed on her, then rolled off.

"God," she said, raising her arms above her head.

"Amazing," he replied. He stroked her breast with a loving touch.

She wanted to scream how much she loved him but held back. Something had changed between them. He'd taken over her heart completely. Afraid of giving her love to someone who could crush her with his pinky, she resisted.

Loneliness had resided in her since her father died. Now, Skip had arrived, bigger than life, filling up every inch of space in every room he occupied. He took her breath away. She hadn't known such tenderness since before her mother had died when she and her parents had been a happy family.

Skip wrapped his arms around her.

"Get over here. Past my bedtime."

She snuggled into him. He pulled the covers over them.

"Goodnight, baby. Thank you. I feel great."

"Goodnight. Sleep well." She brushed her lips against his and snuggled into him. His even breathing signaled he was asleep. There was nothing better in the world than sleeping tucked into Skip Quincy's embrace. Francie muttered a silent prayer of thanks before falling asleep.

SKIP AWOKE FIRST IN the morning. A bad dream that plagued him during the night vanished with the sunrise. Next to him, Francie stretched but didn't wake up. He seized the opportunity to gaze at her without her knowing. She was lovely. She had beautiful skin, lustrous, dark, brown hair. Her body was slender, but her breasts were plenty big enough to fill his hands. Her hips tucked perfectly under his.

Lovely, that's the word his mother would have used. His biological mother—she would have liked Francie. Her artiness, sense of style, and color impressed him. Her drawing blew him away. She had more talent in her little finger than he had in his whole body. Was he jealous? No way—he admired her ability. Why did she choose him? She did, didn't she? She'd be staying with him, wouldn't she? And what about this Paris school thing—did that mean she'd leave him?

Choosing not to face unpleasant questions for which he had no answers, he simply shoved those thoughts out of his mind. He had enough negativity to deal with. Down, two games to one in the World Series was plenty to cope with.

He eased out of bed quietly. Stress built in his shoulder. He needed to go for a run. Almost silently, he gathered clothes, and headed for the living room. After putting up a pot of coffee, Skip downed a bottle of apple juice, and laced up his shoes. If she woke up and he was gone, he'd hate to think how she'd take it, so he wrote a quick note, then hit the pavement. There was a high school three blocks away. It was before the school day started.

Running cleared his head. Exercise had been his go-to fix for everything, and it had never failed him. Breathing heavily through his mouth, he ramped up the speed. After the second lap, he stopped, bent over, breathing deeply.

"Hey! Look. It's Skip Quincy!" He heard a young man's voice and looked up. Shit. High school kids. They were on him before he could escape. Peppered with questions, he simply smiled and signed whatever they shoved at him.

"Do you live near here?"

"Are you going to win today?"

"Don't you want to kick Boots McGuffin in the nuts?"

"Are you gonna beat the Lions?"

"You gonna win the series?"

Skip laughed and eased his way through the small crowd. A few of the boys followed him, until a whistle blew, and the young men were called back by their coach. Guess early morning practice was popular everywhere.

When he returned to the apartment, Francie was in the kitchen, a towel on her head and one around her chest as she stood at the stove, where a pan of eggs sizzled.

"Hungry?" she asked.

"Yep. Water," he said, heading for the fridge. He popped open two bottles of water and downed them. The frying eggs smelled good.

"Sit," she said, scooping the food up with a spatula.

"Looks great. Thanks," he said, grabbing two forks. Francie added a little butter to the hot pan and cracked two more eggs.

"Aren't we sharing?"

"You need them all today. Mine'll be done in a minute."

When they finished eating, they cleaned up together. Skip's mind wandered back to baseball. Could his team compete? Had they simply been lucky in the first game? He paced, slowly, going over the game in his head. Where had they messed up? Then he got it. They had been tight. When a ball took a bad bounce, if you were loose, then you rolled with it, accommodated it, compensated for it. Tight meant stiff, unyielding so when the ball came where you didn't expect it, you were too rigid to realign.

They had to loosen up, get back their rhythm. He took a deep breath. Having a handle on what was going wrong helped. However, now they had to correct what wasn't working. Knowing where you are fucking up isn't enough.

Tension coiled in his muscles, causing cramps. He sat down and massaged his calves. That helped, but the rest of him was tight as a drum. He needed to calm down. He turned and glanced at Francie.

"Do you have to paint today?"

"Why? Did you have something in mind?"

"I don't have to be at practice until four. I'd like to go back to bed...with you."

She smiled. "That could be arranged."

"I need to sleep, too. But first, Miss Francie's relaxation method," he said, taking her hand and heading for the bedroom.

AT THREE, SKIP DROPPED Francie at her apartment. She wished him luck, kissed him goodbye, and headed inside. Although she loved her cozy apartment, there was something missing when she returned. Without Skip in the room, there was a chill, a loneliness that sank into her bones. He filled up a room, completed the picture. She wanted him in her life, wanted to be with him, and that was unsettling.

Although she knew how she felt, she had no clue where he stood, even though he'd agreed to exclusivity. How long would that last? After hearing him declare himself a confirmed bachelor when they first met, she didn't hold out much hope that he returned her feelings

She hung up her jacket and donned her smock. There wasn't much time, and she had seven pictures to get outlined and painted. Professor Stark was sure she'd get the Paris slot and be invited to do a show.

"And if you don't get these paintings ready and you do get it, you'll be unprepared for the private show. It will go to someone else. You'll miss your big chance. And if you don't get it, so what? You'll have seven great paintings you can show and sell. Sounds like a win/win to me. If you're willing to do the work."

She couldn't argue with his logic. She pulled out the canvas and put it on the easel. Seven paintings of Skip's body. She grinned. Staring at naked pictures of him day-after-day wouldn't be hard to take at all. She propped up one of his back and went to work.

One-by-one each canvas received an outline of the athlete's body in a different pose. By seven, when she had to leave, she had three done. Coupled with the three she had done the week before, the first step was almost completed. She smiled as she headed for the subway. As she rode, she prayed the Nighthawks would win this game. They needed it. Skip needed it. And she needed him. The equation was simple.

She settled into her seat next to Elena. The women bowed their heads for a moment, then stood for the national anthem. As he loped off the field, Skip stopped to face in Francie's direction. Their gazes connected, and he doffed his cap before heading to his position.

Hunger gripped her guts.

"I'm starving," she said.

Elena signaled for the hot dog girl. The women ordered food, then flagged down the man with drinks and got two large sodas. Francie wanted to be sober to watch the game. As they munched, the first Lion came up to bat. With fingers crossed and her heart in her mouth, Francie kept her gaze glued to the infield.

Proud of her man, she watched him field expertly, throwing out batter after batter at first, then at second and even at third base. Skip appeared to be on fire. Even his bat had improved as he bounced the ball into the stands for a ground rule double, and hit a single.

With a sigh of relief, the final out was made. In an intense competition, the Nighthawks won, five to two. Elena and Francie made their way out of the stands to the parking lot.

"You coming to Freddie's?"

Elena shook her head. "You know, Bobby likes to go home after a game. He's tired."

Francie snickered, "Yeah, but not too tired. Right?"

Elena blushed. "Shh."

"It's okay. I get it."

"I hope you do!" Elena laughed.

Now it was Francie's turn to get embarrassed. She didn't wait long. Bobby picked up Elena and swung her around before they headed for their car. Skip crushed Francie against him.

"It was a great game," she said.

He nodded. "We were on fire. Loose, focused. No one could've stopped us."

"You were awesome. I'm so proud of you."

"Thanks," he said, glancing at the ground then back at her. "Things came together. Time to celebrate. Can you stay tonight?"

She nodded.

The art show was scheduled to open the day after tomorrow. She'd received a text from Professor Stark during the game. There had been a prejudging. Francie's painting of Skip had made the top five. She had an excellent shot at the top three, meaning she'd have a place in the Paris program. And a decision to make.

Excitement flowed through her veins. She'd have to keep the news to herself. Right now, she had no idea if she'd opt for the school or going to Florida with him. She hadn't made up her mind. After all, it's not like she definitely had the slot, she didn't need to decide. As much as she loved Skip, this was the chance of a lifetime, an opportunity she'd worked hard for, one that might impact the rest of her life.

If she lost Skip while she was away, that would impact the rest of her life, too. Would he wait for her? She'd be gone five months, at least. Maybe more. Trying like hell to push it out of her mind, her nerves tightened. Lying didn't come naturally to Francie. But she had to keep this from him, not distract him, so he could win the Series.

"Now, if we can just win tomorrow, we'll be ahead a game and the pressure'll be off."

"Off?" she asked.

"Not off completely. But a shitload less than it was today."

"I know you can win."

"We just need to keep playing like we did today," he said.

Francie pushed all thoughts of her art show out of her mind and concentrated on Skip. She listened, keeping her comments limited during dinner. When they returned, they made love. Wrapped in the cocoon of his arms, Francie knew what to do. With the decision, came peace.

Chapter Seventeen

Skip had noticed how quiet she'd been the night before, but he didn't question it. If there was trouble brewing between them, he had to put it off until after the Series. He couldn't afford to get distracted. Making love last night had calmed his fears. Things between them were as passionate and loving as always. No matter what happened, he was the luckiest guy in the world to have a loving woman like her. He straightened his cap and loped over to take his position as the pitcher warmed up.

Skip didn't expect the Lions to come back twice as strong after their loss. He'd hoped they had lost their momentum, their energy, and confidence. But he'd been wrong. In fact, their loss appeared to have had the opposite effect. Their hitting was spot-on, and they made no errors in the field. Their pitcher went a full seven innings, keeping the Nighthawks to only two runs. Skip had struck out twice and hit a long fly ball to the right fielder for an out.

Now the Nighthawks were behind two games to three. Skip was quiet in the car as they drove to the apartment. Neither he nor Francie felt like dinner at Freddie's.

"What time does your plane leave tomorrow?"

"Noon. We have to be at the stadium for the bus to the airport at eleven."

Francie nodded. "I have to get an early start tomorrow, too."

"We're in the same place then."

His shoulders sagged as he shrugged off his jacket and plunked his keys down on the side table in the foyer.

"Come on, I'll give you a massage," she offered.

"Hot bath first. Why don't you join me?" He wiggled his eyebrows.

"Food?"

"Oh, yeah. How about we order pizza?"

"I'll do it. What do you want?"

Within an hour, they had eaten their fill, and were stepping into a tub filled with hot, sudsy water.

Skip got in first, Francie followed. He spread his legs open and she stretched out, leaning against his chest. He joined his hands together underneath her breasts. The water worked on his muscles. Slowly the tension drained away.

She folded her hands over his. "You okay?"

"Yeah. Just bummed."

She sat up and turned around. "Can you put your back to me? No, wait," she said, hopping out of the tub and getting back in behind him. "There. That's better."

She soaped up her hands and placed them on his shoulders. Digging her fingertips into his flesh, she loosened the tightness with a warm massage.

"Oh, God. That's amazing," he moaned. "Almost as good as sex."

After the massage, Skip added more hot water and lifted Francie up. She straddled his lap and they made love in the tub. When they were snuggled together in bed, Skip drew her closer before speaking.

"Is everything all right?"

"Uh huh."

"You've been kind of quiet. Preoccupied. Are we okay?"

"Yeah. Sure. Why wouldn't we be?"

"I don't know. You're just not you, ya know?"

"Got a lot on my mind with the art show coming up."

"Yeah. When is that?"

"It opens tomorrow afternoon."

"Shit. Fuck! I'm gonna be in L.A."

"It's open for two weeks."

"Good. I can see it when I get back, then."

"Right."

"Will you take me?"

"I'll be there every afternoon. It's open from five to nine, every day. I'll text you the address."

"I'll come by as soon as I get back. After we win."

"After you win. Yep."

Skip spooned her, resting his chin on the top of her head. Her body was warm against him, exactly the right level of heat, making him drowsy. Pushing the images of the nights in L.A. without her from his brain, he drank in her scent. He stroked his thumb over her shoulder, enjoying the soft smoothness of her skin. Her presence soothed him. Skip had a hard time believing she really loved him because he'd never considered himself loveable. When he was with her, he'd swear he was two inches taller or his muscles had grown stronger.

The smile she wore when he came into view, the hugs, the belief he could do anything, warmed his heart. Was it love? He guessed it must be. And if it wasn't, it was so much more than he'd ever had. He was grateful. Francie was in his blood. He needed her like an addict needed a fix. That was close enough to love for Skip.

THE NEXT MORNING, FRANCIE kissed Skip goodbye and sent him off with prayers and good luck wishes. Now it was time to face her own life. She hopped the subway home, changed into her best clothes, and headed for the gallery. The artists were expected to be there to assist with the display of their work. Three classmates of hers were also exhibiting and being considered in the competition.

A young assistant greeted her and brought her to the choice spot she had landed. Her canvas rested against the wall. Together they hung her piece.

"Yours is outstanding. The best of them all. Really," the man said.

"Thank you. That's quite a compliment."

"I'm a runner. I compete in races. You've captured, perfectly, his expression, the relief of the cold water after being hot and sweaty. I can almost feel it. It's magic. Really. I love it."

"That's so wonderful."

"You're sure to win a place in Paris. If they don't pick you, someone is totally blind."

With that, he walked away and was recruited to help another team of two that was having trouble mounting a large canvas. His words blew her away. Could he be right? She wandered over to a table where there were glasses of white wine. She took one and a piece of cheese then returned to her work. Standing back a bit, she trained a critical eye on the painting. She couldn't find any flaws. Always her harshest critic, not this time.

The man was right. It was good. The picture was titled "Relief." She could feel exactly what he had mentioned. She almost felt the wetness of the drops of water flying off the painting. It was realistic without looking like a photograph and captured his joy at winning the game and cooling off. She smiled. He was such a great model. Was it him or how she felt about him that came across from the canvas to a viewer? She didn't know and didn't care. Whatever it was, the painting was magic, and it had a good chance of placing.

She finished the beverage and strolled through the gallery, checking out the competition. There were a few mighty fine works of art on display. It was five, the doors opened, and people started filling the place. Her stomach clenched, and her nerves kicked up. The judges would be there by six and the winners would be announced at eight. Someone tapped her on the shoulder.

She whirled around to face Professor Stark.

"See what I mean," he said. "Yours is the best of the lot."

Heat seeped into her face. "Thank you." Sweat broke out on her palms. She wiped them on a napkin. This required more wine. She and the professor headed for the refreshment table.

"Whatever you do, don't get drunk. Misbehaving could cause you to lose."

"I thought they'd base their choice solely on the merit of the work."

"They will. But bad behavior by an artist can get their work disqualified."

"I see," she said, nodding. She made a mental note to make this her last glass.

She followed her professor like a puppy dog as he greeted other students and faculty members.

"You should stand by your work, Francie," he whispered. "It's not that I want to get rid of you, but let people see who created that masterpiece."

Giving a quick shrug, she ambled over. The judges came by. They asked her one or two questions and looked at the painting from different angles. They made notes in little notebooks, then left without a word. Francie hit the hors d'oeuvres table and filled a small plate. She needed sustenance.

By seven thirty, there was a dense crowd in the small gallery. When the judges appeared, Francie went to the back to stand with Professor Stark. Her pulse raced. She could hear her heartbeat in her ears. Her mouth went dry, and her palms got damp.

The gallery manager called the crowd to attention and introduced the judges. There were a few words said, but Francie didn't listen. Finally, they announced the awards. First, they gave lip service to the basis for their decisions. All Francie heard was *blah, blah, blah.*

They started with third prize. It wasn't her. Now her heart rate doubled if that was possible. Second prize was announced, and, again, it wasn't her. Panic set in. Sweat broke out on her forehead and upper lip. She wasn't going to place at all! Oh my God! She hadn't realized how much she had counted on winning. And now it wasn't going to happen. Her breathing became shallow. Tears pricked at the back of her eyes.

"And the grand prize winner is...drum roll, please. "Relief" by Francine Whitman."

Stunned, she stood still, her feet cemented to the floor.

"Francie, that's you!" Professor Stark said, giving her a little nudge. "Go on, dear. Go up and get your prize."

She stumbled forward, then found her stride, wending her way through the crowd.

"Here you go, my dear. And you are guaranteed a seat in the Paris art program. Congratulations. Awesome painting. Truly a master-piece," the woman said, placing a ribbon around Francie's neck. A round of hearty applause bounced Francie out of her reverie. First prize—she'd won first place. Her work had been the best of all. She could hardly believe it.

A small, dark-haired woman scurried up to her.

"*Bon soir.* I am Madame Saucier. I must talk to you about Paris. Professor Stark said you have seven paintings, all of this quality, for a private showing at our little gallery at the school, *non?*"

Francie stared at her for a moment, then nodded.

"*Bon.* When are you coming to France, eh? The sooner, the better. We have wonderful studio space for you. You can work there, and it will be safe. Tell me, how soon can you come?"

The idea of finishing the paintings in Paris intrigued her. Having quiet space just for her work would be a dream come true. But what about Skip? Did her enthusiasm for the woman's plan mean Francie was going to Paris?

Mme. Saucier handed her a business card. "Call me when you have made plane reservations. I will have a small flat there for you, too. It's not big, but it's charming and all you will need. Congratulations. I look forward to seeing you in Paris," the woman said, then kissed her on each cheek before leaving.

Little Francie Whitman, a French artist, with her own flat in Paris, and a one-woman show. Could all this be possible? Now, if the Nighthawks would win the World Series, her life would be perfect, wouldn't it?

THE NIGHTHAWKS CHECKED into the same hotel as last time. They had arrived a day early to allow for the time change. Being down a game to the Lions made the team jumpy. No raucous kidding or dirty jokes on the plane to break up the tension. The ride had been quiet, the atmosphere subdued. The men read, slept, or played cards.

Alone in his room, Skip stretched out on the bed, lacing his fingers behind his head. He went over each play of the last game, looking for the spot where the 'Hawks went wrong. The team had tightened up. There were errors. How many times had Cal Crawley said, "Errors lose games"?

A knock broke him from his musings.

"Dinner!" It was Matt.

"Coming."

He dragged his ass to the dresser. There he put everything back in his pockets, including the room key, and joined his buddies in the hall. Their faces looked no more cheerful than his.

The men got in the buffet line in their private dining room. Murmurs of conversation, interrupted by the clinking of knives and forks, were the only sounds in the room. A heaviness in the air weighed on Skip. This game was it—the all-important one. If they lost, the Series would be finished with the Lions victorious. If they won, they'd tie and have another chance.

He showered and hit the sack. One glance at the clock and he realized it was too late to call Francie. He sent a "goodnight, love you" text, instead. Grateful to disappear into sleep, he rested soundly and awoke refreshed.

Today was a day of practice. Tomorrow would be the game. Before breakfast, he dialed his girl.

"How are you?" she asked.

"Okay. You?"

"Good."

"Tomorrow's the game. Do or die."

"Yep. The gallery opened."

"Oh? How'd it go?"

"Great. I won first place."

"First place! Wow! That's awesome, baby. Now, can I see your picture?"

"Yep. As soon as you get home."

"I've got it on my calendar."

"Do you even have a calendar?"

"In my head."

She laughed. "Okay. I'm going to text you the address."

"Throw in the time you want me there, too."

"Okay."

"I'm proud of you, honey. First place. That's fantastic."

"It's a picture of you."

"What? What's a picture of me?"

"My painting. The one that won first prize."

"Me?" His eyebrows rose.

"You're my favorite subject."

He chuckled. "You're mine, too."

"Good luck in practice and for the game tomorrow." She blew a kiss into the phone.

"Thanks. It's a must win. I know we can do it."

"I know you can, too."

The next day the team ate and boarded the bus for the stadium. They trash-talked the Lions and bucked each other up. He did deep-breathing to settle his nerves, then hit the dugout.

In the bottom of the eighth, with the score tied, Boots McGuffin came smokin' down the line from first when Eduardo Lopez hit a bouncer through the hole between first and second. Bobby Hernandez, at second, chased down the ball. In one motion, he scooped it up and tossed it to Skip, covering second. Skip had his foot firmly planted on the back of the bag, but the throw went a little wide, forcing him off the base. He lunged to trap it in his glove, pulling both feet off second base.

McGuffin came in, cleats flying, aimed directly at Skip's groin. Instinct took over. Skip twisted sideways to protect his privates, dropping the ball. Boots was safe at second. In the meantime, the runner on third headed home. Skip recovered enough to get off an anemic throw to home, but it was too late. Matt crowded the plate, preventing the Lion from touching it for as long as he could. But the runner barreled into him, knocking him on his ass and the ball out of his glove.

Run scored, man safe at second, and blood dripping through Skip's socks at the shin where Boots had gored him. Pain seared through him, forcing him to clutch his leg and roll on the ground. He directed every curse word he knew at McGuffin, who almost looked sorry he had inflicted the injury. Play was halted as two men helped Skip limp off the field. They taped him up, gave him a local for the pain and sent him back out on the field.

He returned in time to see he'd been charged with an error. While he was gone, Boots had scored. Now the Nighthawks were down by two, with a score of six to four. They had one more at-bat. Nat was scheduled to start the inning. Then Bobby, then Skip. He prayed his leg would hold out until the game was over.

After Nat homered, the Lions retired their pitcher and brought out a fresh reliever—one of their ace closers. Even with Nat's solo homer, the 'Hawks were short one run. The pitcher struck out Bobby, and Skip sent a long fly ball to the warning track where a Lion caught it and held on when he smashed into the wall at a gallop. He rose, gripping the ball in his glove and holding his shoulder. Jake struck out, and the game was over. The Lions won the World Series, four games to two. Skip's error and failure at the plate lost the game—that's the way he saw it.

Pandemonium broke out as the Los Angeles fans celebrated and the Lions bucked, jumped, chest-bumped, and hugged each other. The Nighthawks' crawled away, up the chute to the locker room, in total silence. After the local anesthetic wore off, Skip's leg throbbed, and his head pounded, too. He'd done it. Lost the World Series for his team. He wanted to crawl into a hole in a corner and never come out.

HIDING UNDER THE SHOWER did no good. His teammates were waiting for their turns, too. Vic stopped by to take a look at Skip's leg. He applied more antiseptic and a fresh bandage. He gave Skip advice on how to take care of it when he got back to New York.

Once everyone was showered and dressed, Cal Crawley gathered the players around.

"Look, we lost, but we played hard. Remember the Lions had a much better record going into the series. We were the Cinderella team here, not them. They'd outplayed us all season. Expecting to beat them was not realistic."

"But you said we could do it. We were better than them," someone in the back piped up.

Cal smiled. "Think I'm gonna tell you they have us beat in pitching, hitting, fielding, and base stealing and expect you to play like winners?"

The men laughed.

"Of course not. Hey, I knew it was an uphill battle. But you did fine. It's a more than respectable showing. Hell, some oddsmakers had the Lions taking four straight!"

A negative murmur went up.

"Bullshit! I knew that was hogwash. I knew you had a fighting chance. And I'm proud of the games you played. All of you," he said, pointing to the men, and stopping at Skip. "No one is responsible for our loss. No one! Is that clear? Don't go pointing fingers at a teammate or yourself as being the cause of our loss. God damn it. They were just the better team this year. Just the better team"

The men shifted around.

"And I'm proud of each and every one of you. You played hard. These games were our best games of the season. That's the way it should be. Shit, if you can't play your best fuckin' game in the World Series, when can you? Nobody could have beat the Lions. Nobody. Not the Bluejays, not the Bulls, and not the Bucks."

He rose and stretched. "The media is waiting out there. I'll handle them. If they corner you, just tell 'em you're proud of your team and the Lions played a helluva game. Thanks for your effort. We'll get 'em next year," Cal said.

He finished by shaking hands with each player. Shame seeped through Skip's body. He didn't want to face Cal, but the manager grabbed his arm and pulled him aside.

"I know you, Quincy. You're already blaming yourself for the whole thing, aren't you? Fuck it, man. This is a team sport. Everybody is responsible. Everybody plays a part. Don't go blamin' yourself for that play at second today. At least you still have your balls."

Skip laughed.

"Take care of that leg. I need you in perfect shape in spring training, ya hear?"

Skip nodded.

"Good. And if I hear you taking this all on yourself, I'll beat the ever-living shit out of you."

"Yes, sir."

"Now get on the God damn bus and let's get back to New York. This hot weather beats the crap out of me," Cal said, patting Skip on the back.

Surrounded by his buddies, he shuffled out the door and headed for the bus. They managed to skirt the press, which was busy with the winners.

He was halfway through the parking lot when he heard his name called. His head snapped up. There stood his parents. His mother looked sad, but his father's face was red with anger.

"Skip! Skip! Over here." Could his parents have flown to L.A. for the Series?

He trotted over to where his father stood.

"I'm sorry you didn't win, son," his mother said.

"Thanks."

"You didn't win because you fucked up. You committed the game-losing error. What kind of asshole are you to do something so dumb? Didn't I teach you better? It was a stupid play."

"Look, Dad, I don't need this right now," Skip said.

"Obviously you need something. You brought your whole team down. They could have won. Won the World Series, if you didn't fuck it up."

"Dad."

"It's just the truth. You're not good enough. You've never been good enough," Bart Quincy said.

"Bart, stop. You're being too rough," Ellen said, tugging on his sleeve.

Bart ripped his arm away from his wife. "Shut the fuck up, Ellen."

"Don't talk to her like that," Skip said, taking a step closer to his father.

"Who do you think you are to tell me how to speak to my wife?" Bart said. "You're not even my son. Just some stupid orphan I took in because Ellen wanted you. I never wanted you!" Bart said, raising his voice.

Ellen gasped, covering her face with her hands. A small crowd of Nighthawks began to gather.

"You've never been my father," Skip yelled, pointing his finger at the man. "My father died in a car accident when I was ten. You were just a man forced to take me in. Don't think I don't know that. You made it clear. Every. Day. Of. My. Life."

"You're nothing but a disappointment to me."

"Yeah, well for a man who couldn't father his own kids..." Skip began.

Bart lashed out, slapping Skip across the face. Skip saw red and grabbed him. Bobby and Matt each took an arm, restraining their buddy.

"Don't! Don't do something stupid," Matt said.

"He's not worth it," Bobby said.

"Skip. I'm so sorry," Ellen said, putting her hand on his arm.

"Sorry, Mom. I've had it. He can drop dead, as far as I'm concerned."

Bobby and Matt stood down.

"Don't say that. Don't ever say that," Ellen said.

"You're dead to me. You were a worthless money suck. Wasted my time with you." Bart said.

"It wasn't his fault we lost. You're the idiot here, Mr. Quincy," Nat said.

"That's right. No one player's to blame. The Lions were the better team. So, shove your attitude. Leave Skip alone," Bobby said.

"Why don't you go home," Dan added.

Cal Crawley moseyed over. "The boys are right. It's nobody's fault." Cal put his arm around Skip's shoulders. "*My* boys feel bad enough about the loss without you piling on. I think you'd best be going about your way, Mr. Quincy."

Bart Quincy opened his mouth, then closed it again. He wasn't going to go head-to-head with the coach. He turned and headed for his car.

Skip's blood pressure spiked, anger brought heat to his face. If no one had been there, he might have given his father a beating.

"Come on. The bus is waiting," Jake said, motioning.

The men surrounded the shortstop, escorting him to the waiting vehicle. When the doors opened, a blast of cold air hit Skip. It would take more than air conditioning to reduce his heat and calm him down.

He stepped up and found a window seat. He always grabbed one so he could see the city. Bobby plopped down next to him.

"What an asshole," Skip said, clenching his jaw.

"Leave it here. You've got a great girl back home. Relax. We'll be in Florida soon." Bobby patted his arm. "Everything's gonna be fine. We'll get 'em next season."

Skip shut his eyes. Soon, he'd be on the beach with his buddies, but what about Francie? Would she be going, too? The way his luck was going, that was doubtful.

Chapter Eighteen

Francie's nerves kicked up. Skip was due any moment. The gallery had a decent crowd of maybe thirty people. As usual, four or five people clustered around Francie's painting, discussing it. There was a blue "first prize" ribbon on the wall next to it.

A dozen people nodded their understanding how her piece could take first place. Others shook their heads, frowning their displeasure at her achievement. Every time someone responded in the negative, she bristled. Criticism from her professor was one thing, nasty comments from strangers were quite another.

When she looked up, there was Skip, filling the doorway. She smiled and threaded her way through the crowd to him. He took her in his arms and kissed her.

"I'm so sorry, babe," she whispered in his ear. "How's your leg?"

"Fine. Forget it. It's over."

"I know. But you must be upset."

"Nah. I'm over it. Where's that painting?"

She took his hand and led him over to the spot. His eyes widened. "That's me?"

"Yep."

"Holy shit! I mean, it's great. That's really me?"

"After a game. It was a hot day, and you were cooling off."

"It's beautiful, baby. Just beautiful. First prize. That's awesome."

"Thank you."

"What do you get for first prize?"

As much as she had tried to prepare for this question, now that the time had come, she was at a loss for words. Her heart beat in her ears.

"Can we go someplace? For a cup of coffee or something?" she asked.

"Sure, sure. But don't you want to stay here? People are talking about your work."

She shifted her weight.

"Do you have something to tell me?"

"Sort of."

"There's wine over there. Let's grab a glass and go sit on that bench in the corner. Whatever the fuck that is," he said, gesturing the abstract art on the wall, "no one is paying any attention to it. We won't be interrupted."

"That's modern art, Skip. Please keep your voice down. The artist might be here."

"Oh, sorry. Just my opinion."

"Come on."

They each picked up a plastic glass half filled with wine and wandered over to the bench. After they sat and took a sip, Skip broke the ice.

"Just tell me you're not breaking up with me. And that you're not dumping me because we lost the Series." His face flushed, sweat dotted his forehead.

She placed her hand on his. "Of course not."

"Does this have something to do with Paris?"

She nodded. "Winning first place means I have a fully-paid seat in the art program in Paris."

"That's great, isn't it?"

"Is it?"

"Isn't that what you wanted?" he asked, taking a bigger sip.

"It's a big honor."

"A once in a lifetime chance, right?"

She nodded. Was this going to be a lot easier than she thought? Was he simply going to let her go?

"Well, then what's the big deal? You have to go, right?"

"I was thinking—"

"Of course, you do. You've been working all semester, probably your whole life, for this chance. Don't let a little thing like you and me stand in the way."

"A little thing?"

"I mean, I'll go to Florida, as usual. And I'll be back. When you get back, we can see each other again."

"When I get back?"

"Yeah. If you come back. I mean if you don't fall in love with a Frenchman and get married over there."

"And that wouldn't bother you?"

"Of course, it would. But you have to go. Absolutely."

Confusion stopped her words. She stared at his face, looking for a sign of sadness, something, but there wasn't anything there. So, he didn't care, and she could leave? The sting of tears behind her eyes made her blink. Perhaps she had misjudged their relationship?

"Really?"

"Of course. You didn't think I'd stand in the way, did you?"

"Actually, I did. I don't mean stand in the way. Just maybe ask me to stay or object or look a little sad that I'm leaving."

"How could I do that? After all your work?"

"I suppose." She sighed. He sure was making leaving a whole lot easier. Guess she didn't matter that much to him anyway.

"I'm sorry to see you go. But we can be in touch, right?"

"Right." Her shoulders sagged.

"When do you leave?"

Since he seemed so nonchalant, why wait? She'd considered staying for Thanksgiving, but it didn't look like he'd even be here for that. The sooner she got to Paris, the sooner she could get her seven paintings finished and ready for the show.

"I'm leaving next week," she said, watching for his reaction.

"Oh. Wow. That's soon," he said, his eyebrows raised, but still under control.

"They want me to do a gallery show with seven paintings of my own. Only my work. I have four completed and I need to finish the rest. They have studio space there for me, so I'm going to go early and get it done. This private show is part of the requirements for the scholarship."

"That's really something. Your own private show in Paris. Can't beat that."

She reached out to touch him, but he pulled his hand away. Was he simply making it easier to go, or had he been lying about his feelings all this time? Skip had never been easy to read and now, he seemed to exist behind a thick stone wall.

"You don't seem to care that I'm going away."

"Hey, a loser like me has no rights with a winner like you. This is your own World Series. And you won. You're the top. I'm so proud of you. Go for it, sweetheart."

"You're not a loser."

"Depends on your perspective. Anyway. This isn't about me."

"But I'll miss you so much."

"Honey, if we're meant to be, we're meant to be. And if not, then we can part friends."

That wasn't what she wanted to hear. Where were his words of undying love? Where was his pledge to fly to Paris to be with her during the off-season? Where was maybe even a marriage proposal? Her throat dried.

"Will you email me?" She choked the question out.

"Sure. Won't have much to say."

"Tell me all about Florida."

"Blue water. Sunshine. Alcohol."

"If it's too much bother, then don't," she said. She couldn't stop the coldness in her tone.

He sat back, staring.

"Hey, we're not going to leave it like this, are we?" he asked.

"Isn't that what you want?" Francie's heart squeezed.

"I don't want to stand in your way, sweetheart."

"You're not."

"Good."

She stared at him again, looking for a sign that his heart was as shattered as hers but saw nothing. Tears threatened. She pushed to her feet. Time to make a break for it before she broke down.

"I need to go."

"I'll be here when you get back," he said, rising also.

"Will you?" She faced him.

"What do you want me to say?" He shrugged.

"If you don't know, then..." Her control faded. Time to make her exit.

"Women always say that."

"Sorry to be so typical."

"Why are you being like this?"

"I have to go to the ladies' room," she said. Ah, the old excuse for escape. "Have a nice life."

"What the...?"

She reached behind her chair and took out a tubular package.

"Before I forget. This is for you."

"What is it?"

"The chalk drawing I did at the lake."

He took it. "Oh, my God. Francie. I..."

But she had made it out of earshot before he finished his sentence. In the bathroom, she sat in a stall and locked the door before she broke into sobs. What was she supposed to do—give up the chance of a lifetime for him? That he didn't even ask her to brought a bitterness to her heart. Did that mean he loved her or he didn't care? She was so confused she wasn't even sure she was in the ladies' or men's room, Francie mopped her face with a tissue, then splashed on water, dried off, and peeked outside before leaving.

She didn't spy Skip. On her way outside, she turned once more to look back. There he was, standing by her painting, looking at it. As if he felt her stare, he faced her, their gazes connected.

Tears streamed down her cheeks. He started for the door. Francie shook her head and ran toward the subway. She needed time. One minute her life had been on a positive track. She'd had love, accomplishment, and happiness. Now all that lay ahead was uncertainty. Could she measure up over seven pieces? Or would her talent run out?

A sudden coolness in the late October air chilled her. An emptiness inside gnawed at her. Had she traded one desire for another? In June, she'd become eligible to inherit her father's fortune. By then, she'd be back from Paris. She'd have a whole new set of choices and challenges to face—and face them alone. The prospect left her hollow.

SKIP CHATTED WITH THE owner of the gallery for a few minutes. Three people had recognized him and asked for autographs. Several people whispered about him being the model for Francie's painting. He smiled. No one had ever done that. Well, Mimi Banner had photographed him. Was that the same thing? Not exactly. Francie's picture had taken many hours of work, poring over it with a brush, bringing the image to life.

When she left with tears on her cheeks, her face sadder than he'd ever seen it, his heart broke. What had he done? He didn't mean to hurt her. But she was a winner, and he was a loser. She could do better than Skip Quincy. He loved her too damn much to hold her back from getting the most out of life. Who knew who she'd meet in Paris? Now with distance between them, she'd be free to find another man.

He'd never find another girl to love him like she did. He'd known that for a long time. Resigned to having half a life, he'd rationalized it as providing more time to work on his fielding to prevent the disaster of that last game from ever happening again.

He simply couldn't shake his shame at having committed the game-losing error. None of his teammates said anything. They'd been damn supportive, but when their checks came without the winner's bonus—how would they feel then? He shuddered to think what he'd taken from his best friends.

He'd hoped Francie would be here for Thanksgiving. He'd thought about proposing to her then if they'd won the World Series. But they'd lost and now he didn't have the balls to ask her to commit, maybe give up her Paris opportunity, to marry a loser.

He'd taken the ring with him to Los Angeles. He'd even considered doing it at the gallery until she told him about Paris. Within an instant, it became as clear as the Caribbean Sea that she had to take the course in Paris, and marriage to him would have to wait—maybe forever.

As he headed to his car, he thrust his hands into his pockets to escape the chilly air. His fingers closed around the square box. What the hell was he going to do with that now? Once she got to France, uncommitted to him, available men would be all over her. He didn't find out when she'd be coming back. And he didn't even kiss her goodbye.

Skip went home and made his plane reservation for Florida. He'd hoped to be able to make it for two. Now he'd be flying solo. He ordered in Chinese food and watched a war movie. He didn't have any interest in porno. It would make him miss Francie. He went to bed early.

He no longer considered the Quincys his parents. The next morning, he removed their pictures and replaced them with ones of his birth parents. They may be long gone, but they'd loved him and treated him with kindness.

He called Billy Holmes.

"Hey. Watson here."

"Watson? How the hell are you?"

"Good."

"Sorry about the game."

"Yeah. Whatever. What are you doing for Thanksgiving?"

"Buying a turkey sandwich and watching porn. You?"

"My friends are having a big Thanksgiving dinner. Wanna come?"

"Any chicks there?"

"Might be a few unattached ones."

"Okay. Yeah. What time and where?"

Skip gave him the information and chatted a bit. Billy's news about how well the garage was doing cheered Skip. He guessed he'd get paid back sooner than he thought.

Thanksgiving Day was dreary, overcast, and nippy—echoing his mood. That had been the weather for almost every Thanksgiving since he'd been in New York. At Matt's, Skip ran errands, helped cook, and set the table.

He missed Francie like crazy and wondered if she'd already hooked up with a French guy. Shaking his head, he kicked himself. Francie would never do that. She wasn't a hop-into-bed-with-anyone type of girl. Seeing his buddies with their women echoed his singlehood. Checking his watch, it was fifteen minutes past time to start the meal, and Billy still hadn't showed. They went ahead anyway. He never showed, leaving Skip pissed.

PUTTING OFF HIS TRIP to Florida, Skip gave himself two days to cool off before heading to the garage in Queens to see what had happened to Billy. He drove over on Saturday morning. With Christmas a few weeks away, the weather had turned cold. A bitter wind chilled Skip. He shoved his hands into his jacket pockets to keep them warm as he crossed the street.

In the small office, he spotted a man behind a desk. Skip went in.

"Hi," Skip said.

The man looked up. "Say, aren't you that guy, Quincy, from the Nighthawks?"

Skip nodded. The man reached out to shake his hand.

"I'm Marty. What can I do for you?"

"I'm looking for Billy Holmes,"

"Bill? Nobody calls him Billy."

Skip nodded. "Seen him?"

"He took off a couple of weeks ago."

"Took off?"

"Yeah. Didn't say nothin', just left."

"Did he leave any word for me?"

"Nope. Just a letter for a guy named 'Watson.'"

"Watson? That's me."

"I thought you were Quincy."

"Watson's what Billy called me when we were kids. We were best friends."

"Yeah? You in that orphanage, too?"

Skip nodded. Marty opened a desk drawer and plucked out an envelope. He handed it to Skip.

"Don't be too mad at him. Bill does what he can, ya know? He never means to hurt nobody. It's just him. The way he is. Sticking around ain't his thing."

"Thanks," Skip said, heading out into the cold. He stuffed the letter in his pocket. After returning to his building, he dropped off the car and walked to his favorite diner. Hunger gripped his belly. He ordered a big breakfast before remembering that baseball season was over and he'd better rein in his food intake or he'd bust out of his clothes.

He sucked down coffee, then ripped open the envelope. Marty had been correct, Billy never hung around long. Skip had been surprised when his friend hit him up for a loan to buy into a business. He didn't think twice, and shelled out the money, hoping his friend had found the right path and could settle down. Obviously, that wasn't happening.

Dear Watson,

I know I owe you fifty large and you'll get it someday, believe me. For now, I

got a good offer for my share of the station. A friend I met in juvie offered me

a job in Arizona. It being so fuckin' cold here now, that looked pretty good.

He needed me right away, so I cashed out and hit the road. Sorry to stand you up on turkey day, but you know how it is. Never liked crowds much anyway.

I appreciate what you done for me, giving me this stake. It'll take me a little ways, then I'll figure out the rest, like I always do. You've been a good friend, Watson.

My only friend. I knew I could count on you. If I can't get you the money for a while, at least you won't be hurtin' for it.

Thanks for everything. I hope you're not mad 'cause you're the closest I got to a

brother. Don't know when I'll see you, but I'll be back. I promise. Take care.

Holmes

Skip crumpled up the letter in his big hand and left it on the table. The waitress put a plate in front of him and eyed the letter.

"Want me to get rid of that for you?"

Skip nodded. Anger shot through him at Billy's words. His friend never intended to pay him back. Not that Skip needed the money, but

Billy's lies hurt. Of course, Billy had always been a liar and a manipulator. Skip knew that, had known it since he was ten. In the orphanage, he didn't care. Billy had taken care of him, shown him the ropes, and beat up anyone who gave Skip a hard time.

This time was different. Billy had ripped him off—on purpose. Skip had become just another mark. Although he'd suspected his friend had been jealous when Skip had been adopted, that was a long time ago. Still, he knew Billy could barely contain his envy when Skip hit the major leagues. Billy had athletic ability, but no support system, no parents, bogus or real, to help him make something of himself.

Skip had credited the Quincys for guiding him into baseball, although he had a feeling he'd have ended up there anyway. Once Sal Guardino, his high school coach, got a hold of Skip, he'd been on his way to fame and fortune.

He finished eating, turned up his collar, and went for a walk. He headed to Riverside Park. Angry and alone, he stuffed his hands in his pockets and moseyed down to the river. The Hudson looked as muddy and gray as the sky. Christmas approached, and, despite his mother's pleas, he had no intention of setting foot in the Quincy house.

Matt and Dusty had invited him there, at their rental in Florida. The celebration would be festive—it always was with the Nighthawks. But it'd be hollow. He needed something to fill him up but had no clue what. He returned to his apartment and binged on fast food and porn. He locked himself inside, refusing to think about the betrayal of his oldest friend, his poor performance on the field, and the desertion of his girlfriend. Life sucked. He'd just wait it out. In a couple of days, he'd be heading to Florida to meet up with his buddies.

That wouldn't change anything. His life was in the crapper, depression hung over him like a cloud that refused to blow away. That night, he got a text from Bobby, inviting him to dinner. Why the hell not? He hit the shower.

SKIP PICKED UP A BOUQUET of flowers for Elena. When he knocked, she opened the door and threw her arms around him.

"We're so glad to see you," she said.

Skip nodded. He couldn't remember being glad about anything since the last time he'd slept with Francie. Elena handed him a beer and the three made small talk. She put a chicken and rice casserole, that looked delicious, on the table. Skip couldn't remember the last time he'd had a home-cooked meal. Oh, yes, Thanksgiving.

"How you doin'?" Bobby asked, taking a helping of salad.

"Okay. You?"

"We're great. Can't wait to get to Florida. This winter shit is a fuckin' pain," Bobby said.

"Exactly."

"You're coming right?" Bobby asked.

Skip nodded because his mouth was full of food.

Elena glanced over at him, from under her lashes. "You know, for a few dollars more, you could fly to Paris."

Skip choked. Bobby rushed over to pound him on the back. Once he got his airway clear, he looked up at her. "Why would I do that?"

"Dunno. A little birdie told me that a certain artist over there is missing her man."

"Why doesn't she tell me directly?"

"Because you told her to go and didn't care."

"What do you mean I didn't care?"

"Just quoting the artist."

"Of course, I cared. Who am I to tell her she should miss out on the opportunity of a lifetime?"

Elena frowned. Fury built in her face. "Skip Quincy, don't give me that bullshit! Did you tell her how much you loved her? No. Did you say you'd fly over and stay with her? No. Did you propose marriage? No. Did you write her off, practically telling her to leave and see ya around? Yes!"

"I did not!"

"Yes, you did. She told me all about your conversation."

"She's a winner. She's going places. I'm going nowhere. How could I saddle her with me? The team probably won't renew my contract next year. I fucked up. I'm not in her league."

"That is the biggest crock of crap I've ever heard," Elena said.

"Hey, man, are you kidding? You're the best shortstop in the league!"

"Really? After I lost the final game in the Series?"

"Didn't you listen to Crawley? He said it was nobody's fault. And he was right. Nobody was hitting worth shit. Our pitching sucked—big time! There were three other errors that day. Stop being such a maniac. It wasn't all about you, asshole. We're a team. We win as a team and we lose as a team."

"Francie hasn't found anyone else?"

"What do you think? That girl doesn't give her heart to everyone. She's in love with you, and that's not gonna change. So get your ass over there."

"Yeah. And stop feeling sorry for yourself, dickwad," Bobby put in, taking a forkful of food.

"Your mopey face is a downer. Thanksgiving, I thought I'd burst into tears, just looking at you. You've got it all. Don't be an idiot. Don't lose her." Elena scooped up a piece of chicken.

"I didn't want to lose her. I thought she'd do better solo. I didn't and still don't have the right to go over there, or marry her, or anything."

"That's because you don't want to," Elena replied, eyes flashing.

"Yeah, man. Come on. Act like a man, not a pussy. Go over there and make up with your girl." Bobby took a gulp of beer.

"Is she really mad at me?"

"You broke her heart. But, I think she wants you back," Elena said.

"Yeah?"

"Yeah."

Skip finished dinner, made excuses, and rushed home. He was on the internet in a flash, changing his reservation from Miami to Paris. If Francie told him to go to Hell, so what? At least he'd see the city of love. He had to try. Life couldn't get more miserable for him than it had been, and maybe she'd take him back.

They belonged together. He knew it in his bones. Confusion drifted away, and he saw that she had offered the love he'd been seeking all his life. She was his future. Wherever Francie was would be his home.

He packed a small bag, just in case she told him to take a hike. Elena texted him her address. He sucked in air and climbed into a taxi.

"JFK airport. International departures, please."

FRANCIE TOOK ANOTHER glass of wine. The show had been a success. It was in the second week now. Hundreds of people had wandered through, admiring her seven paintings of Skip. Madame Saucier had been effusive in her praise and support. Things couldn't have been better. Well, it could have. Skip being there would have been the icing on the cake.

She sighed and leaned against a wall. The romance of Paris only made her heart ache more. She hid her feelings from the people at the art school, but every night, in her cozy apartment, she'd shed tears over Skip.

Only a week left until Christmas Eve. She had been invited to two parties. Not looking forward to going, she had accepted anyway because it was good for her career. Having Christmas with strangers depressed her.

She finished her wine. A gust of cold air brought her attention to the front door. A man entered. Something about the way he walked looked familiar. No, it couldn't be. She was having hallucinations. Not Skip, it couldn't be Skip—could it?

He looked around until his gaze settled on her. With a lopsided grin, he strode across the room.

"Francie?" He stood, arms wide, hesitating.

She flew into his embrace. Tears burst forth as he held her tight against his chest. She smothered her sobs in his jacket. Her shoulders shook. He rubbed her back and kissed the top of her head.

"Baby, baby. Don't cry. It's gonna be okay."

Unable to speak, she quieted down and clung to him.

"I love you, baby. I just couldn't stay away," he whispered in her hair.

She pushed away from him and wiped her face with her hands. "I love you, too."

"Is it okay that I came?"

"So much better than okay. I wanted you to come with me."

"Then why didn't you ask me?"

"Why didn't you volunteer?" She stared at him.

"These are all yours?" he asked, gesturing at the canvases on the walls.

She nodded.

"Let me take a look."

Together they meandered through the gallery. There were other people perusing the paintings and discussing them. They stopped behind a couple Francie guessed were married.

"She must love this man very much," the woman said.

"Why do you say that?" the man asked.

"Look at the loving way she paints him."

Skip had heard the conversation, too. His gaze went around the room. He moved them to a quiet corner.

"These are all of me?" he asked.

She nodded.

"Why?"

"Because I love looking at you. Your body. It's just so perfect for painting. And, like the lady said, because I love you."

As they moved from painting to painting, Skip's grip on her hand tightened. She introduced him to Madame Saucier, then she took him home to her little flat.

"This is real nice," he said.

"Madame Saucier found it for me."

"I love you. We belong together. I don't ever want us to be apart. Can I stay here until spring training?"

"I was hoping you would."

He grinned. Drawing something from his pocket, he knelt next to the bed.

"Francie Whitman, will you marry me?" He opened it to reveal a stunning diamond ring.

"Marry you?"

"Yeah. Will you?"

"Oh, I thought you'd never ask. Yes, yes, I will."

Skip drew the ring down her finger. Francie moved as if in slow motion. She could hardly believe her dreams were coming true. With Skip, Paris would morph from a black-and-white experience into full color.

"Come here," he said, crooking his finger.

Feigning shyness, she moseyed over. He started to undress her, but impatience got in the way. She helped as clothing flew through the air. Within minutes they were naked, heading for the bed.

His hands closed over her breasts. "I've missed you, this, these. You know what I mean."

She nodded. Her palm eased up his chest to his neck, then cupped his cheek. He kissed it, then her lips.

"Baby," he murmured.

"Skip, I—"

But he put his finger over her lips.

"We belong together. You're all the family I need."

"I feel the same. As long as I'm with you, I'm safe. I can deal with whatever comes along."

"I'll keep you safe, always. Wife. What a funny word. Wife. You're gonna be my wife." He grinned.

"Yeah. Husband. Never thought I'd say that. I'll love you forever."

"It's an honor to be with you."

He slipped his hand between her legs, starting her motor. She arched her back, pushing her hips into his. His shaft was ready for action. Francie wrapped her arms around his chest. Slipping from her embrace, Skip repositioned himself between her legs and used his tongue to ignite her to white hot.

"Skip, please, please."

"You want it, baby?"

"You, I want you."

"You've got me, honey. All of me," he said, sliding into her.

At that moment, she understood that his heart, as well as his body, belonged to her. As her heart swelled, happiness flooded her. She gave herself to her fiancé with pent-up passion anxious to be released. Shortly after an intense orgasm rocked her, Skip exploded. His groan made her smile.

Afterward, when he drew her to his chest, she snuggled into his arms and watched her diamond twinkle in the moonlight streaming in her window. His voice interrupted her thoughts.

"It's good, so good, to be home."

EPILOGUE

Will Grant had gotten his dream. He was being called up from the minors to play for the New York Nighthawks. At twenty-six, he'd put in four years with the 'Hawks' farm team. Before spring training began, he'd been assigned to handle the two-week baseball camp for kids. The camp took place during the kids' February break from school. Each child came for a week.

He'd chuckled at the way the boys and girls looked up to him. Hell, he was no one—yet. Just a guy who grew up in a small town and played ball. He'd worked with one of his idols, catcher Matt Jackson. Matt and his fiancée, Dusty, ran the program.

This was the first year they'd taken private school kids who could pay. The team had added a week, just for them. Prepared for kids with huge attitudes and a sense of entitlement, he'd been surprised by the group that had shown up. They were good kids.

Try as he might to be impartial, he couldn't help but favor one boy, Mickey Rice. Sometimes you meet someone, even a kid, and you hit it off.

Mickey only had one parent, a mom. Will had been blown away by the gorgeous blonde holding Mickey's hand as they walked through the entrance. The woman had style, beauty, and charisma, a lethal combination.

He'd never do anything to jeopardize his future with the Nighthawks, so he was polite and friendly to Juliet Rice, but no more than that. Still, visions of her in his bed heated his blood. She was older than he, maybe thirty-two or three? But he didn't care. He'd always liked mature women. His dad had said it was due to his losing his mother so young.

He didn't question the attraction, simply worked to keep it in check. He'd be damned if giving in to desire would ruin the program or tarnish his reputation with the 'Hawks. Still, she was damn hard to resist.

THE END

Books by Jean C. Joachim

BOTTOM OF THE NINTH
DAN ALEXANDER, PITCHER
MATT JACKSON, CATCHER
JAKE LAWRENCE, THIRD BASEMAN
FIRST & TEN SERIES
GRIFF MONTGOMERY, QUARTERBACK
BUDDY CARRUTHERS, WIDE RECEIVER
PETE SEBASTIAN, COACH
DEVON DRAKE, CORNERBACK
SLY "BULLHORN" BRODSKY, OFFENSIVE LINE
AL "TRUNK" MAHONEY, DEFENSIVE LINE
HARLEY BRENNAN, RUNNING BACK
OVERTIME, THE FINAL TOUCHDOWN
A KING'S CHRISTMAS
THE MANHATTAN DINNER CLUB
RESCUE MY HEART
SEDUCING HIS HEART
SHINE YOUR LOVE ON ME
TO LOVE OR NOT TO LOVE
HOLLYWOOD HEARTS SERIES
IF I LOVED YOU
RED CARPET ROMANCE
MEMORIES OF LOVE
MOVIE LOVERS
LOVE'S LAST CHANCE

LOVERS & LIARS
His Leading Lady (Series Starter)
NOW AND FOREVER SERIES
NOW AND FOREVER 1, A LOVE STORY
NOW AND FOREVER 2, THE BOOK OF DANNY
NOW AND FOREVER 3, BLIND LOVE
NOW AND FOREVER 4, THE RENOVATED HEART
NOW AND FOREVER 5, LOVE'S JOURNEY
NOW AND FOREVER, CALLIE'S STORY (prequel)

MOONLIGHT SERIES
SUNNY DAYS, MOONLIT NIGHTS
APRIL'S KISS IN THE MOONLIGHT
UNDER THE MIDNIGHT MOON
MOONLIGHT & ROSES (prequel)
LOST & FOUND SERIES
LOVE, LOST AND FOUND
DANGEROUS LOVE, LOST AND FOUND
NEW YORK NIGHTS NOVELS
THE MARRIAGE LIST
THE LOVE LIST
THE DATING LIST
SHORT STORIES
SWEET LOVE REMEMBERED
TUFFER'S CHRISTMAS WISH
THE SECOND PLACE HEART (Coming)

About the Author

Jean Joachim is a best-selling romance fiction author, with books hitting the Amazon Top 100 list since 2012. She writes contemporary romance, which includes sports romance and romantic suspense.

Dangerous Love Lost & Found, First Place winner in the 2015 Oklahoma Romance Writers of America, International Digital Award contest. *The Renovated Heart* won Best Novel of the Year from Love Romances Café. *Lovers & Liars* was a RomCon finalist in 2013. And *The Marriage List* tied for third place as Best Contemporary Romance from the Gulf Coast RWA.

To Love or Not to Love tied for second place in the 2014 New England Chapter of Romance Writers of America Reader's Choice contest.

She was chosen Author of the Year in 2012 by the New York City chapter of RWA.

Married and the mother of two sons, Jean lives in New York City. Early in the morning, you'll find her at her computer, writing, with a cup of tea, her rescued pug, Homer, by her side and a secret stash of black licorice.

Jean has 30+ books, novellas and short stories published. Find it here: http://www.jeanjoachimbooks.com.

Sign up for her newsletter, on her website, and be eligible for her private paperback sales. Sign up for her newsletter here:
https://www.facebook.com/pages/Jean-JoachimAuthor/221092234568929?sk=app_100265896690345